AN ASSISTANT PROFESSOR

AN

ASSISTANT
PROFESSOR

A NOVEL OF SORTS

ADEEB YUSEF SALAM

New York

AN ASSISTANT PROFESSOR
A novel of sorts

© 2016 **Adeeb Yusef Salam**

Published in New York, New York, by Morgan James Publishing. Morgan James and The Entrepreneurial Publisher are trademarks of Morgan James, LLC.
www.MorganJamesPublishing.com

The Morgan James Speakers Group can bring authors to your live event. For more information or to book an event visit The Morgan James Speakers Group at www.TheMorganJamesSpeakersGroup.com.

Shelfie

A **free** eBook edition is available with the purchase of this print book.

CLEARLY PRINT YOUR NAME ABOVE IN UPPER CASE

Instructions to claim your free eBook edition:
1. Download the Shelfie app for Android or iOS
2. Write your name in **UPPER CASE** above
3. Use the Shelfie app to submit a photo
4. Download your eBook to any device

ISBN 978-1-68350-090-2 paperback
ISBN 978-1-68350-092-6 eBook
ISBN 978-1-68350-091-9 hardcover
Library of Congress Control Number:
2016908308

Cover Design by:
Megan Whitney
megan@creativeninjadesigns.com

Interior Design by:
Bonnie Bushman
The Whole Caboodle Graphic Design

In an effort to support local communities, raise awareness and funds, Morgan James Publishing donates a percentage of all book sales for the life of each book to Habitat for Humanity Peninsula and Greater Williamsburg.

Get involved today! Visit
www.MorganJamesBuilds.com

Dedicated to A.J.S.,
and in memory of R. K. Narayan fifteen years after his death,
who died in Madras in the wee hours of Sunday morning on May 13, 2001

PART ONE

PLACES IN
THE HEART

CHAPTER ONE

Reluctantly rising from its pacific repose, the moon melted the darkness. The bright days were growing longer now, bravely curtailing the dense darkness of the nights. In spite of a respectable northwesterly wind whistling through the woods, the Chinese chimes hanging with rigid dignity from a neatly constructed gazebo challenged the moon's obstinacy. The Indian chimes that had hung in the same place for about a quarter of a decade, before the children had all but destroyed them, had been more generous in their liberal response to the breeze's slightest touch.

Reclining under the gazebo on the east balcony of his three-story home, a solid stone villa nestled among the young mountain pine and aspen in the shadows of the ancient Cedars of Lebanon, Thomas J. Sleiman straightened at the first sign of moonlight, as if the moon demanded recognition. And indeed it did. For this night, it appeared much larger than normal, much larger even than the sun, whose radiance it now imitated.

He'd been away on one of his notorious trips, and now was soaking up the sanity of silence after an unusually hectic day at the university. The sound of the flowing river brought with it bits of conversations he'd had during the day. One persisted:

"By the way, did you know Narayan died?" asked Mr. Morrison in his still distinct British accent, though he'd lived in the Middle East, away from Britain, for fifty years.

"No! What? I didn't. When? Where?" Dr. Thomas Sleiman inquired frantically.

"In Madras, I think, or I suppose they say Chennai these days, don't they?"

"Who told you? How old was he? At what time? Where exactly was he?" continued the assistant professor, shocked and bewildered by the news.

"Well, I heard it on the BBC yesterday, May thirteenth, but I don't know the exact day or time or any of the details," said Mr. Morrison with a touch of surprise at the barrage of questions.

Oh my God, I was there in Madras when he was dying, Thomas thought. *I was probably on my way to the airport.* He imagined that the great author of timeless novels such as *The Vendor of Sweets* and *The Bachelor of Arts* might very well have expired at the precise second when he was passing by the author's house to leave India.

"It seems we were both leaving India at the same time," Thomas speculated aloud.

"I do recall hearing that he was ninety-four or ninety-five," said Mr. Morrison, disturbing Thomas's private speculations.

"Oh my God." This time he said it aloud. "I was there, Mr. Morrison. I was there when he was dying . . . ." He was not ashamed to show emotion in front of his colleague and friend, nearly forty years older.

He'd always had much older friends. There was the Catholic priest at his grade school, twenty-five years older, who took him on weekend trips when he was just ten years old; they had "philosophical" discussions sleeping out under the stars with the priest's little nephews. There was the highly distinguished American professor of literature and philosophy, twenty years older, whom he'd befriended at a Trappist monastery where he'd taken refuge for an entire month after leaving the seminary, and, as some of his critics had said, his vocation.

Leaving the seminary had been one of the first traumatic decisions of his young adult life. Another had been the decision to enter. Most everyone was shocked since he'd been a somewhat conceited teenager—his vanity a natural result of being a handsome, broad-shouldered, popular athlete who continually received praise from all quarters. Though disposed to conceit, his general and deeper disposition was one of kindness and almost humility due mostly to the sound characters of his parents, who had given him much affection, and what he always considered the precious gifts of hope and his Catholic, cosmic faith. His first love was shocked as well; she didn't believe he would go through with it, until he did. He was surprised by her reaction since they weren't going together when he made the decision. In fact, he'd kissed her only once, and that'd been a good three years earlier. But she scolded him shortly before he left for not knowing that after that kiss she vowed to marry him, even though she never told him anything about it.

The priest who inspired him to join the seminary at age nineteen was ten years older as well. Excepting celibacy, he'd been quite content with his newfound spiritual road. But when his fellow seminarian and close companion committed suicide by throwing himself into an aloof and raging sea, the young Thomas Sleiman ran away and for two years couldn't bear to look back.

The occasion of this looking back was the momentary solidarity he felt with his dead friend one lonely summer day when the first real love affair of his mature life ended in utter hopelessness. She too had been older, a medical student whom he'd met at the university in his home state in the Western United States. She was an artist of sorts, an iconographer who'd fled an oppressive Eastern European regime at the risk of her own life. He admired her courage and was captivated by the suspenseful stories she told of how she was almost detected, not once but three times as she fled Romania via Poland. He admired her intellect too. She was virtually all alone in a strange country, and Thomas too felt all alone after leaving the seminary so suddenly. For a time, they'd been a perfect match. When she left him, his first experience of despair, he realized what his friend must have felt the moment before he jumped.

Instead of jumping, Thomas held on and withdrew into long periods of silence and pathetic attempts at prayer during which he counted on the more efficacious prayers of those who loved him. He eventually returned to the seminary, although he left again a few years later after earning degrees in philosophy and theology from a reputable university in the capital city of those same United States.

When the full moon had ascended to the middle of the sky and the wind had died down to no more than a tender breeze, Thomas retired. As he dozed off, he heard again, "By the way, did you know Narayan died?"

The first person he saw at the university the following morning was Mr. Morrison. Entering in while knocking, as was his custom, he found Thomas reclining in his favorite corner chair, gazing out the window, lost in his early morning contemplation.

"Well, did you see the news last night? Narayan's death made world news for the second night in a row."

"So it's world news, is it?"

"Why, of course it is. He not only won the National Prize of the Indian Literary Academy, India's highest literary honor, but he was awarded the A.C. Benson Medal by the Royal Society of Literature in 1980, and was made an Honorary Member of the American Academy and Institute of Arts and Letters."

"I know, I know, Mr. Morrison, I meant it as a confirmation, not a question." His thoughts ran wild. *I have long known that he was great,* he mused, *and I have lately known that in some small but significant way my life was somehow to be affected by his. May thirteenth . . . May thirteenth . . . my father's birthday, the attempted assassination on the Pope's life, the Pope, my other father, the world's father, May thirteenth, the day of the apparition of the Virgin Mary to the children in Fatima in 1917. May thirteenth. Why did he die now, just as I have returned from my first trip to India, a trip that has changed me on the inside? And why was I introduced to him when and how I was?*

He went back to May thirteenth of the previous year when Graham Greene's famous novel, *The End of the Affair*, fell fatefully into his hands. That book offered redemption, of a sort, after his second extramarital love affair ended so abruptly. It'd lasted only four months, and they'd never consummated the affair, but it was as intense as anything he'd ever before experienced. And so was the guilt and pain afterward. He was indebted to Greene for this atonement and became a loyal disciple. He vowed to read everything Greene ever wrote, but struggled for months to get through the first chapter of *A Burnt Out Case*. As his lover's plane departed for India on June seventeenth, he hurriedly read the final note she'd placed in his hand before she left:

Don't feel too bad about what happened, my sweetheart; we haven't done anything so terribly wrong, have we? In fact, maybe, just maybe, God himself reserved these days for us in heaven from all eternity, for without you, I would have surely died and would have had no chance of ever returning home. You've given me another chance, another life, for I was planning to take my own. Don't you see? Don't lose heart, my heart, for if you lose heart—you, the Prince—what will happen to us, your servants? Don't worry; be strong. God will bless you and your family and give you all a long life.

A bottomless pain emerged from deep within him; it even prevented him from crying. The introductory quote from Greene's novel escaped from his mouth: "Man has places in his heart which do not yet exist and into them enters suffering so that they may have existence." It was from the great French thinker Léon Bloy, the same Bloy whose last-minute intervention into the lives of Jacques and Raïssa Oumansov Maritain prevented them from carrying out the suicide pact they'd entered into shortly after their marriage. That'd been a remarkable intervention, especially since Maritain went on to become one of the most influential philosophers of the twentieth century. But as he climbed into his jeep to leave the airport, Thomas wasn't thinking about philosophy or literature, Bloy or Greene; he was coping with the pain under the crushing sounds of departing airplanes.

"And who introduced you, Thomas, to the novels of Narayan?"

"Graham Greene," he said at once, adding thoughtfully, "they were close friends you know."

"Yes, I think I've heard that before. Greene was indeed a great writer himself, of course, but he's a bit too depressing for me."

"I really wouldn't know. I've read only one of his novels."

"And which one was that?"

Thomas feared that Mr. Morrison had been reading his mind.

"*The End of the Affair.* Have you read it?"

"A long time ago," said Dr. Morrison, as he struggled to remember the plot.

Thomas capitalized on his friend's momentary lapse, lost all inhibition, and imposed himself excitedly upon his cornered listener by recounting for him the main movements of the story. When he got to the crucial part, his friend was astonished at how animated the assistant professor had become.

He tells the story with such expression, he thought to himself.

Thomas described with great precision and accuracy all the events that unfolded in the novel on the crucial day. He repeated the date three or four times, twice in one sentence. "On June seventeenth, it was on June seventeenth that the affair ended." He explained how Maurice, one of the main characters, had found his ex-lover's journal and had read in the entry for June seventeenth the whole story of how and why she had left him and vowed never to see him again. It was a deal she had struck with her God. She'd promised her Lord that she would do anything, even give Maurice up, if, as he lay dying in front of her, God would somehow bring him back to life.

It wasn't the first, nor would it be the last time that Dr. Thomas Sleiman told the story to anyone even appearing to be interested. And each time he recalled with incredulity how it was that that novel had slipped into his hands during the very same time of his own affair and how his affair had also ended, unbelievably, on the seventeenth of June, though in quite different circumstances: in a noisy, foreign city called Beirut, which he had learned to call home. It was no wonder that the assistant professor thought of Greene as a kind of prophet whose every word had to be taken seriously and whose every novel had to be read.

This belief was only strengthened when he came across tributes paid to Greene by important critics such as Alec Guinness, who wrote upon Greene's death in April of 1991 that Greene "was a great writer who spoke brilliantly to a whole generation. He was almost prophet-like with a surprising humility." William Golding said, "Graham Greene was in a class by himself. . . . He will be read and remembered as the ultimate chronicler of twentieth-century man's consciousness and anxiety." And then there was William Faulkner who, after reading *The End of the Affair*, wrote, "For me one of the most true and moving novels of my time in anybody's language."

Thomas felt confident in his worship of Greene. So confident, in fact, that he began to share his new love with many of his colleagues in the English department and insisted that Greene's novels be added to the syllabi of the relevant literature courses at the university.

"Why don't you read any Greene in your twentieth-century literature course?" he said one day to a female colleague, a visiting professor from America.

"I haven't read anything by Greene," she said almost proudly.

"You haven't?" he blurted, hardly able to conceal his aversion.

"Is he that important?" she asked, astounded at his response.

"Yes, he's even more important than that."

"Than what?" she asked.

"Well, I mean that he's not just important; he's very important. And not only that, he's a Catholic author, and this is a Catholic university."

"Oh, you mean that we should include him simply because he's Catholic?"

"Of course not, that's not what I said. Listen, just read him and see for yourself."

"All right," she said. "And which book would you recommend?" she added sarcastically.

"*The End of the Affair*."

"Oh, I saw the movie."

Thomas nearly gave up in despair.

"That's too bad; your imagination may have already been damaged beyond repair."

"Oh, don't be ridiculous, Thomas; lend me the book."

He went back to his office and reverently took down the book from its shelf. He handled it as if it were a relic and carried it in procession to the altar of his colleague's desk where he feared that it might be scourged and sacrificed. His worst suspicions were confirmed the following morning when he found the book lying on the dusty floor of his office. As he picked it up and dusted it off, he regretted that he'd lent it to her.

"That's what I get for casting my pearls before swine," he mused, and prepared himself for an attack. Within minutes, she appeared at his office door.

"Thomas," she bellowed, "it's just like the movie. I'm sorry, but I just don't see why people think he's so good."

"You read it awfully fast," he said challengingly.

"I'm a fast reader."

He wanted to ask her about the June seventeenth entry in Sarah's journal, but he prudently restrained himself and made an excuse to get away quickly.

Before he could escape, she proclaimed sonorously, "Thomas, maybe you should stick to philosophy and let us in the English department, who are trained in literary criticism, deal with literature."

"Maybe so," he said, trying to be a good sport, and after excusing himself, hurried off to the bathroom. He felt sick to his stomach, but the feeling subsided. When he returned to his office, he saw to his horror that she was still sitting there waiting for him.

"Still here?"

"Yes. I wanted to talk to you about something."

"Feel free."

"One of my best students, a girl, of course, came to my office clearly confused and conflicted over what you've been teaching them in your philosophy course."

Thomas, though listening, noticed for the first time how radically short her hair was, and wondered secretly whether she'd always had such a repellant appearance. It wasn't just the hair, or the lack thereof, that put him off, but her entire manner; in her presence, he somehow felt guilty of his masculinity.

"Did she get specific?"

"Yes, she did. I'll tell you in a moment, but in short, she said that your assessment of good literature is entirely at odds with mine."

"Well, we all have different tastes," he said casually to avoid an argument.

"It is not about tastes, Thomas. She is my best student, and I have spent a lot of time forming her mind."

You mean brainwashing her, he said inwardly.

"It seems your principles are entirely opposed to mine, and this is causing undue stress in this poor girl's soul," she said somewhat arrogantly, and this time not without some anger in her voice.

Well, at least she believes there are such things as principles and souls, he mused silently. *Perhaps there's still hope for her.* Thomas looked at her with pity and said, "I do admire your candor, Pauline, and appreciate that you have brought this up with me directly instead of discussing it behind my back or with the dean, as another colleague of mine, who has the same complaint, often does."

She knew to whom he was referring. "Well, for your information, we have brought it up with the dean."

"We?"

"Yes, you've just admitted that others are upset as well."

"I know of only two, and you are one of them," he said confidently. Thomas was not at all threatened and thanked God there were only two against him; at his university in America, nearly the entire faculty, except two, had been against him. The Middle East, at least in this regard, had proved to be a saner place for Thomas to live and work. Pauline, who had no real long-term commitment to either the country or the university, but who had simply wanted a change from the monotony of her dull academic life in America, and so had taken a position as a visiting professor in Lebanon for a few years, was now fully agitated by Thomas's calm and confident behavior.

"You said that she got specific, correct? Will you please tell me what exactly is bothering her?"

"I've had enough agitation for today, Thomas. I don't feel like continuing this conversation. The next thing you're going to tell me is that we should be reading the complete works of Jane Austen."

Now there's a real woman, Thomas thought to himself. "You mean you don't?"

"Of course we don't."

"In heaven's name, why not? She is a woman, you know."

"We're willing to defend our reasons," she replied archly, ignoring his challenge to her brand of feminism.

"How can you deprive them of a heroine like Fanny Price of Austen's *Mansfield Park*?"

"*Mansfield Park*?" she cried. "You see, this is exactly what I'm talking about, Dr. Sleiman," she said sarcastically, refusing now to call him by his first name. "Are you not aware of the fact that critics as prominent as Kingsley Amis say that Fanny Price is 'a monster of complacency and pride,' and that Lord David Cecil once said that Fanny Price was 'a little wooden, a little charmless, and rather a prig'? And others have said worse things about her and about the novel as a whole."

"Why don't you let the students make up their own minds?"

"We've only a limited time, and I want to make sure they get the best."

"What could be better than Austen's masterful writing on the moral implications of priestly ordination as a masculine fulfillment of personal vocation and as influencing the morals of a nation at large?" said Thomas, refusing to drop the subject.

"You can't be serious, can you?"

"Of course, I'm serious. Have you ever read *Mansfield Park*, or have you just read what your critics say about it?"

"Well, if it's anything like *The End of the Affair*, I'm sure I will loathe it. And, again, please take my advice: stick to philosophy and leave literary criticism alone. It's not your field."

Nearly forgetting that she was a woman, which wasn't entirely difficult to do with this particular female, Thomas approached her to physically escort her out of his office, but he managed to compose himself, and said politely, "I'll take that into consideration, Pauline. Thank you. Now if you will excuse me, I have a class to teach."

On the way to class, he had to walk by the office of Pauline's ally, who was waxing eloquently on the superiority of the analytical tradition in front of a few students who'd gathered around him: "You've got to get that awful word mystery out of your vocabulary, or you'll never become critical academicians," he declared authoritatively. Thomas walked past unnoticed, entered his classroom at the other end of the hall, greeted his students, closed the door, and said with conviction, "Today we shall continue to gaze together at the doctrine of the angels, which conveys the awesome mystery, splendor, and unity of the cosmos itself."

Halfway through the lecture, a student raised his hand and asked deviously whether angels wore clothes, at which the whole class burst out laughing, ruining the atmosphere that Thomas had worked so hard to create. He wanted them to take angels seriously because he believed they played a crucial role in the human struggle for eternal salvation and everlasting happiness. He was just about to lose his temper when he reminded himself not to take the insult personally. *Anger is one of the seven capital sins*, he privately reminded himself. *This is exactly what the fallen angels want. If I get angry now, I will ruin everything. Anyway, I'm prepared.*

Thomas forced a smile and retrieved from his briefcase a large print of one of Raphael's famous paintings of angels. "I knew you were going to ask that, James, and actually, I'm glad you did because I must say that, as much as I admire Raphael, I do think he has done an enormous disservice to angelology."

"To what?" a biology major exclaimed, not able to control her dismay. "You mean this constitutes an entire branch of theology?"

"Yes, of course it does. I mentioned that before, didn't I?"

"But you've also been telling us that theology is a genuine science, and when you were talking about Aristotle's *Metaphysics* and *Natural Theology*, you almost had me convinced, but now I'm confused again. First of all, you've said that angels are invisible—if, that is, we assume for the sake of argument that they even exist, of which, by the way, you haven't convinced me. Secondly, how does anyone dare to imply that we can scientifically study angels, regardless of whether they are always naked or not," she said sarcastically, throwing a look of impatience at James. "I mean no disrespect, sir," she added sincerely, "but I have tried for two months now to see that theology is, as you claim, a science, and at times, as I've said, you've almost convinced me, especially when we did Natural Theology, but at other times, I feel like you're dragging us back to the Middle Ages. My biology teachers think that some of what we do in this class is a little strange."

"That's no surprise coming from biology professors, Joan," he said, not a bit put off by her comments, as she was one of his best students. "What is really troublesome, my dear, is that some of my own colleagues in the religion and philosophy departments, not to mention the English department, think I am a little strange too."

They all laughed spontaneously, which created the right moment for Thomas to continue. "Look at these ridiculous-looking angels." He held up the print of Raphael's chunky, nude, babyish angels. "These symbols have inspired still worse ones." He took out more prints of nineteenth-century angels, disgustingly girlish, soft, skinny, and forgiving, without an ounce of real authority necessary for genuine forgiveness.

"I suggest, rather, that these images are much closer to the truth." He turned out the lights and projected Fra Angelico's paintings on the classroom screen. When he turned on the lights, he saw that the mood he'd worked so hard to create before, and which James had destroyed in a reckless moment, had returned.

His thoughts raced. *I must act now to expose the demons for what they really are: egomaniacs, swollen, bloated spiritual spiders, always eating, never satisfied, forever sucking into themselves other selves in an attempt to destroy the human creature's genuine individuality.*

And act he did. Before long, nearly the entire class was open to what he was saying.

One student sitting in the back of the class looked visibly moved by the horrifying description of how the fallen angels sought literally to devour souls for spiritual food. "Sir," he proffered, "didn't you tell us before that the two great temptations of the devil and his legions were either to convince us that they didn't exist, or to convince us to give them too much attention?"

"Yes, very good, exactly."

"Then why, may I ask, have you spent so much time on the fallen angels; what about the angels of light, and what about God?"

"Thank you for asking, Dominic. I think you're ready to hear about the angels of light, and about that God whom they serve and adore. You see, whenever we are talking about the angels of light, and especially about God himself, it is always better to begin with describing what they are not. This is called, in the Christian theological tradition, the *via negativa*, the negative way. If we begin with the positive terms, we are bound to miss the point. For when I affirm something about God, as in the statement God is good, it's highly misleading because our grasp of what's good falls so infinitely short of God's actual goodness. When we deny, however, our language is more meaningful."

"And this goes for the angels of light as well?" Dominic asked.

"Yes, but in a different way, of course, since the angels of light, as powerful and beautiful and awesome as they are, are still creatures. And I've told you a number of times now that they are not physical at all; they are pure spirits; pure intellects if you will."

Dominic was ready to interject, but Thomas stopped him with a slight movement of his hand.

"Just bear with me a little longer, Dominic. I want to draw your attention to one more thing. I think that what we are going to look at now will really interest you, especially you English majors; about half of you are majoring in English, right?" A number of students began talking enthusiastically about Milton and Goethe, anxious to show off their knowledge of the theological and philosophical elements in *Paradise Lost* and *Faust*.

Thomas allowed them to talk freely, as it encouraged the other students, and because his plan was working. "I'm very impressed with what you're learning in those courses; your teachers ought to be praised, but may I suggest a few things here?"

The entire class was now open to what he was about to say.

"As much as I admire Goethe's *Faust* and Milton's *Paradise Lost*, I must side with one of my favorite writers, C. S. Lewis, against them, at least in the following respects." He moved slowly to the board and wrote in large letters, "The demons are incapable of genuine humor, authentic civility, and common sense. This is why Goethe's image of evil in the character of Mephistopheles is so harmfully misleading. The much better image is the character of Faust himself—incapable of laughter—real laughter from the heart, that is, since he is so insidiously caught up in himself."

He moved to the other side of the board and wrote in similarly large letters, "Devils and demons are not capable of high poetry or splendor of any sort whatsoever. This is why Milton's images of the devils are so deceptively confusing." And, finally, moving to the center of the board, he wrote in even larger letters, "Ruskin was right. Read Dante!"

CHAPTER TWO

"O h yes, now I remember," said Mr. Morrison. "It was a very moving and powerful novel, wasn't it? I do admire Greene, don't get me wrong, Thomas, but as I have said, his novels tend to depress me, given my disposition to introspection, that is."

"I agree with you somehow, Mr. Morrison," Thomas said in a conciliatory manner. "I had a similar experience while reading *A Burnt Out Case*." He painfully recalled that he had not yet finished it nor even come close to fulfilling his vow, though he intended to. In preparation, he read everything he could find on Greene's personal life. That's how he was first introduced to Narayan.

"How did you know they were such good friends?" Mr. Morrison asked.

"I read it somewhere. He dedicated *The Man-Eater of Malgudi* to Greene to mark more than a quarter of a century of friendship. That novel was particularly special to me because he wrote it the year I was born, in 1961."

"You mean you are barely forty? I'm nearly twice your age, you know."

"Yes, I know, Mr. Morrison. I only hope that when I am seventy-five, I'll have your zest for life and sharpness of intellect."

"Thank you. You're very kind, but age is just a number; it's all in the mind, Thomas."

He'd often heard his father say this, and he repeated it to others, but he had reservations about just how true it was, as the enigma of time always perplexed him. In his present circumstances, time seemed to drag; he sometimes experienced despair and wished he did not have to live another forty years. He was ashamed to admit this, and confessed it to the priest periodically. In his mind, it was due simply to his own selfishness and immaturity. At times, he didn't know how he would manage to live through so many more days when lately he was struggling just to get through another Sunday.

Sundays had been particularly difficult after he'd left America and moved to the Middle East. His wife, born and raised in Lebanon, had never been fully happy in America and had long looked for an opportunity to get back home. Thomas also wanted to live there as he'd enjoyed his periodic visits, beginning with the first one when he was married. He had fond memories of that first boat ride from Cyprus to Lebanon. The airport was closed in those days due to the war, but it didn't stop the young lovers from going there to get married, especially since her answer of yes to his offer of marriage was conditional on getting married back home.

Thomas was all for it. He had loved Lebanon from the moment he had heard the name as a young boy, and each time he heard it, his heart beat with a mysterious longing for something he felt he'd once had but somehow lost. He had always wanted to visit the land of his grandparents, and what better occasion than a wedding to do so. After the wedding, they went back to America, where he began teaching and working on a PhD in Philosophy. A few children and a few years later, he took a position as an assistant professor at a Catholic university in Lebanon. But he soon found out that visiting and living in a place were two totally different things. It wasn't that the assistant professor wasn't happy in his new post and country; he was, but something was missing, and that something became more pronounced in a foreign environment. He had a deep love for life, and perhaps that was one of his problems, for he always expected so much more than it usually gave him. His students and colleagues often told him he was idealistic, but instead of taking it as a criticism, he took it as a compliment.

Though his fields were philosophy and theology, he had lately come into the world of literature. He had always read, of course, and he liked to preach to his children about the importance of reading good books, but it had slowly dawned on him that the most effective medium of communication was literature and not pure philosophy, as he had previously thought. He was proud of the fact that at age twelve he had finished Tolkien's trilogy. Each time he mentioned this fact to his twelve-year-old son and eldest child, his son surprisingly reminded him of details concerning where and with whom he had read it, details that he himself had almost forgotten.

"So what exactly was it that attracted you so much to Narayan?" said Mr. Morrison one cool morning during his regular visit to Thomas's office a few days after Narayan had died.

"Well, it's hard to put a finger on it; it's not just one thing."

Mr. Morrison sat patiently waiting for an answer with a gentle smile on his face. Thomas got up from his favorite corner chair, went to his desk, and picked up one of Narayan's novels that he'd been looking at earlier in the morning. The office was filled with morning light. "For one thing, I cannot pick up one of his novels without being transported immediately to South India."

"Well, now that you've been there, were his descriptions accurate?"

Thomas moved to the end of his chair, visibly animated, and said with great seriousness and joy, "Mr. Morrison, you may think this odd, but while in India, I experienced many things that I could swear I've experienced before. On May tenth, for instance, I climbed up St. Thomas Mount in Madras. The locals call it Peria Malai in Tamil. I experienced tremendous peace on the Mount where tradition says St. Thomas, one of the twelve apostles of Christ, was martyred. On the way down, I had a great urge to look toward the southwest at some open fields with much greenery interspersed in between. I heard some voices, oddly familiar, but couldn't get a clear view of what I knew I wanted to see. Once I got to the right position, the view finally opened up, and I saw some young boys, aged ten or eleven perhaps, playing cricket. The characters of Narayan's very first novel, Swami and friends, unexpectedly came to life. But more than that, I too became a little boy again. An overwhelming gratitude at being part of the great mystery of life and death gripped me tightly and would not let go. I knew I had been there before—I knew it. I was fiercely happy and acutely sad simultaneously."

Mr. Morrison listened attentively. Thomas realized that he'd gotten carried away and directly got hold of himself. He felt he may have crossed the borders of propriety with his passionate speech. But even so, he'd also wanted to tell Mr. Morrison that the key to understanding the entire experience was to be found in the most momentous fact of all, a fact that Thomas couldn't bring himself to reveal—namely, that someone was by his side on the Mount. To reveal that this someone was a woman whom he loved profoundly, and that she'd originally been his maidservant Jhansi when he and his family had first moved to the Middle East, would have been much more than just crossing the borders of propriety. But it was true. She'd arrived in their home on August 15, 1996, one of Thomas's favorite feast days, the feast of the Assumption of Mary into heaven, body and soul. Jhansi's sister, Shivani, who had arrived shortly before her, was originally assigned to the house of Dr. Sleiman, but as fate would have it, the agency assigned her at the last minute to another house, and thus Jhansi's destiny was to be forever bound up with the destiny of Thomas Sleiman.

The agency amounted to nothing more than a cog in the machine of the organized crime industry of domestic slavery. In India, the girls had been informed that they were going to work for two years as nannies taking care of young children. It was respectable work, they were told, and the money was excellent. Little did they know their passports would be confiscated, and they would be at the mercy of their owners as live-in maids for two or three years depending on their contract. It was big business. The lucky ones, like Jhansi and her sister, ended up in Lebanon, where they could count on some degree of civility, and the really lucky ones ended up in quite decent households where they were treated as human beings; those not so lucky ended up being raped, beaten, unpaid, or just generally abused.

The sisters thought they would make enough between them in two years to pay for four dowries. They were a family of six girls, no boys. Only the eldest girl was married, and her marriage had put a tangible strain on the household economy. Financially, it made a lot of sense for them to work abroad, but their father was dead set against it. After sustained pressure from the girls, their mother, and many of their relatives, he finally gave in and agreed to let them go.

When Thomas grew reflective, his friend interrupted the silence.

"I've not experienced anything quite like what you experienced on St. Thomas Mount, but I did have an interesting occurrence in 1982. When I was working for Radio-Free Lebanon, I had a powerful dream that took me back nearly twenty years to 1963 when a Judo partner threw me down so hard that I ended up a few hours later walking around West Beirut in Judo attire, not knowing where I was. That happened in '63, mind you, and I'd forgotten all about it until the dream of '82. Since then I have had the same dream every so often. I am wandering around West Beirut, which turns suddenly into England, and then back again into Beirut."

"That's interesting, Mr. Morrison. You know, when I was young, I used to dream about Lebanon, as my grandfather liked to tell us stories about what he called the old country. We would sit with him for hours to hear over and over again how the Ottomans tried to recruit all the boys of his village into their army around the time of the Great War. We found out later that this was World War I. He always called it the Great War. We loved to hear the part about his escape out of a window while wicked soldiers shot at him as he rolled down the hill out of harm's way. We fell in love with Lebanon then. I don't quite know why, since it sounded so cruel. He told us about the famine of locusts that darkened the sky and caused mass starvation in the country, and about the attack on his village from the neighboring Muslim village, wherein some of the prominent old men of the village were hanged in their own Maronite Catholic Church. The hangings really scared us, but as he spoke, he seemed to forgive. I don't know, it was all so cruel, but I guess it also sounded mysterious and beautiful, for whenever he spoke of Lebanon, there was always magic in his voice, especially when he spoke about the Cedars of Lebanon. We were proud to be Lebanese Americans, though we understood little about Lebanon. Anyway, I used to have these dreams about living in Lebanon, and now, here I am. Recently, I have been having those same dreams, but Lebanon turns suddenly into America and then back into Lebanon."

This led them into an interesting discussion about dreams, roots, imagination, Bergson's explanations of memories, primitive art, impressionism, Proust's

Remembrance of Things Past, and about the relationship between ideas and pictures—each of them providing in turn for one another the needed intellectual stimulation without which the morning would have been more intolerable than it already was.

"Time to get to work, my friend. I'll look forward to hearing tomorrow what else it was that attracted you so much to Narayan."

"Sure enough, Mr. Morrison; thanks for the visit."

Thomas hurried back to his favorite chair, situated so he could gaze eastward toward the green valleys and steep mountains crowned with old monasteries at each peak. The mountains were old, the valley historic.

He spent the rest of the day meeting with students, correcting exams, and lamenting over the sad state of affairs in academia. This was one of his favorite themes in his civilization course.

"There is no such thing as liberal education anymore," he preached with conviction. "The Greeks sometimes afforded education for their slaves, but it was illiberal education—that is to say, not for the sake of itself, but for the sake of something else. Never did they provide liberal education for their slaves since liberal education was for man qua man to free the mind and develop the soul for virtue, to make men more human, more free."

"Are you saying, Dr. Sleiman, sir, that our high tuition is for slave education?" cried one of his students.

"Of course that's what I'm saying."

"You mean we are slaves?"

"Well, you could put it that way, yes."

Inevitably, he said to himself, "So what does that make you, Thomas?" He knew that some of his brighter students wanted to ask the same thing, but out of respect they refrained from doing so, a respect that Thomas rather enjoyed as a welcome change from the overly casual attitude of most of his university students in America.

"You see, the nineteenth-century European reformers made a huge mistake, as well intentioned as they might have been, when they made education available to everyone."

"Why is that?" was the retort.

"In making it universal, they had to cheapen it and bring down standards."

"Well, a little bit is better than nothing," they argued.

"You are absolutely right if you are talking about bread and beans, but when you are talking about liberal education, you are dead wrong. Have you never heard the saying that a little learning is a dangerous thing? No, if you are going to drink from the well of knowledge, you had better drink deeply; if you don't, you are likely to get the stale and polluted stuff on top that will eventually poison you. You must keep in mind that this educational reform was taking place during the Industrial Revolution. So the idea was to make education more practical. In other words, perhaps without knowing it, the reformers bought into the agenda of the industrialists: Don't train thinkers; train slaves for the factories. And not much has changed since then. Big business determines the curriculum of the major universities. The university is just another cog in the machine of a so-called free world-market economy that has run wild—with the worldwide weapons industry calling most of the shots."

Thomas often continued in this way unchecked until one of his students politely raised a hand to remind him that time was up. Begging their pardon, he'd continue to rant and rave about how the medieval universities had been real universities: "A study of the universe, a universe of studies . . . liberal education . . . the University of Paris . . . theology as the queen of the sciences with philosophy her handmaiden . . . ."

PART TWO

THE WOODS
ARE LOVELY

CHAPTER THREE

T homas called Mr. Morrison the following morning to inform him that he would not be in his office for the usual morning visit, as he had to attend to the duties of his other administrative position at the university.

"Very well, I'll see you tomorrow then. We'll have a lot to talk about. I still want to hear all about your travels to Iran and India."

"Yes, yes, it was an extraordinary trip. Let's talk tomorrow. Today I'm swamped."

"Of course, and by the way, I've finished the two Narayan novels you lent me. His English is delightful. I'm really beginning to see why you admire him so."

"Yes, and the more you read, the more you'll see."

Thomas went from meeting to meeting all day long, as he had no classes to teach that day. There were deans from important Western universities who had to be received and entertained. The day, as usual, was spent in discussions about possible exchange programs, joint ventures, academic affiliations, and a host of other things that Thomas had long lost interest in. When first appointed to the position, he enthusiastically proposed all kinds of exciting joint ventures with universities abroad that were committed to genuine liberal education, but he soon wearied of all the petty idiosyncrasies of academic bureaucrats and eventually just went through the motions of his job.

Sometimes he felt guilty at the end of the month when he picked up the extra compensation, but he appeased his conscience by reminding himself that the administration who paid him was the same one that had ultimately been responsible for killing his ebullience; he rationalized that at least he was not neglecting his duties. On top of this, the new administration's ostentatious modus operandi was killing the alacrity with which most of the faculty members had begun the new semester. At home, he was constantly dropping hints of his recent dissatisfaction with the academic profession in general.

At times, he thought about giving up academia altogether to become a writer just as his latest hero, Narayan, had done. "But it's so impractical," he said to himself. "It's self-deception to think I could earn a living through writing. Anyway, I ought to count my blessings. Academia has been good to me. Many of my classmates from the States still don't have tenure-track positions, whereas I'm already up for tenure next year and should be promoted to the position of associate professor."

The thought of being called an associate professor, however, scared him to death. "I don't deserve the title," he said to himself. "The professors who taught me would laugh at the idea of me being called an associate professor. No. I think I shall remain an assistant professor forever; it fits me." Many of his colleagues respected immensely his teaching ability, and his students were quite vocal about the positive impact his courses in human thought, philosophy, theology, and world religion had on them. In addition to this, he had published books and articles of fairly good quality, and was continually presenting papers on a variety of topics at reputable international conferences. And although he was becoming disillusioned with academic activity in general, he was successful in the academic environment. He knew that, given his family responsibilities, he couldn't just give it all up.

Not a few of his students practically worshipped him, which at times proved to be near disastrous, especially when these students were young, beautiful, intelligent, tall, slender, and female. His family and friends joked with him about it, and he didn't take it very seriously either until he found himself very involved with a particular young lady, who unexpectedly and mysteriously entered fiercely into his life and soul. It was the first time in thirteen years of combined teaching in America and the Middle East that such a thing had happened with one of his students. She fell in love with him, as she later told him, while he was giving a lecture on the epic of Gilgamesh. He had been drawing a comparison between it and Homer's *Odyssey* and claiming that both epics dealt in similar ways with the necessary tension between the wilderness and domestic life. Enkidu, the wild man, in the older Akkadian epic, was somehow analogous to Calypso in the Greek epic, he argued.

"I've read Homer," she interjected, "but I don't see your point at all, sir."

"What I mean is that Enkidu is the one that first prevents Gilgamesh from settling down to a domestic life of marriage and children, and Calypso, as you know, also threatens the domestic life of Odysseus. Both Enkidu and Calypso represent different dimensions of human instinct, which are not simply negative realities, but necessary ones for the taming of human instinct. In other words, the forces that endanger us are the very same ones that sustain and refurbish us."

"What exactly do you mean, sir?"

"Well, some of you are still familiar with rural living, so think about it in terms of our cultivation of the earth, in terms of the farm and the wilderness. I think it was Sir Albert Howard who said something like 'to learn the fertility of the farm, we must study the ferociousness of the forest.'"

At this, a favorite poem spontaneously came to mind, which, to his mind at least, cleverly connected the related themes. With unaffected conviction and ample expression, he recited it for them:

Whose woods these are, I think I know
His house is in the village though
He will not see me stopping here
To watch his woods fill up with snow
My little horse must think it queer
To stop without a farmhouse near

Beneath the woods and frozen lake
The darkest evening of the year

He gives his harness bells a shake
To ask if there is some mistake
The only other sound's the sweep
Of easy wind and downy flake
The woods are lovely dark and deep
But I have promises to keep
And miles to go before I sleep
And miles to go before I sleep

There was a general quiet in the room once he'd finished, and a few even had contented smiles on their faces. Thomas was pleased that he'd delighted them and genuinely satisfied that they'd learned something important. But his delight turned hastily to anguish when one student hooted out, "Sir Albert . . . ? Who wrote the poem, Dr. Sleiman?"

"No, no, the poem was penned by Robert Frost, the eminent American poet."

"Sir Frosty, sir?"

"No! Sir Albert Howard was . . . oh, never mind."

"Should we know those names for the test?" complained another student.

"No, no. My only point here is that there's a lot of wisdom in these ancient epics; the people who wrote them were positively intelligent, and we can learn a lot from their insights; they were remarkably advanced."

"As compared to what?" fired back an engineering student without even raising his hand. "You surely don't want to compare our advanced civilization to theirs, do you, sir? I mean, they knew nothing about science."

And neither do engineers, he thought privately. "Wait a minute. First of all, please raise your hand. Second, before I can respond meaningfully to your interesting and important comment, we need to have an entire session on how the meaning of that term science has changed over the ages."

"But we have automobiles and television sets," he insisted, all but ignoring his teacher's remark. "We have things those ancient societies couldn't even begin to conceive of."

The student's tone was rather mischievous, causing some of his friends to chuckle. Thomas was ready to launch into his tirade against what he considered the two most destructive inventions of the modern world, but he constrained himself and wondered whether it would make any difference, especially since he had not yet given up either his own car or television, though he wanted to desperately. "If it were up to me, I would give them up in a heartbeat, but I must live in this oppressively modern mechanized world," he said under his breath.

He wondered at times like this whether his teaching vocation had any meaning. The misconceptions and prejudices were so deep-seated in so many of his students, and even in so many of his colleagues, that he doubted whether they could ever be overcome. Inevitably, however, a savior would take flesh in the form of another question put forth by another student that would lift him out of the distress of his disheartenment.

"Could you give us another example of the kind of wisdom you are referring to, sir?"

"Why certainly, Juliet. Notice the sustained meditation on the different kinds of love in these epics. And notice how this meditation is connected to another meditation on the beauty and wisdom in nature, a meditation that has all but ceased due to the way in which modern technology has tried to master nature."

Actually, she couldn't recall precisely if it was during his explanation of the different kinds of love or during his recitation of the line from Frost, "the woods are lovely dark and deep, but I have promises to keep," that she actually gave herself up to him forever, but she knew that it'd happened sometime during the Enkidu presentation.

"What do you mean by the different kinds of love, sir?"

"Well, the ancients had different words for different kinds of love. First there was *storge*, or family love, the natural and mutual affection of parents and children and brothers and sisters, which was sometimes expanded to similar relationships such as that of a king and his people. Then there was *philia*, the happy love of intimate friends, usually, but not exclusively, between members of the same sex. Then they had *eros*, a passionate and wild love between a man and a woman with an energizing fecundity that leads to a deep and joyful renewal of life leading back to *storge* in the reality of their child. And finally, *agape*, a radically transcendent and incomprehensible divine love whose sacrificial immanence unites, orders, and perfects all of the other loves in totally unpredictable and mysterious ways. This latter word for love, although in use in Greek before the Christian era, was immortalized by the writers of the New Testament when they used it to express the essence of God as revealed in Christ crucified."

Many of his students became notably interested while others drifted away.

"Now just how this ordering and perfecting of all the other loves by *agape* takes place is one of the great Christian mysteries and can never be explained fully or defined. The best way to say something meaningful about it is to turn our attention to the Christian teaching on the Holy Trinity, wherein we are given a glance into the secret essence of God's inner life. There we find that God is a community of persons who love one another infinitely and eternally. That is to say, God is not simply one person, with different masks, but three distinct persons whose eternal ex-change of knowledge and love is so dynamic and so fast that it can never be measured. Thus it is outside of time if we understand time to be a measure of change."

At this point, one of his Muslim students, who had become restless, firmly stated, "This means there is multiplicity in God, in which case Christianity is not a monotheistic religion like Judaism or Islam."

"Precisely, Ahmed, very good." Some of the Christian students were puzzled by their teacher's answer and were visibly irritated.

"Dr. Sleiman, sir, with all due respect, I think you're wrong. Christians believe in one God just as Jews and Muslims do. Everyone knows this. What do you mean by confirming Ahmed's statement that Christianity is not a monotheistic religion like Judaism or Islam?"

"I mean that God is not a community in Judaism or in Islam; in Christianity he is, that's all. To be sure, Christians are not polytheists. They believe that the three persons each equally possess the one all-good, all-knowing, all-powerful, all-beautiful, indivisible nature—one nature in three persons! Or, if you prefer, one what and three whos! But these three whos, that is to say, three persons, have relations with one another. They have a communal life."

"Can we get back to love, sir," said one student.

"We've never left it, Nadima. Just be patient and you'll see the connection soon enough."

The idea of diversity or multiplicity in God was so foreign to Ahmed's mind that the strain began to show on his face. "For us Muslims, it is an outrage to say that God is more than one."

"It is for Christians too, Ahmed."

"I don't get it, sir. Is God three or one for Christians?"

"God is one what but three whos."

"So, three equals one and one equals three?"

"Not at all; three persons possess the same numerically one nature."

"I see; three persons make up one nature."

"No, wrong again. This would mean they share it, which would mean that the divine nature has parts, but the Christian doctrine teaches that God has no parts and is not divisible; God is one. This is why theologians insist on the term possess—God in three persons possessing a singular nature."

By this time, nearly half the class had lost interest; the other half were arguing among themselves.

"Please, let's have some order. And let's go back to the original subject. Nadima has been awfully patient."

"Thank you, sir."

"Now, we were trying to get at the way in which *agape* orders and perfects all the other loves, right? Well, I brought up the Trinity because there we find that love is a person. In fact, love is three persons who love one another so perfectly and completely, according to a sacred order, that they not only enjoy unity, but they are that unity; they are one; they have the same nature."

"What do you mean by 'according to a sacred order,' sir?"

"I mean according to a hierarchy."

"I thought you just said that they were equal, didn't you? And now you're suggesting that there is hierarchy in the Trinity?"

"In a way there is, but it isn't a hierarchy of nature; it's a hierarchy of relation, just as in a family. In fact, God is a family."

"Now you've really lost us, sir. We don't know what you are talking about."

"Look, in each and every meaningful relationship, there is an exchange, right? Persons exchange knowledge and love with each other. But these exchanges take place according to some sort of order, don't they? It's happening right here, right now. You listen to me, or pretend to listen, because I'm the teacher. My relation to you is primarily active and yours is primarily receptive. But sooner or later, I must become receptive, and you must become active. Otherwise, no real teaching or learning takes place. This accounts for a kind of order in our exchange. All relationships follow this order: parents and children, men and women, even friends take turns in activity and receptivity."

"But what does this have to do with how *agape* orders all the other loves, sir?"

"Well, the persons of the Trinity exchange knowledge and love according to this eternal pattern, which all the other loves somehow reflect. Now, of all the human loves, *eros* is the most divine. God himself has made it thus. When true lovers embrace, they enter into a realm that is outside of time. Their exchange of knowledge and love is so vibrant and immediate that one becomes the other person for a moment. This surrendering of self to the beloved in *eros* finds its perfect fulfillment in *agape*. This is why I argue that in one respect the divine in Christianity has more in common with the divine in Hinduism than it does with the monistic understanding of the divine in Islam, or even in Judaism. For in Hinduism, there is community among the gods. And these gods sometimes make sacrifices for one another. More than this, so many of the stories about the gods in this tradition are deeply connected to *eros* love. For instance, Shiva put Ganga on top of his head and hid her in his hair from his wife Parvati so that Ganga, who was mad with love for Shiva, would stop destroying the earth."

"Are you saying, sir, that you prefer an anthropomorphic paganism over the great monotheistic traditions?" asked one of the brightest and most thoughtful students in class.

"All I'm saying is that I think the concept of a divine reality that is dynamic and down-to-earth is more commensurate with the Christian concept of the divine than one that is radically transcendent and static."

"But the ancient mythologies that depict the gods getting all tangled up in sexual love seem so silly," one of the students said, and a few concurred, giggling.

"That's only because in your immaturity, you're still somewhat silly," Thomas said with a straight face. "At any rate, the point is that the ancient Greeks and Hindus understood the profound connection between *agape* and *eros*. I think this is related to what St. John meant when he wrote in the Bible that 'God is Love, and anyone who lives in love lives in God, and God lives in him.'"

Only a few of his students had managed to follow him to the end of this mini-course on love, and when he realized this he surrendered and dismissed them. Before they could get out of class, however, he informed them that their weekend assignment was to go through the epic and pick out passages referring to the different kinds of love. Then they were to write a two-page essay on how these different kinds of love were related to one another. A few students complained politely, but the assistant professor acted as if he didn't hear them and went back to his office. A few of the more inquisitive students followed him to his office to ask about Hinduism.

"Look, if you really want to get a good idea of what I'm talking about here, I would suggest you read the novels of R. K. Narayan."

"Who, sir?"

"Narayan. Here, borrow this one, *The Vendor of Sweets*. I'll be interested in knowing what you think about it."

"Thank you, sir, but do you have any standard introduction, something more scholarly?"

"Yes, but they're all so misleading when they're disconnected from the ordinary lives of ordinary people struggling with ordinary problems."

"Is that what you meant in class by dynamic and down-to-earth?"

"Yes, in a way. Listen, do you have a moment?"

"Sure."

He grabbed Narayan's *The Dark Room* off his shelf and read to them a passage describing a platform that a young boy and his two sisters set up in their home for the Hindu festival of Navaratri:

In an hour a fantastic world was raised: a world inhabited by all God's creations that the human mind had counted; creatures in all gay colors and absurd proportions and grotesque companies. There were green parrots which stood taller than the elephants beside them; there were horses of yellow and white and green colors dwarfed beside painted brinjals; there was a finger-sized Turkish soldier with not a bit of equipment missing; the fat, round-bellied merchant, wearing a coat on his bare body, squatted there, a picture of contentment, gazing at his cereals before him, unmindful of the company of a curly-tailed dog of porcelain on one side and a grimacing tiger on the other. Here and there out of the company of animals and vegetables and mortals emerged the gods—the great indigo-blue Rama, holding his mighty bow in one hand, and with his spouse, Sita, by his side, their serenity unaffected by the company about them, consisting of a lacquered wooden spoon, a very tiny celluloid doll clothed in a pink sari, a sly fox with a stolen goose in its mouth, and a balancing acrobat in leaf-green breeches; there stood the great Krishna trampling to death the demon serpent Kalinga, undistracted by the leer of a teddy bear which could beat a drum. Mortals and immortals, animals and vegetables, gods and sly foxes, acrobats and bears, warriors and cooking utensils, were all the same here, in this fantastic universe conjured out of colored paper, wood, and doll-maker's clay.

CHAPTER FOUR

O nce his student declared her love for him, his life turned upside down. He found himself lying to his wife, finding excuses to be away from home, and desperately in need of the love his young lover so abundantly and ardently offered him. He did not try to sleep with her, but he knew he would if it continued. They both knew that it was wrong, but neither could find the strength to stop. They tried a number of times but took turns giving in, and sometimes ended up back together on the same day they'd broken up. His confessor told him it was an addiction, very much like alcohol addiction, and that he would just have to go through the pain of withdrawal.

"But it's more complex than that, Father."

"Yes, I suppose so, in that the reasons you are addicted to her are more complex, but it still boils down to an unhealthy addiction, and you're going to have to give it up," his confessor stated bluntly, but with compassion.

The confessor also pointed out that in all three of the inordinate and sinful relationships he'd had in his lifetime, they had all been a matter of getting involved with a subordinate.

"Jhansi was your maid; Shivani, Jhansi's sister, was like your maid once you rescued her from the police and immigration officials and fixed her legal papers, and Juliet is your student. So what does that tell you, Thomas?"

"I honestly don't know, Father; you tell me."

"It means that all three were just classic cases of hero worship. And you like being worshipped as a hero, don't you?"

Tears welled up in Thomas's eyes, and he was barely able to say his act of contrition. "O my God, I am heartily sorry for having offended you by my pride, by my inflated ego, you, O my God, whom I should love and adore above all things and above all people. I firmly intend with the help of your grace and the prayers of the Virgin and all the saints, to sin no more and to avoid the near occasions of sin. Amen."

For many weeks afterward, Thomas wondered what hero worship really was and why the priest had said that his three love affairs were just cases of hero worship.

"Were none of these loves genuine loves after all, but simply cases of hero worship?" Thomas questioned himself. "In that case, perhaps every love is just a matter of hero worship. And perhaps our love for God is a matter of hero worship. What's wrong with hero worship anyway? Isn't it the most profound of loves? Don't we worship God as our Divine Knight in shining armor?"

During this period, Thomas Carlyle's treatise *On Heroes, Hero-Worship and the Heroic in History* coincidentally wound up on his desk. When he noticed that it had been published in 1840 on May 8, he marveled at the coincidence. *It must have a particular meaning for me*, he thought, as he raced through it looking for an answer to his latest perplexity. He didn't find exactly what he was looking for, but as he read the treatise, he was struck by Carlyle's insights into what it was that constituted a great man, a hero. Thomas had always had heroes, and he believed it was a good thing to have a hero.

"After all," the professor finally concluded, "to have a hero means simply that we love the hero; this is why we take them as heroes. So we ought not to make a distinction between love and hero worship, especially not the kind of sharp distinction that the priest was making. I must take this up with my confessor the next time I see him."

Thomas reflected deeply on who his heroes were and why. He had had sport heroes, music heroes, spiritual heroes, and literary heroes. He was captivated by Carlyle's descriptions, especially as they reminded him so much of Narayan, who, even before his death, had emerged as one of his literary heroes. He read and reread with the greatest attention the following section in Carlyle's treatise:

I should say sincerity, a deep, great genuine sincerity, is the first characteristic of all men in any way heroic. Not the sincerity that calls itself sincere, ah no, that is a very poor matter indeed; —a shallow braggart conscious sincerity; oftenest self-conceit mainly. The Great Man's sincerity is of the kind he cannot speak of, is not conscious of: nay, I suppose, he is conscious rather of insincerity; for what man can walk accurately by the law of truth for one day? No, the Great Man does not boast himself sincere, far from that; perhaps does not ask himself if he is so: I would say rather, his sincerity does not depend on himself; he cannot help being sincere! The great Fact of Existence is great to him. Fly as he will, he cannot get out of the awful presence of this Reality. His mind is so made; he is great by that, first of all. Fearful and wonderful, real as Life, real as Death, is this Universe to him. Though all men should forget its truth, and walk in a vain show, he cannot. At all moments the Flame-image glares-in upon him undeniable, there, there! I wish you to take this as my primary definition of a Great Man. A little man may have this; it is competent to all men that God has made: but a Great Man cannot be without it.

That's what made Narayan great; the fact of existence was great to him, Thomas mused. He thought about the remarkable way in which Narayan's descriptions turned ordinary facts about ordinary people and places into what they really were: great facts of existence, universal truths, full of meaning, full of value. The experience of Srinivas in Narayan's Mr. Sampath came to mind. He reached for the book and quickly found what he was looking for:

Srinivas shut his eyes and let himself down in the luxury of inactivity. Mixed sounds reached him: his wife in the kitchen, his son's voice far off, arguing with a friend, the clamour of assertions and appeals at the water-tap, a peddler woman crying "brinjals and greens" in the street—all these sounds mingled and wove into each other. Following each one to its root and source, one could trace it to a human aspiration and outlook.

The vegetable seller is crying because in her background is her home and children whose welfare is moulded by the amount of brinjals she is able to scatter into society, and there now somebody is calling her and haggling with her. Some old man very fond of them, some schoolboy making a wry face over the brinjal, diversity of tastes, the housewife striking the greatest measure of agreement, and managing thus-seeing in the crier a welcome solution to her problems of housekeeping, and now trying to give away as little of her money as possible in exchange—therein lies her greatest satisfaction. What great human forces meet and come to grips with each other between every sunrise and sunset!

Srinivas was filled with great wonder at the multitudinous-ness and vastness of the whole picture of life that this presented; tracing each noise to its source and to its conclusion back and forth, one got a picture, which was too huge even to contemplate. The vastness and infiniteness of it stirred Srinivas deeply. "That's clearly too big, even for contemplation," he remarked to himself, "because it is in that total picture we perceive God. Nothing else in creation can ever assume such proportions and diversity."

Yes, thought Thomas approvingly, after reading the passage for what must have been the hundredth time. He thought of Chandra's temporary disillusionment with love and friendship in Narayan's *Bachelor of Arts*, and how, after the one he loved married another, he had to train his mind not to think of her anymore because she was a married woman. He thought of Savitri's futile and heart-rending struggle to be semi self-reliant in Narayan's *The Dark Room*. The last episode of this novel had so affected Thomas that he remained speechless for a good ten minutes while his son, reviewing his science lessons, questioned him in vain about the origins of clouds and earthquakes.

He thought also of the heroic Nataraj in *The Man-Eater of Malgudi*, a novel for which Narayan gained great distinction. "My God, what a great writer, what a great man," he had said to himself after reading the last line of that novel. Other literary heroes came to mind: Mircea Eliade, Jane Austen, Marie Corelli, Graham Greene, Fyodor Dostoyevsky, Evelyn Waugh, Umberto Eco, Boris Pasternak, Kamala Markandaya, V. S. Naipaul, Irene Nimarovsky, Aldous Huxley, Iris Murdoch, Anton Chekhov, John Updike, Thomas Hardy, Chinua Achebe, Maiteryi Devi—and even Henry James, whom Thomas had originally disliked, but whose writings had lately so impressed him that he posted an excerpt on his office door one semester:

> Life is, in fact, a battle. Evil is insolent and strong; beauty enchanting but rare; goodness very apt to be weak; folly very apt to be defiant; wickedness to carry the day; imbeciles to be in great places, people of sense in small, and mankind generally unhappy. But the world as it stands is no illusion, no phantasm, no evil dream of a night; we wake up to it again forever and ever; we can neither forget it nor deny it nor dispense with it.

"The great fact of existence . . . Carlyle was right," he reflected, as he taped the quote from James on his office door.

CHAPTER FIVE

After four months of seeing one another nearly every day, a concrete opportunity forced Thomas and Juliet to be apart for ten days. Thomas was invited to Iran to deliver a paper at an important international conference on human rights, a paper that he ended up dedicating to her. They literally attacked one another with kisses and hugs a few hours before he departed as they clandestinely met in one of their usual hideouts. She begged him for the last time not to go to India after the conference in Iran, as she now knew all about Jhansi.

"I've told you a thousand times, *hyatee*, I'm just worried about her. She refuses to marry, and her father won't allow her to become a nun, as she had originally wanted to do before she came to Lebanon. She never wanted to get married."

"But it's not your business anymore; what are you going there to do?"

"I thought that perhaps I could talk to her father and convince him to let her enter the convent."

"Do you have to go there to do that? You like playing the hero, don't you?"

Thomas was silent for a moment and became a bit angry. After two or three minutes, he said rather harshly, "I've told you already. I'm also going there to establish contacts with some important universities. And you know that ever since I worked with Mother Teresa's Missionaries of Charity sisters as a young seminarian, I have always wanted to visit India. It's a dream of mine."

"So is she, but either you don't realize it yet, or you're not telling me about it."

"You're my dream, sweetheart," he murmured as he reached out and brought her close to him.

"For how long?" she said desperately.

Thomas sometimes regretted that he had ever told her about Jhansi. He recalled vividly the night he had done so. They had met at an old monastery near his house, the second time they had met there.

"How long do you have?" he asked, as she climbed into his vehicle.

"Just fifteen minutes; my parents are waiting for me."

It would prove to be a familiar dialogue over the next four months as they precariously sought to find a few minutes each day just to hold one another tightly and whisper intimacies into each other's ears. They were in the same spot that night that they'd been in when she'd first hugged him and told him she loved him. She'd told him once before in his office, and he was completely comfortable hearing her say it, but the circumstances were quite different then. For one thing, he still looked on her as his student, and therefore did not feel *eros* love when she said it. That day in his office, she was listening to him explain how, according to the speculation of certain Catholic theologians, obedience and freedom were the same thing before the original Fall of Adam and Eve. These remarks had followed her comment about never wanting to get married, which surprised him based on what he thought he knew of her personality.

"Why not?" he asked her.

"I want always to be free."

"But true freedom is found in obedience."

"How so?" she asked challengingly.

"Well, you're a Christian; you know the words of Our Lord: 'The truth shall set you free.'"

"Fine, but he also said, 'I am the truth,' so this means that Christ shall set me free, not some lazy husband who can't be trusted to remain loyal."

Thomas was amused and attracted by her intelligence and valiancy. He had always thought of her as a rather shy girl who was somewhat unsure of herself.

"Well, just make sure you marry someone who isn't lazy and who will remain loyal," he said rather casually.

"Such a man doesn't exist, sir," she said respectfully this time, as if she had suddenly realized that she was addressing her teacher, who was also a man.

"Really?"

"I know of no happy marriage. And . . . I have . . . just recently learned," she said, choking back tears, "that the only man I trusted to be totally faithful, my . . . my . . . father, has . . . turned out . . . not to be."

"Anyone can make a mistake, Juliet."

"What?" she said, returning to her challenging tone that bordered on impoliteness. "You men are all the same," she all but shouted.

Thomas grew silent, stunned by her abrupt upheaval. After a few moments of dead silence, she collected herself and apologized.

"I am sorry, sir. You didn't deserve that. I don't have a right to speak to you like that."

"Not at all—don't worry. I'm not offended," he said calmly and seriously. "You've been hurt deeply, Juliet, that's evident, and not only by your father."

At this, the tears poured plentifully down her full cheeks as she grasped for the tissues to hide her wounds.

"You're right, we men can be ruthless at times. I am sorry."

Past feelings of guilt stung him sharply. He thought of his own daughter, only six, and vowed never to hurt her like this, and prayed that no man would ever bruise her in this brutal way.

"I know of no one who is happily married, sir," she said again.

"I am," he said.

At this, she composed herself and brought the conversation back to speculative theology.

"So, you were saying that there was no opposition between obedience and freedom before the Fall?"

"Yes, that's right, and not only that, but neither were virginity and fecundity opposed."

"You mean before the Fall I could have been a mother and a virgin at the same time?"

"Precisely."

"Now that's appealing. I have always wanted children; it's just a husband I don't want. And given today's in vitro fertilization technology, I think I could pull it off," she said half-jokingly.

"Well, it wouldn't have worked quite like that. You still would have had to have a husband, but the marital act would have been such a perfect expression of love and selflessness that there would have been no rupture to soul or body."

"No rupture?"

"No. Only rapture! Perfect ecstasy. Perfect unity. The woman's body and soul, in complete harmony, would have received man's body and soul, also in complete harmony: woman perfectly receiving man in a giving sort of way. Man perfectly giving himself to woman in a receiving sort of way. And even when bearing children, there would have been no rupture to woman's body."

"You mean without pain?"

"Well, only with the good kind of pain—you know, the kind of pain you experience after a good workout or a morning stretch. That's why the book of Genesis says, 'I will intensify your pains at childbirth.'"

"I see. I see. I think I'm beginning to understand. Tell me more."

"Okay. Then God says to the woman, 'Your urge shall be for your husband, and he shall be your master.'"

"Stop it! If that's what our Holy Scriptures say, then I no longer find them holy."

"No! You don't understand. It wasn't God's idea for man to be the master of woman. It's a result of the Fall, of sin, of disobedience; this is a description of the disordered world. God's idea was, as the Rabbis say, for woman to be man's partner, equal in dignity, created not from his foot, to be lower than him, nor from his head to be higher and rule him, but from his side, his rib, from his very heart to be his companion. In fact, the Rabbis play on the word for rib in Hebrew as it is similar to the word for heart."

At this, she began to believe in him and to see his beauty more deeply than before, and almost in spite of herself, uttered inadvertently,

"Sir, you know what?"

"Yes," he said gently.

"I love you." She voiced it with such purity that Thomas felt remarkably gratified and simply looked at her and said "thank you."

But the circumstances in his car on that first night they were alone outside the university, in the lonely monastery parking lot, were quite different. She had reached out then and embraced him.

"Now I am happy. Now I am finally happy. I love you. Do you love me?"

He was puzzled by the question and wanted to say, "I hardly know you," but instead asked, "Can't you feel it?"

"Yes," she said joyfully. "I do. I do. Never leave me. Promise that you'll never leave me."

"I promise," he said fortuitously. And so on this second night in the same lonely parking lot when she told him she only had fifteen minutes, much had changed. He leaned in to kiss her, but she stopped him.

"I have to know something first."

"What is it?"

"Have you ever been with another woman besides your wife?"

"What?"

"I mean since you've been married." She looked at him with a level gaze.

Thomas felt cornered. "Why do you ask?"

"Because I have to know if you really love me."

Thomas was perplexed. *Have I initiated everything*, he wondered, *or has she?*

He was ashamed to tell her about Jhansi, but for some inexplicable reason he believed he must. He was also ashamed that at thirty-nine years of age, he had tried to kiss his nineteen-year-old student.

"I'm waiting," she said, as if she were his wife.

He told her that Jhansi had come from India not expecting to be a maid. She had been deceived. She was educated, patient, strong, self-giving, feminine, great with kids, had a job at a bookstore, knew computers, was extremely intelligent, and beautiful.

"It sounds as if you're in class posing an argument of some sort. What are you saying?"

"It's a complicated story."

"I'm listening." She settled back in the car seat and waited.

"There's no time now to tell you everything."

"Just a simple yes or no is enough; you'll tell me the details later."

Thomas was getting more and more flustered, and resented that she had cornered him.

She has no right to ask me such a question.

"Well? Yes or no?"

"What do you mean by have I ever been with someone besides my wife?"

"Have you ever made love to another woman since you were married?"

"No," he said firmly, "but I . . . kissed Jhansi."

"Did you love her?"

"I suppose I grew to, yes."

"I have to go now. My parents are waiting."

"Wait, that's not fair. I didn't explain the circumstances."

"Maybe tomorrow you will. Goodnight."

With that, she got quickly out of his car and into hers, and sped away. Thomas grew angry.

"She thinks I am a hypocrite now. I teach one thing and do another," he said aloud.

Perhaps you are, came another voice from he knew not where.

"And not only that, she gets me to desire her, and then she hits me with all of this," he whispered to himself.

Thomas sat in his car for a long time, confused and angry.

"What's wrong with me?" he asked aloud, as an old familiar pain returned. He finally got out of the car, the intensity of his own thoughts suffocating him.

"Perhaps I just need to walk a bit."

The view of Beirut was stunning from the mountains; the flickering lights of the ancient city, as it jutted out into the Mediterranean, seemed to be floating on that timeless sea. Hundreds of small fishing boats were sparkling in the wet dark harbor not far from the ruins of one of the earliest law schools in civilization:

the Roman law school, destroyed long ago by a massive earthquake. The city had been built and destroyed seven times, and boasted of being the second oldest inhabited city in the world, second only to Byblos a few miles north. The latest restoration of Beirut had sought to undo the damage of a brutal and insane war, commonly referred to by outsiders as a civil war, though most Lebanese knew it was much more complicated and controversial than that. The person whose rise to power and international fame destined him to take on the massive job of rebuilding Beirut, also turned out to be quite complicated and controversial as well because the reconstruction brought insurmountable and scandalous public debt. People from around the globe marveled at the restoration, but the wounds of war festered beneath the surface.

Refreshed by the night air, he made his way back home. Everyone had gone to bed, and so he decided to sleep in the front room so as not to disturb the family, who were all enjoying the restful sleep of the just and the innocent, but not he. As soon as he lay down to sleep, the suffocation returned. He sat up on the couch wondering what he would say to her if she ever consented to see him again. He replayed the conversation over and over in his thoughts.

"Why did I tell her anything?" he questioned himself. "And why am I so empty? How can I need her so much so soon?"

He then seized the crucifix from a little altar in the corner of the room next to a half-consumed candlestick and, holding it close to his face, poured out his frustration to his Lord.

"Day after day I tell my students that you are the lover of mankind, that you are the divine groom who satisfies the human heart in ways that no human being ever can. I quote one of your saints who said that our hearts were made for you alone, and they are restless until they rest in you. I tell them that you are the fountain of love, the source of joy, and that human loves are just flickering sparks of light compared to the sun of your tender and divine love, but I don't know if I really believe that, Lord. If it's true, why am I starving to death? Why this abstruse loneliness? Why do I so severely need the love of this young woman?"

The next day they were able to meet outside the university in an isolated spot that became a favorite over time. It was a beautiful place in the woods overlooking the river. He apologized for trying to kiss her the night before and assured her that he wouldn't do it again. He surprised himself as he told her about the details leading up to that first kiss with Jhansi.

"You see, I'm used to a lot of love. My former confessor and very close priest friend in America once told me that I have a great capacity to love because I've been loved so much. He warned me against vanity and selfishness, though, and often told me I had a strong tendency toward inordinate self-love."

"What does inordinate mean here?"

He treasured the way the words sounded in her questions. They reminded him, as she sometimes did too, of his younger sister, Marie, to whom he had always been especially close. Happy to play the role of teacher, as it gave him security, he confidently said, "That's a good question; it means the bad kind of self-love, which is always turned inward instead of orientated toward others." Even as he was speaking, his thoughts went back some months earlier to another student who'd followed him to his office after the mini love lecture to ask him about the place of self-love among the other loves.

"You've got to read the latter part of Aristotle's *Ethics*," he had told him, "where Aristotle considers directly the relation of self-love to the other loves."

Juliet could tell that he wasn't completely with her in his thoughts.

"What are you thinking about, sir?"

"Oh, about a conversation I had a while back with a student on the subject of self-love."

"A boy or a girl?" she asked with noticeable jealousy.

"A boy, a very good student."

"That's good," she said, relieved.

Her need for him at this point was intense. She called it love, but it was more like hunger, and it had been growing in her for a long time. She wanted to possess and consume him, and he sensed it; it awakened in him the desire to do the same to her, unleashing a hunger that he had never known before, and which, before long, he also would call love.

"But I still don't get it. You've confused me. Doesn't self-love necessarily have to be directed toward the self?"

"Yes, yes, good, but . . . you've got to read Aristotle's *Ethics*, and then you'll see that—"

"Fine, I will, but can we please get back to Jhansi?" she said, cutting him off.

"It's all related, Juliet; don't you see?"

"Please, my dear teacher," she said sincerely.

"I'm just answering your questions, my dear student." They both laughed and he continued.

"To make a long story short, I guess I've been unusually lonely since I left my life in America." He'd surprised himself with how open he'd become with her.

"Don't you like it here?"

"It's not that, I do like it. I like my job, I'm happy with our neighborhood and the schools; my children are learning three languages. I'm glad that my wife has her family close to her. And the landscape is beautiful. Just look at this valley." They gazed at the historic riverbed far beneath them.

A wild river, born beneath the passion of an equally wild winter in the snow-covered mountains, made its way for the tired Mediterranean Sea. It wasn't a long journey at all, just a few miles and a few hours west, and the lonely river found its home in the same place it originated.

"Where else can you see the snow and the sea at the same time? If you stretch out your arms, you can nearly touch them both at the same time. This valley has witnessed the likes of Alexander the Great and the Crusader armies, you know."

"No, I didn't know."

"Oh yes. And just thirty miles to the south over there," he said, pointing as if he could see it, "is the famous city of Tyre."

"You mean Sur, right?"

"Yes, of course. Did you know that from there the Cedars of Lebanon were exported to the great and wise King Solomon, or Suleiman, as they say here, to build the first Jewish temple to Yahweh?"

"I've never heard that."

"You haven't? Why not?"

"We were taught nothing about Jewish history in school. In fact, I recently learned that the twenty-four books of the Hebrew Bible are all recognized by us Christians as the inspired Word of God. I went all through Catholic grade school not knowing anything about the Old Testament. When we did refer to it, it was always in terms that were semi-derogatory."

"What a pity. Is there anything in this country that isn't politicized? Now don't tell me you're not aware of the fact that Jesus was raised just about another thirty miles south of Tyre, over there," he said, again pointing as if he could see the ancient village of Nazareth.

"I guess I knew that what people call the Holy Land was somewhere around us, but I never knew it was so close."

Thomas looked at her as if unable to comprehend what she was saying.

"I told you," she said defensively, "we were taught nothing about that region; we ignored it as if it didn't exist. You know the history and geography of this region better than most of us natives do."

After a few seconds of silence, she said, "So this Jhansi took away the loneliness, huh?"

The discomfort of the previous night returned, and he tried to get back to the subject of Tyre.

"Speaking of Tyre, did you know that Shakespeare had a story about a prince of Tyre named Pericles? Did you ever read it?"

"I'll read it for your sake someday, but now will you please answer my question?"

Thomas was put off and feared something similar to the night before was about to happen, but said in spite of himself, "Yes, I suppose she did, but must you refer to her as 'this Jhansi'?" no longer feeling guilty about his affection for his former maid. "Can't you simply say her name?"

"I'm sorry. I didn't mean to be rude."

Thomas's desire for Juliet vanished, and no longer caring what she thought of the whole matter, he said in a rough tone,

"Are you of the same opinion as my wife simply because she was a maid?"

"What do you mean?"

"When I told my wife all of this, she was more upset about the fact that it was our maid than she was about the actual kiss of disloyalty. She even said it wouldn't have been so hard had it been one of the beautiful girls at the university." He added mentally, *someone like you, I suppose.*

Juliet was still and quiet.

"But the fact that she was our maid, and black, and from India . . ."

"What? You told your wife. Why?"

"I couldn't hide it, and she sensed it. It was the first time in over ten years of marriage that I'd kissed another woman, although she would never consent to the fact that she was a woman; she insisted on calling her the maid."

Juliet now took her turn at playing teacher and said pontifically, "I think you were wrong to tell her, and I think she was wrong in feeling worse simply because Jhansi was a maid."

Thomas looked at her seriously and deeply.

Weakened by his presence, which had become unusually strong now, she added, "After all, if you were attracted to her, she must have been. . ."

"Been what?"

"Very, very special," she said shyly, giving herself away.

"Thank you. It's good to hear you say that. I ceased to look on her as a maid. We'd become friends over the course of two years. We often played word games together with the kids, which she always won, even though English was her fourth language after Tamil, Hindi, and Kannada. We prayed together, and we were silent together, especially in the mornings, as my wife likes to sleep in. She could anticipate my needs, small and large ones."

"Do you think she loved you from the beginning?"

"No, of course not! She wouldn't allow herself; she knew it wasn't proper."

"And so how did these massive walls of propriety finally collapse?" she asked sarcastically.

"Actually, I asked her that same question, and she explained it all in a letter; would you like to read it?" he fired back sardonically.

"Just tell me," she demanded, and she came so close to him that he could feel her breasts.

Weakened by her presence, and with the desire for her returning, Thomas obeyed.

"Well, after she had been with us for about two years, our baby son took ill one cold New Year's night and was hospitalized due to a severe case of bronchitis; he almost died. For about a month, Jhansi and I were running the household together as my wife stayed with our son. It was a difficult time for everyone. My wife suffered a lot, poor thing; thank God, she had her family next to her. Jhansi too was extremely worried as she thought of the baby as hers and loved him dearly; after all, she helped raise him. I came home late from the hospital one night and asked her to give me a massage, which she was in the habit of doing for my wife, but not for me."

Thomas paused. He was amazed that he was telling her so much about his personal life and wondered what had come over him.

"Go on. Please go on," she implored.

Thomas obeyed. "I asked her to massage my feet, which she'd never done. Then I showed her how to do it by reaching out and massaging hers. I thought nothing of it, really, but as she later told me in her letter, something changed inside her in that moment. She wrote—rather dramatically, I thought—that she felt as though she'd died only to be reborn in a better and more real world. She even remembered the date and the time. I think she said it was January twelfth. I knew nothing about it; she hid it for seven months."

"And why did she finally reveal it?"

"Are you judging her?" he snapped, and he stepped away from her.

"No. Absolutely not! Poor girl, I can feel . . . almost . . . what she felt," and she added hesitatingly, "minus three months."

At this, he looked deeply at her again. She reached out and kissed him passionately. "I love you. I really love you," she whispered. "Tell me more. Go on. What happened?"

Thomas was beside himself. He was happy that she had secretly loved him for so long and overwhelmed at the way her mouth so genuinely expressed it.

"That's about it," he said, no longer thinking about Jhansi, and still taking in the wild power of Juliet's kiss.

"What do you mean, that's about it? Why and how did she finally reveal it?"

Thomas surrendered and forced himself to recall the events of that summer day when his wife and children were thousands of miles away. "I picked her up one day from the house of my wife's relatives. She had been moving all week from one relative's house to another for house cleaning. When I picked her up, she was tired and down; it was the first time I had seen her like that. She missed our children. She missed our house. She missed my wife. And I soon found out that she missed me too. We had to go back to the house so she could do some washing and cleaning. When we got there, I suggested that she rest a bit, which she did. And then somehow it came out that she liked me."

"Somehow? That she liked you?"

"Yes, we had been joking about something when she suddenly got serious and told me that she was happy to be back home. I told her that I was happy to hear her refer to our home as her home. She said it was me who made it a home for her. It was then that I began to look at her differently. I really don't know what happened."

Before Thomas knew what he was saying, he dreamily continued, "We gently held each other, and I could feel, without touching them, her swelling breasts beneath her white and lavender sari. Then I felt them and kissed her softly; it was her first kiss. She was twenty-two years old."

"And did you tell her that you liked her too?" whispered Juliet, feeling the swelling of her own breasts now.

"Yes, I did tell her that. In one instant, everything changed for me. I tasted her goodness from the inside, and I liked it. Soon I began to love it. I began to love her."

Juliet was listening attentively, and now, for some reason, without any jealousy.

"Are you still in love with her?"

"What do you mean by love? I don't know. I haven't seen her for nearly two years now. We all agreed that it was best for her to go back before her contract was up, which she did, on May eighth. I can still see her standing there at the airport. She stared at me as if she were dead. I wanted to look at her and say so much to her, but my wife was there."

"Are you still in love with her?" she repeated.

The feeling of being kissed so strongly and with so much affection just a few minutes earlier overwhelmed him again. He looked directly at her swelling breasts with her nipples nearly bursting through her blouse. He gently placed his left hand on her breast and the other on her face. She closed her eyes and groaned agreeably. And without answering her question, he authoritatively took her tightly into his arms and kissed her from the depths of his being, overpowering both her young, firm body and her tender soul.

CHAPTER SIX

From that moment forward, Thomas found a way to see her each and every day until his departure to Iran. And without fail, she asked him at least once a day whether he loved her.

"Of course I do," was his standard response. At which her response was always, "How much?"

Moments before he left for the airport was no exception: "Do you love me?"

"Of course I do."

"Say it."

"I love you."

"Again."

"I love you."

"Again"

"I love you. I love you."

"But not like I love you. I love you more than any woman has ever loved you, more than your wife does, more than Jhansi does, even more than your mother does. Please don't go, my love. Please don't go to India. Just go to the conference in Iran and come back early. Don't tell anyone you're coming back early, and we'll spend the time together. Please don't go."

"Try to understand, Juliet. I explained it all to you during our boat ride yesterday, remember?"

"How can I forget those moments? I'll treasure them forever."

"Wait for me. I'll be back in ten days."

"Ten days? I can't live without you for even one day, and you know that. How can you leave me so easily, and for ten days? Don't go, *elbee*. Don't go."

He called her from the airport before departing, and the conversation was much of the same. He kept her picture next to him on the airplane. When he arrived in Qatar, somewhere in the sands of the desert, where he had to stay for a night before catching the connecting flight to Iran, he put it next to his bed in his lonely hotel room. Each time he looked at her picture, he kissed it and pressed it to his heart. He'd become recklessly close to her and wondered how he would ever leave her.

That night, bits and pieces of the conversation he'd had with Juliet the day before played over and over in his mind: "I've told you already, I'm also going there to establish contacts with some important universities. And you know that ever since I worked with Mother Teresa's Missionaries of Charity sisters as a young seminarian in Washington, DC, I have always wanted to visit India. It's a dream of mine."

"So is Jhansi, but either you don't realize it yet, or you're not telling me."

"You're my dream, sweetheart."

"For how long?"

Thomas did dream that night in his lonely Qatar hotel room, but not about Juliet. He was walking in the evening on the shores of Lake Victoria in some East African country when a beautiful black maiden approached him from behind, whispering his name and urging him to follow her. They walked together in silence for a while; the only sound was the supple and smooth splash of the lake's waves on the shore. Eventually she broke away and went up a steep hill; he followed her on a red-dirt road for a long time, gradually moving farther and farther away from the lake. He watched her body from behind, and her graceful walk mesmerized him. Most of her back and waist were exposed. She had only a white silk cloth tied around her lower body that just barely covered her well-defined buttocks.

The white cloth perfectly complemented her smooth black skin in color and form. Her hips moved back and forth with gentle seductive power. This consistent sway of feminine movement gave him ecstatic comfort and even happiness. She entered her hut and turned around without smiling, her dark, black face now aflame with such light that he couldn't make out who it was. He fell to his knees in front of her and slowly pressed his chest against her thighs and his head against her waist, wrapping his arms around her lower body. He wept tears of pleasure and felt great peace when a scream startled him. He jumped up and saw a young boy running toward him with blood streaming down his face from a cracked skull. The boy was shouting pathetically, "My father, they have killed me . . . my father, they have killed me." Thomas awoke with horror and stayed awake for the better part of an hour trying to remember where he had heard or read those words before. He thought they were in a novel he had read recently, but he wasn't sure.

When he finally fell asleep again, he was back with the beautiful East African maiden. The same scenario by the lake unfolded. He followed the maiden up the steep hill, the same desire for her growing stronger with each step; this time when he entered her hut, he tried to seduce her. He thought it was Jhansi, but was startled to see it was not when she turned around. The shock nearly jolted him out of the dream. Half-conscious now, he tossed and turned fearing that the horror of the little boy crying "My father, they have killed me . . . my father, they have killed me" would return; but sensing he was safe from the dreadful sound of the little boy's voice, he gave in and fell back into deep sleep once again. The beautiful black face, bathed in light, appeared again in the hut, which had now been transformed into an Indian ashram. She took him by the hand and lovingly led him to a small wooden table in the corner of the room on which lay an old book with a handsome binding. A half-consumed candle was struggling for life. There were no lights. The entire planet seemed plunged in darkness.

He picked it up and struggled to read the title: *The Complete Literary Works of Thomas Sleiman*, edited by A. S. Jhansi Rupali Kaloor on January 12. Published in memory of the seventh anniversary of her death.

He opened the book and read the table of contents: *Short Stories*: The Turtle of the Sea or the Net; That Man in His Car; January 12; On Precious Stones; Just a Small Miracle; Lake Victoria; Slightly South of the Equator. *Critical Works*: The Darkness Drops Again; The Brilliance of Marie Corelli: A Critical Study of the Romances of Marie Corelli. *Poems*: The Rain; My Blistering Lips; The Horse; The Wedding Feast; But I'm a Woman; Good Morning. *Novels*: An Assistant Professor.

Someone had handwritten at the bottom of the page: "T. S. apparently never finished or published the one novel he spent his life on." He slowly thumbed through the book, his eyes roaming the pages, searching for the short story titled "January 12," which he found on page forty-three, and began reading:

January 12
(A short story)

It began as most other days. She sat up in bed, made the sign of the cross, and whispered a soft "good morning" to her mother, who had awoken her. Rays of white light were just beginning to lighten the darkness of her room when the date suddenly dawned on her. When her mother left the room, she sighed and said to herself, "January twelfth again; another year gone by. Oh well, I'll celebrate alone, I suppose."

"With whom are you speaking?" said her mother from the little kitchen adjacent to her room.

"Myself, Amma."

"About what, dear?"

She wanted badly to tell her mother everything, but prudently refrained.

"Nothing," she barely managed to say, encouraged by the sudden thought of sharing it instead with her best friend at work. This new hope helped her jump out of bed to choose the white and lavender sari, the very one she had been wearing on that day.

"Coffee's ready."

She appeared a few moments later, took her seat on the floor mat next to her mom, and gladly received from her loving hands the hot fresh cup of coffee.

"Mmm . . . smells so good. I don't know what's better, the taste or the smell."

"Well, they go together, don't they? One completes the other. So are you going to tell me why you were talking to yourself so early in the morning?"

"Oh, would it have been less unusual if it'd been later in the day?"

"Why yes! As the day progresses, so does the madness; by evening, I suspect most people are talking to themselves. Or if they're not, they should be."

"It's nothing, Mom, really, I was just . . ."

"Please, daughter, spare yourself the trouble. I know something's on your mind. It has been there ever since you returned here to India. I wonder if it was wise for us to send you abroad to work as a nanny in the first place."

"Oh Mother, must we begin with all this so early in the morning?" She quickly changed the subject to enjoy the rest of her coffee in peace.

"Bye, Amma. Have a good day. See you this evening."

On her way to work, she rehearsed precisely how to bring up the subject with her friend.

"Surely she will think it not only odd, but perhaps even immoral," she murmured to herself. "On the other hand, maybe not—after all, it wasn't immoral, I don't think; it just happened, that's all. If she's really my best friend, she'll understand. Of course she will; she knows me," she assured herself.

The forty-five-minute bus ride had come to an end, but she'd hardly noticed because her thoughts were too full of him. She barely made it off at the right stop and found her friend waiting for her in the usual spot. Her friend Sita came from quite a distance as well, but regularly arrived before Rupali did. They had met in the same place for nearly two years. They would then get on an express train, arm in arm, for the second leg of the journey, a twenty-minute slash through town that brought them within ten minutes' walking distance from the office where Rupali worked as a receptionist and Sita as an accountant.

"Wow," Sita said this morning when they first met. "Are you getting married today? You look absolutely gorgeous; what a beautiful sari."

"What do you mean getting married? I am."

"Oh, I see," she said giggling, "and where is he hiding?"

"Over there," Rupali said, pointing toward the northwest, as a new and fresh light appeared in her face.

"Must be quite rich then since that's the affluent part of Chennai, isn't it?"

"Well, yes. He is rich, but not financially, and he's not in Chennai," she declared emphatically. "He's further north and further west."

"Oh, further northwest, then. Let's see," Sita said teasingly, enjoying what she took to be a little game. "If we keep going north and west, we end up in . . . oh, I've got it, perhaps he's in Bombay, I mean Mumbai. Right?"

"Wrong. Further west."

"I see. He's not in India, then? Okay, I give up. Who is he, and where is he hiding? And more importantly, I suppose, does he know he's married?" They both burst out laughing until Rupali composed herself, took a deep breath, and announced with a perfectly straight and serious face, "He lives in the Middle East, and was once my boss."

Not taking her seriously, Sita began to joke again, but Rupali remained solemn.

When she noticed that Rupali wasn't laughing, Sita got serious too.

"What?" she finally blurted out. "You can't be serious?"

"And why can't I be?"

"Because he's already married, and he is a Christian, and he has a number of adorable children, from what you've told me."

"Thanks for reminding me; I already know all that. Listen to me, my dear and best friend, we are secretly married; we pledged our love to one another two years ago today. And we are now making plans to see each other, but as yet it is unclear as to how we're going to manage it."

"Rupali," Sita said sternly in a raised voice, "he's a married Christian man."

"I know that! That's why we're unsure as to how to make the proper arrangements."

"Proper arrangements!" her friend said in dismay. "Are you out of your mind?"

"Are you scolding me as my mother would?"

"Of course I am. I am sure you haven't told your mother anyway, have you? It's a stupid, silly plan, and it will lead nowhere. I'm amazed at you!"

Rupali quickly crumpled up the yellow notepaper she'd been planning to share with her friend and threw it down onto the railway tracks where it took its place next to an already existing pile of garbage that decorated the train station.

"What was that?"

"It was the stupid, silly poem I'd wanted to show you today," she cried, exploding into tears. "I thought you, of all people, would understand, or at least hear me out."

"Understand what, my dear friend? Understand that you're planning to take a man away from his wife and children—something that would destroy him, his family, and you?"

On hearing these words, Rupali violently broke away from her friend's arm and took a seat on a lonely public bench. She waited all alone for the express, but kept her eyes focused on the pile of garbage next to the tracks where her rejected poem lay abandoned on a twisted piece of fading yellow notepaper. Her friend eventually followed her and sat down gently by her side. Rupali got up abruptly and said rather rudely, "Go sit somewhere else, please. I didn't invite your company."

"This is a public bench. I've no need of an invitation."

The long two-minute silence that ensued was obscenely interrupted by the sound of the oncoming express train they'd been waiting for. In a flash, Rupali dashed toward the tracks and jumped down, casting herself across them in such a way as to clutch the twisted piece of paper with her right hand. A threatening horn sounded as the conductor saw the figure of a woman on the tracks.

"Rupali, Rupali!" Sita screamed wildly. "Get up, I beg you, get up, get up!"

Rupali lay deathly still and braced herself to be cut in two.

"Rupali, Rupali . . . get up, I beg you, get up, for God's sake, get up my friend, get up!" But it was as if Rupali heard nothing but the deafening sound of the oncoming train. Others began shouting and screaming as the whole station was by now in a horrible uproar, for it was clear that the train could not stop.

"Rupali, my friend," Sita begged savagely for the last time. "If you die, how will you ever see him again?"

At this, Rupali's despair vanished instantly, and with a hope that knew no limits, she heroically moved herself off the tracks and extended her arms to the outstretched hands of her friend. The screeching steel blades of the angry express slightly tore the hem of her sari as the two girls fell hard on the ground above. They wept in each other's arms, until so embarrassed by the crowd that'd gathered around them, they got up and made their way slowly to the train to take their seats. Still clutching the paper desperately, Rupali placed her head on Sita's shoulder.

"Let me read it now, my dear Rupali," she said with the utmost tenderness and sincerity.

Rupali surrendered it, closed her eyes, and fell fast asleep. Sita unraveled the crumpled paper, smoothed it as best she could, and read the title: "Secret Marriage." Its depth transported her into another world; its beauty brought her to tears.

Thomas awoke. The image of the hut was still vivid in his mind; it now dawned on him that the words "My father, they have killed me . . . my father, they have killed me" were from one of Chinua Achebe's novels, but he couldn't remember which. He also tried to remember what had happened in the hut, conscious now of having slipped into the same dream after being startled out of it by the screams of the little boy. When he remembered the hut transformed into an Indian ashram, he then remembered the book, and the whole dream came back. He went over it: the hut, the book, the table of contents, the editor, A. S. Jhansi Rupali Kaloor, the mention of her death, January 12. He began to recall the storyline of January 12 . . . the coffee . . . the lavender sari . . . the train ride . . . the yellow notepaper . . . the screeching train . . . and then he fell fast asleep yet again.

In this dream, he was in his office looking up at a little white convent adorning one of the many hilltops decorating the canyon that climbs up to the snow-covered mountains from the sea. The convent became bigger and bigger as if it were moving toward him, and then he was hovering above it and gazing down into one of its rooms where Jhansi was sitting at a desk writing a letter. The words of the letter were sparkling and coming off the page for him to read line by line, as if floating in midair. He began to read. . .

This very late response to the generosity of your last letter, my dearest friend, is a source of great shame. My only excuses are that the remoteness of the convent in which I stay precludes the consistent flow of mail, and the gardening and janitorial work with which I'm occupied keeps me extremely busy during the day, not to mention that it finds me perfectly exhausted at night. The nuns are awfully sweet, but they are too old to help out much. By the time I've finished my work, said my prayers, and read his poems, which he manages to slip to me from time to time, I am lucky just to make it to my bed.

My consolations are few but sustain me: I live in a beautiful setting in the mountains overlooking the sad sea. There are plenty of red, white, yellow, peach, and pink roses everywhere. I watch the sun as it rises and sets each day. On some days, when it rises, it's like a bridegroom dressed in golden white and yellow attire coming out of his tent to meet his bride. And when it sets, it's as if he consummates his union anew with his sea-bride, dressed in her silver and blue sari, driven to ecstasy by his touch, an ecstasy that forces even the clouds to blush. Oh, those clouds, like so many guests at a secret marriage, light up with reddish orange joy as soon as he moves close to her. The wind is the priest; the rainbow their wedding ring, appearing only now and then after the thunder has played its wedding march. The sun sets, in fact, right over the university where he works, which I can see from my bedroom window, and once in a while, I even see him, my greatest consolation—that is, when he can arrange his schedule to come to the public liturgy. We slip from time to time into one of the empty parlors where we hold each other and dream about being alone together someday, somehow.

At times, I'm quite lonely and am tempted with feelings of rancor, but they dissipate when I pick up my prayer beads or read one of his poems. On rare occasions, like today, I find some time for myself, and I write some letters. I had begun today to write to my mother, but when I realized the date, I changed my plans and immediately wrote to you. I think of you often, my dearest of friends, and shall never forget January twelfth, three years ago, when your loving wisdom rescued me.

Your friend forever . . .

Thomas awoke as the sun began to rise. He could still see the sparkling words of the letter and Jhansi's face as she wrote it, as if the sun were rising in her eyes. A great sense of joy overwhelmed him, and he fell back into a deep and peaceful sleep once more, which lasted deliciously until early afternoon. On his way to the airport, he was struck by the way in which the Gulf States had all so suddenly emerged from the sands of the desert. The heat and desert dust were oppressive, even in the air-conditioned taxi.

CHAPTER SEVEN

H e arrived in Tehran as scheduled only to discover that no one was there to pick him up, as there had been a mix-up due to the airline strikes. A fellow passenger, and newly found friend, graciously helped him find his way to the hotel, and he got settled just in time for the opening dinner of the conference, wherein he found the conversation elevated and stimulating. His friend's Khuda Hafez when they parted reminded him of just how genuine and hospitable most Iranians were.

He thought of his Persian university friends whom he'd studied with in America. He could still hear the anguish in one student's voice, devastated by the bad image of his country portrayed in a popular motion picture. He tried to remember the title of the film, but could only come up with the word daughter. The absence of sensational advertising coupled with the natural beauty of the snow-peaked mountains surrounding Tehran was refreshing, especially after spending a night and day somewhere in the sands of the desert. It reminded him of his own hometown in the Rocky Mountains. He was thrilled to be there. Unlike most visitors to Iran, he had not been affected by the biases of the Western media, which had made that country out to be a backward place better fit for the Dark Ages than for the modern world.

"After all," he'd told many of his students and colleagues, "it's ancient Persia, isn't it?"

Thomas constantly fought against the modern tendency to divide history between the Dark Ages and the Enlightenment, and often argued that there was probably more light in the so-called Dark Ages than in the so-called Enlightenment age. He deplored, of course, the scandals and crimes of past societies committed in the name of religion, but to claim that such insanity was the result of religion seemed to him ludicrous and unsubstantiated. He agreed with Auguste Comte's law of human progress when it came to such things as the development in medicine, but rejected his claim that the theological/religious stage was synonymous with an undeveloped and fictitious state of intelligence. He was ever in the habit of telling his colleagues and students that most of the great thinkers of the past from Plato to Copernicus were theists of some sort, and he was constantly heard saying that "in the East, you know, all of the great intellectuals were spiritual figures."

He laughed as he read in one particular tourist guide, obviously written for foreigners, that "in this embattled country, buses are partitioned for men and women, while married women are confined to the four walls of their domestic arena, in strict observance of fanatical Islamic laws." It wasn't that there wasn't any oppression of women or religious fanaticism; there was, but there was also plenty of religious sanity and genuine intellectual activity as well. And he knew that one could find fanaticism and oppression of women, both religious and irreligious, for that matter, anywhere.

On the way to the hotel in Tehran, he remembered how his students and colleagues had been surprised that a conference on human rights was being held in Iran, of all places.

"Isn't it a contradiction in terms to have a conference on human rights in Iran?" some of his students ignorantly asked him, as they confusedly referred to religious fundamentalism and the Iranian revolution of 1979. He was surprised that the same kind of prejudice against Iran that he experienced in America was also present in Lebanon, at least in the part of Lebanon he was in.

"Wait a minute now," he shot back. "You sound a lot like many of my American students and colleagues."

"You tell them, Dr. Sleiman," said Mr. Morrision, who just happened to be there for his usual morning visit, cheering him on.

"How's that?" they said.

"Haven't you ever heard of Mohammed Mossadegh and Operation Ajax?"

Not surprised at all that they hadn't, he continued. "Have you never wondered about the cause of the 1979 revolution in Iran, and why the religious fundamentalists came to power?"

"That's how those Muslims are," said one outspoken, ignorant Christian student, who had spent all his life in one isolated area of Lebanon. "They are all fanatics."

"And you're not," Thomas murmured to himself, but finally said with some compassion, "My friend, I believe you are guilty of an informal fallacy."

"And which one is that?" he answered back somewhat disrespectfully.

"The fallacy of hasty induction. You can't say such things about more than one billion people based only on your experience of a half dozen or less, can you?"

"I know at least a dozen Muslims, and they're all fanatics," he snapped back stubbornly.

Thomas gave up on him and turned to some of the students who were really listening. "In the early 1950s, the United States ran an operation against Mossadegh and accused him, quite falsely, of being a communist even though he was democratically elected."

"Well, the British were in on it too, you know," said Mr. Morrison, "and were probably the ones who were really behind it, since they were extremely bitter that they'd lost control of the Iranian oil industry. In fact, I believe the British gave false information to the United States by accusing Mossadegh of moving closer to communism and the Soviet Union. This is how they dragged the US into the dispute; they couldn't handle the new prime minister alone. One must remember that this was at the height of the Cold War."

"That's right," said Thomas. "In fact, it's common knowledge that the final strategy of the US-British plot was planned right here in Beirut."

"Yes. I believe Kermit Roosevelt, the son of the US President Theodore Roosevelt, was here in Beirut for those meetings. Poor chap, he later committed suicide. Anyway, power politics are ugly no doubt. The whole thing was pathetic, especially since Mossadegh tried over and over to reach a reasonable settlement with Britain."

"Yes," said Thomas, "and the whole bloody thing almost failed because the Shah nearly backed out at the last minute."

"Whatever happened to Mossadegh?" one student asked.

"Who was the Shah?" asked another. Mr. Morrison and Thomas began to speak at the same time. Thomas addressed the first question; Mr. Morrison addressed the second.

"Well, Mossadegh was unjustly tried for treason and sentenced to prison."

"The Shah was Mohammed Reza Pahlavi, the monarch of Iran, whom the US and Britain turned into their puppet. All of this needs to be understood as leading up to the Iranian revolution of 1979."

"We've never heard about this before," said one thoughtful student.

"We've been led to believe that it's simply a country of religious extremism, lacking real culture."

"On the contrary," retorted Thomas, "if you would interact more with your fellow Shiite students from Lebanon's other universities, or even with the few that are here at our own university, you would know this isn't true."

To keep their attention, Thomas quoted a journalist friend of his from Nigeria who was an expert on Iranian affairs and who regularly kept Thomas up-to-date with developments in African literature and journalism:

"Iran's spiritual heritage and cultural values are far more enduring than the faddish secularism of a postmodern occidental culture." This immediately got the attention especially of his American colleagues, who had been forced to pass by his office due to its central location, and who now paused to listen.

"Just listen to this," he said, gathering up the Nigerian daily spread out on his desk, concealing a great heap of clutter.

Among the clutter were two precious pearls that Thomas had just begun to discover: Chinua Achebe's *Arrow of God* and *Things Fall Apart*, two novels that his friend from Nigeria had recently sent him. His colleagues at first were all ears as he read the following passage:

Iranians, as the embodiment of the Persian culture, speak of humanistic development rather than concrete, material technological advancement, although with respect to the latter, they can hold their own. They share with authentic Africans a humanism that ascribes attachment to nature as a paradigm of integral development. The Iranian woman, on her part, is homely and naturally graceful as any actualized woman can be. In her maternal elegance, she seems to endow femininity with a sensuality that demands veneration. The air is ambient with a simplicity so sophisticated that it would make the New Yorker look inferior. Something tells you that the fragmented egoism and the atomized existence of bubbling Western cities are absent here. Here, there seems to be a focus you do not understand. And the probable reason becomes clear: as you look around, peering at the numerous billboards hanging on high-rise buildings, you are arrested by a post-Revolution Iran that makes hagiolatry a means of social mobilization. The larger-than-life billboards seem to be a medium for national conscientization.

On the walls of buildings and on the rooftops of high-rise residential apartments, the brilliantly illuminated paintings of Iranian men in military fatigues stare at you continuously like deities in constant want for sacrifice. When it is not a painting of agonizing soldiers, it is the painting of Ayatollah Khomeini, adorned by well-crafted panegyrics in Persian calligraphy. The ubiquitous billboards seem to be a constant reminder that the labors of the Iranian heroes, whom they call martyrs, must not be in vain. And the message is clear: Iranian nationalism is founded on the Islamic religion and the Persian culture. Owing to this, there are two things you will never find in Iran. One is an advertisement of alcoholic drink and spirits; and the other is an advertisement that exploits the female anatomy as selling points for essential commodities. However, it is in this area that the Western world finds Iran wanting. According to the cultures of the West, a society is truly free when people are allowed to express themselves and air their views the way they feel. Based on the psychology of individualism and uniqueness, the freedom of expression, seen as its own foundation, becomes the theoretical basis for the politics of difference, which the post-modern world attempts to propagate. True, the freedom of expression has a different meaning in Iran. While there are a few privately owned newspapers, the electronic media are government-controlled. This is because the Iranian government makes a distinction between what should be expressed and what people tend to express; and as a result, journalists who are too critical of government policies often find themselves in jail. Yet, of all the various aspects of the freedom of expression, the most vulnerable to western attack, apart from press gagging, is the sartorial state of the Iranian woman. Unlike her counterpart in the West, the Iranian woman has to dress up in headgear and a one-piece cloak, called a chador, that makes her look like an Ursuline nun. Wrapped up in this black attire, her sumptuous curves and erotic privacy become a spectacle for the visual nourishment of her husband, while it at the same time discourages the commercialization of her anatomy.

"That's sexist," cried one of his female colleagues from America.

"I think it's beautiful," fired back a female student from Lebanon. "I wouldn't mind wearing a veil. At least it would prevent men from looking at me as simply an object of pleasure."

Still another girl remarked, "I like to be looked at as an object of pleasure."

"Perhaps we could have an open discussion on the issue," suggested the assistant professor, as he quickly began reading again, wanting to avoid a heated dispute so early in the morning, and trying hard not to gaze at the extremely sexy young woman who had made this last comment.

There seems to be a symbolism attached to the black ankle-length chador. By its size, it tells you that the female anatomy is not a commodity to be exploited by the boardroom grandmasters of advertising. On the other hand, its monotonous blackness fills you with sobriety and pensiveness. Beyond this, others who think that the sartorial state of the Iranian woman is only emblematic of the deeper sexism against her. For instance, Mrs. Zaria, a member of a Canada-based association of Iranian women, tells a story of the public suicide of one Dr. Mrs. Homa Darabi as a demonstration of "all the injustices against a woman." In March of 1983, Mrs. Darabi, an Iranian university professor and activist against the Islamic regime, walked into a public square, doused herself with petrol and set herself ablaze. She was said to have protested against the Islamic Republic, which had continued with the subjugation of women. But some others will not agree with Zaria. Mrs. Fatimah Mosavi, a lawyer, sees it differently. "I won't say the Iranian woman is being suppressed. I will not say also that there is a case of inequality," she said. "The Iranian society is only trying to put the woman on her natural position." When you overlook the internal crisis over personal differences, the Iranian woman, at a glance, is a symbol of motherhood and innocence. In her sartorial elegance, she radiates a feminine grace that evokes a feeling of honor and respect. In her modesty, she lashes out at the myopic viewpoint that tends to see equality on the basis of interchangeability, as she exposes the foolishness inherent in Western feminist activism. While the feminist of the West wants to become a 'man' in order to demonstrate her equality, the Iranian woman wants to show her equality by becoming truly woman.

Thomas paused for a moment.

"That's an insult," protested one professor, who'd come over to see what all the commotion was about. Though he didn't show it, Thomas was perturbed by her presence since just the week before this same professor had shot down his suggestion to begin committee meetings with a profession of faith, a prayer, and some silence. She had lectured him in front of his colleagues on how unprofessional that would be, and managed to convince the other members that she was right. She'd ended her mini-lecture by reminding Thomas that it wasn't a meeting in the Religion Department. Explaining himself, Thomas said that such a crude separation of faith and reason could not be justified in a private Catholic institution.

"It is precisely this kind of secularism in education that is responsible for the deadening departmentalization which has all but killed the genuine university spirit," he had rebutted.

"Catholic means universal; thus Catholic education must be open and all encompassing. It must be cosmic. It must have a unity—or else it can have no beauty. Of course, it must have endless diversity, but it can't be divided into a million and one pieces of disconnected branches of knowledge."

He also told them that one of the reasons he'd left America and come to the Middle East was to get away from that kind of secularism. Unmoved by his arguments, she insisted that it would still be unprofessional. Thus, he had launched into an etymological analysis of the term professional and showed convincingly how the term was related to the term professor, which originally referred to how the instructors in the first medieval universities in Europe professed their faith in the Nicene Creed.

"To say it is unprofessional for professors to profess their faith in their official capacity as professors at a university is a mindless contradiction in terms," he concluded. One colleague had gotten his point, but the others didn't quite know what to make of him.

And so when this same professor claimed that she was insulted by the news article, Thomas stopped reading and simply stared at her. He wanted to tell her that no one had invited her over to listen, but he prudently restrained himself and said instead, "Would you rather that I read quieter, Dr. Carey?" His tone was conciliatory.

"Go on, continue reading as loud as you wish; it's not your fault that your office is so close to the lounge. Anyway, I need a good laugh this morning," she said sardonically.

Thomas didn't bother to respond to the slur, and continued reading.

Western feminists want to leave the family and go to the faceless public; the Iranian seems to build her stronghold around family to exhibit her equality with the man. While the Western feminist has shattered the mystique of womanhood by the propagation of a bare-it-all culture, the Iranian woman glorifies the woman by her sartorial comportment. While the feminist's bare-it-all culture demystifies womanhood, the Iranian embellishes the mystery that makes her woman by nun-like resplendence. . . .

As these last sentences were read, Dr. Carey could bear it no longer and walked off rather rudely.

"I guess she disagreed with some of this," Thomas said to those around him still listening. "Shall I continue?"

"Please do."

"Very well. Let me read to you what he has written about the city of Qum and Iran's intellectual heritage."

Qum is Iran's citadel of learning as well as its national sanctuary. It is a city of shrines and grottoes, museums and libraries, universities and seminaries. Here, where the patron saint of modern Iran (Imam Khomeini) has his resting place, is the holiest city in Iran. On the streets of Qum, every graffiti is a prayer or an inscription of divine exultation. Women roam around like cloistered nuns on a free day, while every man seems to be a professor, a scholar, or a cleric. Almost every gathering of young men in Qum is a rendezvous for philosophical analysis or a peripatetic academy for comparative religious studies. In Qum, you go to bed arguing over Kantian theory of "Is" and "Ought" and you wake up to continue the debate. Decked in suits and gowns like the president himself, the turbaned and heavily bearded clerics and professors litter the streets of Qum in their quotidian preoccupation. Clutching books and encyclopedias as they race from one library to another, their magisterial candor seems to be an act reminiscent of medieval scholasticism. However, it is in Esfahan that you behold the panoply of Iran's grandiloquence. Esfahan is a city of warm, accommodating, outgoing and proud inhabitants. It is a city of magical beauty and material prosperity; a pleasant mélange of realist West and surreal Persia. Like the poems of its worthy son, Omar

Khayyam, Esfahan is the gracious counterpoint of cultural opposites. Here, Farsi and English, Persian and Western, jeans, pants, and chador never come into conflict. It is a city of towering minarets and smoking oil-rigs. It is a city of lavishly ornate mosques and mausoleums as well as hi-tech manufacturing car plants. If the West genuinely wishes to dialogue with Persia, the symbolic convergence should be at Esfahan. Intellectually, the Iranians have a flourishing depth that makes those of younger civilizations look like neophytes. Long before the West came to know Aristotle, the Iranians had read him inside out and had deduced various approaches to his works. As a matter of fact, the works of Aristotle and other pioneers of Western intellectual culture came to the Western world through the Iranian scholar Ibn Sina (Avicenna).

"Enough, enough, Dr. Sleiman, you've won us over. We won't ever again say that Iran is a backward country."

"No. Please continue," said Mr. Morrison, who had lit up another bowl of pipe tobacco, amused by the morning's happenings.

"Did I hear that this piece was written by a Nigerian?"

"That's correct; he's a friend of mine and was a student of Chinua Achebe."

"I only wish our own British professors could write such enchanting English," Mr. Morrison said with authority.

As an expert in English, who had taught the language for nearly fifty years and published important books in the field, his word meant something.

"I've insisted for years now that some of the best English authors of the century are not from America or Britain, but from Ghana, Nigeria, and India. I wouldn't be at all surprised if an Indian wins the Nobel Prize for Literature one of these days. Please finish the article for us, Dr. Sleiman."

"By all means, Mr. Morrison."

Not only is Iran the intellectual center of the oriental world, it remains the most flourishing civilization in arts and literature; and the reservoir of this intellectual heritage is far from being tapped for the optimal benefit of the human race. Just as the West parades its intellectuals from

Plato to Aquinas, Shakespeare to Einstein, likewise do the Iranians flaunt their great minds from Zoroaster to Ibn Sina, Omar Khayyam to Mullah Sandra. Ibn Sina, who flourished in the tenth century, was the link between ancient philosophy and medieval Western philosophy. His treatises on medicine as well as his translations and interpretations of ancient philosophy were works the world depended on for some time. Until the early 18th century, Ibn Sina's books and medical encyclopedia, which he started writing at the age of eight, were some of the most influential text books in Europe. Iran also seems to have the most enduring poetic tradition in the literary world. Despite the influence of other cultures and civilizations at different points of its history, Iranian (Persian) poetry remains unchanged. The Shahnameh (The Book of Kings), a national epic composed by the tenth-century Iranian poet, Ferdowsi, still lives forever in the heart of every Iranian. Every revolutionary movement in the world has a line of Khayyam's poems for inspiration. What is problematic for Iran, however, is the cultural tension presented by generational differences. The young want to be American and secular; the old want to be Persian and Islamic. The young desire a society that dances to the tune of a pop culture; the old desire a society guided by the leadership of the Ayatollah. Along these lines, the influential generation of Iranians want to go out to the world, they want to be accepted, they want the world to open its hands toward them. While this is a genuine desire for global socialization, the gesture calls for caution. This is where President Khatami's call for dialogue among cultures and civilizations makes sense.

"Is this the sort of thing you're going to be involved in when you travel to Iran, Dr. Sleiman?"

"That's right. The title of the conference is Human Rights and the Dialogue of Civilizations."

"What is your paper about?"

"The title is 'Christianity and the Universal Declaration of Human Rights.'"

"What is your claim, sir?"

"I claim that the philosophical and theological presuppositions of the UN Declaration of Human Rights in 1948 are primarily Christian ones. More specifically, I try to show that Roman Catholic Popes and intellectuals, such as Pope Leo XIII, and the great French Catholic philosopher, Jacques Maritain, and the Lebanese statesman Charles Malik, all played key roles in the eventual formulation of the document. I also show that, to its great credit, the 1948 declaration moves away from many of the humanistic tendencies in earlier rights documents such as the French Declaration of the Rights of Man and the United States Bill of Rights."

"What do you mean by humanistic? I thought humanism was a good thing, sir."

"It is, but it's much too simple to claim that there's only one kind of humanism; in the past, there were in fact different kinds. There is what Aleksandr Solzhenitsyn defined some years ago at Harvard University in his famous commencement address as rationalistic humanism, or humanistic autonomy, which he defined as anthropocentricity, that is to say, the 'practiced autonomy of man from any higher force above him . . . wherein man is the center and measure of all things.' This worldview was born in the Renaissance and found its political and social expression in the so-called Age of the Enlightenment. It became the basis for many of the political and social doctrines that flourished in Europe in the eighteenth and nineteenth centuries, and it is still a prevailing Western view that has been exported literally to the entire planet. Anyway, you don't want to hear a lecture on humanism, do you? You guys must be tired."

"No, sir, please continue; you can't stop now."

"Very well; if you insist! Let's see, where was I? Oh yes, there is also in the past what could be defined as a biblical humanism, or a Judeo-Christian humanism, which takes its starting point from the question the psalmist put to God: 'What is man that you should be mindful of him, or the son of man that you should care for him?' And then it was developed in the light of the answer that the psalmist gave to his own question: 'yet, you have made him a little less than a god, and crowned him with glory and splendor, making him lord over the works of your hands, setting all things under his feet.' This was a humanism thus characterized by a delicate tension between man's absolute nothingness and his awesome grandeur as a creature just a little less than a god. Very much unlike the rationalistic humanism described by Solzhenitsyn, this Judeo-Christian humanism presupposed that man, who was paradoxically both radically insignificant and at the same time infinitely valuable, could only be understood in terms of his relation to God.

"We may also speak of an exclusively Christian humanism, which began when St. Paul related the words of the psalmist, 'you have made him little less than a god, and crowned him with glory and splendor,' to the meaning that Christ gave to the words glory and splendor. As St. Paul put it in his letter to the Hebrews, 'But we do see in Jesus one who was for a short while made lower than a god, and is now crowned with glory and splendor.' And why was he crowned with glory and splendor? Because, as St. Paul goes on to tell us, 'he submitted to death; by God's grace he had to experience death for all mankind.' This may very well be the essence and beginning of what came to be recognized later as Christian Humanism. In the patristic period and early Middle Ages, this was developed implicitly within the tension of two competing views of man: one that saw man in all his beauty, power, and majesty, created for dominion over this present world, to which he was vastly superior, and one that stressed the need for man to deny the world since both it and he were deeply disordered and wounded by sin. The former tended to focus on man's semi-autonomy; the latter, on man's total and utter helplessness, but both views took their start from the belief that man had been created in the image and likeness of God. John of Salisbury in the twelfth century developed this theme explicitly, and by the time of Ignatius of Loyola in the sixteenth century and Pascal in the seventeenth, these great thinkers tried to preserve and develop the delicate balance in this Christian humanism against two extremes. One extreme was what we might call the Reformation extreme, in which humankind and the physical world had been radically and deeply corrupted by sin. Therefore, resisting finding God in all things was a pointless endeavor. The other extreme was what we might call the Renaissance extreme. This view tended to deny that man was a sinner, and preferred to speak only about his magnificence and autonomy."

Bits and pieces of all these conversations that he had had before he left Lebanon occupied his mind that night while lying in the bed of his hotel room.

Thomas's thoughts eventually turned away from ancient Persia, modern Iran, humanism, and human rights, back to Lebanon, which seemed so far away. But she was as close as ever. When he called her, she could hardly breathe due to excitement.

"My God, I love you. I'll always love you. You are my light."

"I'm not the light, *habebtee*, I'm just. . . ."

"Stop it. I know what I'm saying. If you're not my light, then I prefer to live in darkness. I can't live without you."

"I love the way you love me, Juliet. Will you stop loving me one day?"

"What? Are you serious? I can't. I won't. Did you call your wife and children?"

"Yes."

"Are they fine?"

"Yes, thank God, they're all fine."

"Good. Do you know something?"

"What is it?"

"Maybe you won't believe it, and I know it may sound strange, but I love them dearly—all of them, including your wife."

"But you don't even know them, and I'm sure she wouldn't say the same if she knew I were talking to you now."

"I know, but I love everyone related to you and everything connected to you; can't you see this?"

Thomas was astounded by this statement, and wonderfully gratified.

"I love you too, my love. I'll try to call you tomorrow night after the conference."

He had trouble getting through at first, the following night, but finally got connected. He sat up in his bed once he heard her voice on the telephone.

"For hours I've been waiting for your call. How are you? I miss you. How was it? I was praying for you."

"Thank you, *elbee*, it was great. I had your picture up at my place in the conference room all day long. Two young men and a middle-aged woman saw the picture and had to say how beautiful you were. They thought you were my wife."

"I want to be."

Thomas remained silent for a moment then changed the subject.

"How are things at the university?"

"Everything's the same; how did you do?"

"People seemed to like the paper, and there were positive responses from some very important people."

"I knew you would be brilliant."

"I don't think I was brilliant, but one person, a man whom I respect immensely, insisted on getting copies of my paper immediately, well before the conference proceedings are published next year."

"Congratulations! What was the setting like?"

"Oh, it was grandiose, almost pretentious. The hall was spectacular, and the Islamic art, touched slightly as it was by a Persian brush, was quite edifying. I even found myself enjoying the chanting of the Koran before each session; it was prayerful. I was interviewed a few times by some local television stations that employed, I must say, some really top-notch interviewers who knew English well."

"So who were these important people?"

"One was a Muslim cleric who argued lucidly for religious freedom in Islam. You could have heard a pin drop when he gave his intervention. He said that Islam ought not to force people to stay Muslim by imposing the death penalty on those who decide to leave, claiming that such force undermined the true power of religion, which comes from personal conviction and from the will."

"Do you know what else comes from personal conviction and the will?" she asked.

"What's that?"

"My love for you, *elbee*. I miss you. I can't live without you. When do you leave for India?"

"Tomorrow evening."

"Please be careful. Try to call as soon as you get there."

"I'll do my best; I still don't know where I'll be staying or where I'll be going exactly."

"Just take care of yourself, please."

"I will, don't worry. Wait for me."

"I'll wait forever."

"I love you."

"Not as much as I love you, *hyatee*. Hurry back."

These were to be the last intimate words exchanged between them. She would never again call him *hyatee*, at least not to his face, and he would never again call her *elbee*.

PART THREE

THAT RARE AND FAIR
ROMANTIC STRAIN

CHAPTER EIGHT

A s he stepped off the plane, he feared she wouldn't be there. He doubted whether she'd received the one-line note he'd sent a week before, announcing his coming, as there had been no way to confirm its reception; her phone had been disconnected for weeks.

What timing, he thought as he walked between the many dark faces lined up behind two ropes that formed a narrow walkway just outside the terminal. *It's just not meant to be. I shall never see her again. But it's May eighth*, he reflected, trying to console himself. *It couldn't just be a coincidence that I am arriving here on the very same day that she left two long years ago. I didn't plan it this way. It must have a meaning. Too many things had to fall into place for me to be here now.*

He looked around in vain to catch a glimpse of her. *Will she wear a sari? Which color will it be? Has she gained weight?* He strained his neck and stood on his toes looking for any sign of her as he let himself get pushed about by the elbowing crowd. *Will she be with her parents? Will they think it odd that I've come to India without my family? Surely, they will question my motives. What are my motives anyway? Perhaps Juliet was right. Maybe I am still in love with her. Has she told anyone about us? Where is she, for God's sake?* He was assailed again by the same doubts. *She didn't receive my note. I have no way of calling her. I have an address, but maybe they've moved; after all, why is their phone disconnected?*

Though it was an extremely hot and humid morning, the sights, sounds, and smells somehow delightfully comforted him because of their unfamiliarity.

"I'm finally here in her India, in South India, the most Indian part of India," he said to himself a moment later, as a feeling of hope returned to rescue him. "There's a reason I'm here now. I shall find her, that's all."

All of his doubts dissipated; at once she appeared, as radiant as the sun, her white and pink sari flowing brightly and majestically around the dark skin of her long and strong feminine arms. She walked briskly toward him, gracefully embraced him, and said with all the charm of a twenty-four-year-old innocent young woman ardently in love, "Welcome to India," and with her mouth next to his ear so that no one else could hear, added tenderly, "My great king."

After two long years of waiting, not knowing whether such a day would ever arrive, she confidently took hold of his right arm and led him to a car waiting to carry him to her home.

"This is my father, my mother, and my grandmother."

"It is a pleasure to meet you. I've heard a lot about you. But you all look so much younger than your pictures," Thomas said sincerely.

There was an instant bond between him and her family. They were all calmly aware of a genuine mutual affection. She sat on his left side with her leg slightly touching his. He couldn't keep his eyes off her face and checked himself a few times for staring so conspicuously.

"My grandmother was on her way back home to Bangalore when your note arrived yesterday; she changed her plans so as to see you."

"Thank you. It's an honor to meet you, Grandma."

"She was married at age ten," volunteered Jhansi.

"What?" he said, unable to contain his surprise.

"And my mother at thirteen."

"No wonder you both look so young," he said, trying to conceal his shock. They laughed approvingly.

They both seem very happy, and yet they were forced to marry men whom they didn't know, whom they didn't choose, he reflected. He thought affectionately of his father's mother, whom he had been with at the moment of her death.

She too, in fine Lebanese fashion, had been forced to marry at a very young age. She loved her husband and was heartbroken when he died. Maybe the older way of arranging marriages early on was better, he thought. But after reconsidering it for a moment, he changed his mind. *No*, he said to himself, *these were the lucky ones*, remembering all the horror stories he'd heard from the old-timers and the ever-present neurosis of his mother-in-law, an effect of being forced to marry her much older cousin. He momentarily gave up his natural tendency to idealize the past.

"So when did you get the note?"

"It arrived yesterday shortly after I returned from the church. I literally begged Our Lady during the Mass to let me see you," she said in a low voice that only he could hear, "and within a few minutes after I got back home, your note came."

"She nearly fainted when she read it," her mother added, able to hear the last part of her daughter's sentence. "She has missed you and your family dearly these two years," she added with a smile. "How are your wife and children?"

"Fine. Everyone is fine, thank God."

"Jhansi went through severe depression when she first left your family. She especially missed your youngest son. Is he better now?"

"Yes. He is fine, praise God!"

"And how do you find Jhansi? Does she look different with more weight?"

Thomas now felt he had permission to indulge himself and took all of her in slowly and affirmatively.

"She looks fine, very fine. She has bragged a lot about your cooking, and it seems she was right. I think her complexion has lightened a bit as her face has become fuller."

"Yes, indeed it has. You see, Jhansi, what did I tell you?"

Thomas had not taken his eyes off her for even a second, as if in a trance. When she felt his gaze, she finally looked directly at him. He stared intensely into her dark, black eyes. Streams of joy and light were exchanged in a flash.

They were led into a sweet and agonizing rapture wherein time stopped only to begin again when the car suddenly swerved to miss a beast of burden that unexpectedly turned in front of it. The swerving of the vehicle brought her onto his lap, increasing his happiness sevenfold. The driver apologized, and the small talk resumed.

Thomas had thought that Middle Eastern cities were disorganized and crowded, and they were compared to the American cities he was used to. But Madras made Beirut and even Cairo seem calm, clean, and relatively uninhabited. In no other city in the world did cars, cows, bicycles, bulls, trucks, horses, auto-ricks, and an occasional tiger or bear come together in quite the same way as they did in that Indian city, and it all seemed to move naturally together as one—in and out of the scores of human beings walking, running, and crawling to wherever they needed to go. Her father sat in front with the driver and occasionally asked Thomas questions about his family and his work. He felt relieved to be speaking to her parents.

My, how they seem to like and respect me, he thought. *Would they continue to if they were to find out that I had . . . I had done what?* he argued with himself. *I didn't make love to her, though I certainly could have. And even if I had, I loved her, and she loved me. What would have been the great crime in this?* Juliet's words came instantly to mind. "Loved? Is it over? Maybe not? Surely not! But what if they knew I had tried to . . .?"

Thomas prevented himself from thinking this latter thought, as the guilt was still too deep. He had to get her forgiveness. He had confessed in a letter, but he had to face her with this.

Maybe this is why I have come to India—to face her with this. What would she say? What does she think of this? Judging by the way she greeted me, this confession has changed nothing, nothing at all.

Half an hour later, he climbed the poorly lit steps to the second floor of a one-bedroom apartment that she had called home for many years. She put an arm around the shoulder of a good-looking, stout middle-aged woman at the top of the stairs.

"This is my maid," she bragged, as if to recover some of the dignity she'd lost in working as his maid for nearly three years.

She had told them once that her family had a maid, and that she never would have left her country if she had known that she was going to work as a maid. But Mrs. Sleiman had her doubts about the story, especially after she found out about Jhansi and her husband; she began to think that the entire story had been made up to gain sympathy and extra money. Thomas never doubted Jhansi. He recalled her shyness in serving their company, and remembered distinctly her habit of disappearing whenever visitors arrived for fear of having to serve them as a common maid. He looked lovingly at her as she entered her humble home and introduced the other members of her family. Thomas was borne away by happiness; he felt at home.

"So, my daughter tells me you were in Iran?" her father said, as they removed their shoes and sat down.

"Yes, I was invited to deliver a paper there at an international conference on human rights."

"And what was the topic of your paper?"

"The UN Declaration of Human Rights," he said casually, not expecting much of a response.

"You mean the one of 1948?"

"Yes."

"Well, what did you have to say about it?"

A bit surprised by his interest, he said, "I tried to show that it was deeply influenced by religious rather than by secular forces."

"Oh, that sounds important. India is struggling now with this whole question of secularization."

Now very surprised by his interest, Thomas said much less casually, "You see, the earlier human rights documents were associated with the French and American Revolutions, and were quite secular in their approach."

"I studied those revolutions in school, but I can't recall much about them; the name Rousseau comes to mind though."

Although tired because of the trip, Thomas now became very interested in the conversation, and said enthusiastically, "Yes. Well, basically, I argued that beginning especially with Rousseau's thought, the West started down a road of secularism that has been causing havoc ever since and, ironically, hasn't helped the cause of human rights at all."

"What do you mean exactly by secularism, sir?" asked Jhansi's sister Meena, who was studying political science at the University of Madras. "It's a much trickier word than most seem to realize, don't you agree?"

Thomas was delighted to receive such a question, and didn't expect to get into such a discussion so soon after his arrival.

"Well, let me first tell you what I don't mean," he said, assuming his didactic mode of communication, which had become so much a part of his nature due to his profession. He began his lecture at once.

"The etymology of the term secularism is. . ."

"Excuse me, uh . . . sir . . . but don't you want to rest and eat something?" said Jhansi, as she took her position on the floor in front of him and handed him a glass of water.

She had wanted to call him my love or my king, but everyone was too closely gathered around him. The neighbors had come in to look at him; some were introduced, others just stayed in the background, pointing and laughing quietly. The mood was festive.

"He was about to teach us something," said Meena, clearly disappointed.

"There will be plenty of time for that, my dear sister; let him rest now." Jhansi loved to listen to him and was slightly irritated that he had been about to begin a discourse without her present.

"By the way, you are planning to stay for at least a couple of weeks, aren't you?" asked Jhansi, getting right to the point of what was most on her mind.

"I'm afraid not. I must leave at the end of the week. It's nearly a miracle that I've made it here at all, believe me."

"What?" Jhansi cried. "Don't say it! You must stay longer than that. It cannot be. Impossible! You've come all this way for five days—it's nothing."

"Nothing? It's one hundred and twenty hours."

"You must change your plans."

"Jhansi! What is wrong with you?" her father said in a loud voice. "The man has just arrived, and you already speak about his departure? Is he a child who needs you to plan his life for him? Show him some respect, my daughter, for heaven's sake, and make him more comfortable." To Thomas, he added, "I hope she wasn't always like this while your employee, sir."

"No, no, not at all, not at all! We all miss her, especially the children. They still mention her often and continue to pray for her by name."

"That's nice to hear, sir. Come now, what can we get you, Mr. Sleiman? You don't look comfortable. Would you like some coconut juice? I've just bought some."

"Thank you, Mr. Kaloor; that sounds refreshing."

As her father left the room to get the juice from her mother, who had already prepared it, Jhansi stole a look at Thomas that showed her acute pain and disappointment upon learning that he planned to leave just as suddenly as he had arrived.

I cannot live without him next to me, she mused. *I cannot live without his love.*

She had written these same words in her last letter to him, which he'd received about a month earlier.

"I know that you can live without me," she had written, "but I cannot live without you, without your love."

That sentence had penetrated him deeply, and he could now read it in her eyes. Before long, her father appeared with the coconut itself from which Thomas slowly drank the delicious juice.

He looked around at the tiny one-bedroom home adorned with a Christian shrine that was cluttered with pictures of the Virgin, the Christ Child, and various saints—and before which, as he was to discover the following morning, her father would light incense and perform his daily prayers. There was also a shrine of sorts in the kitchen, but this one was decorated with Hindu gods and goddesses. No rituals were performed in front of it; Jhansi told him that her parents merely liked the colorful images. A picture of his youngest son caught his eye. It was in a place of prominence as if a member of the family. The large icon of Christ the King that he'd given to Shivani before she left hung also in a place of prominence.

He had imagined her house so much bigger than it was. *How were seven people raised here?* he wondered.

"It's small, isn't it?" Jhansi said, as if reading his mind.

"It's adequate," he said, not wanting to offend.

"We can get you a hotel if you want," she hastened to add.

"It's not necessary unless you and your family would feel more comfortable."

Jhansi laughingly assured him that they were perfectly at ease with him staying there.

"We all sleep on the roof at this time of year, you know."

"That's fine by me."

"Well, before you say so, let me show it to you."

Her parents protested that he might be tired, but he assured them that he was fine, so they motioned her to take him up. Everyone else stayed inside, as the sun was quite strong. When they reached the top of the stairs, right before the entrance onto the roof, they noticed the few feet of privacy that the space compassionately offered them, and they embraced at once, overcome with passionate fervor.

"Oh, Jhansi, my angel," he murmured into her hair.

"My great king, I can't live without your love. I won't. You must bring me back with you. I've told my parents you would."

"What?" he asked in confusion, pulling apart.

"About a month ago I told them you would be coming in May to arrange my marriage, perhaps with someone in your family. This was the only way to prevent them from forcing me to marry."

"But how did you know I was coming?"

"I didn't, but I literally begged heaven that you would come in May, and you did. I can't believe it. Thank you. Thank you for coming, my king. I can't live without you. I cannot."

"Stop it, Jhansi. I'm not a god. I'm a man."

"You're my god; can't you see that?"

"Listen to me," he said firmly, as if mildly reprimanding one of his children or students. "You're a Christian, aren't you? Jesus is your God, Jhansi, now stop it; don't be silly."

"You're my Jesus; why don't you comprehend this? I've written it repeatedly in my letters."

Thomas didn't know how to respond. *This is idolatry*, he thought. *How can she say such things? Surely she doesn't really mean them.*

"Hold me tighter, please, tighter," she moaned.

"You mean they think you are going back with me?"

"Yes. Or at least they are waiting for you to tell them about my future."

"Oh my God, Jhansi, why didn't you tell me this in your letters?"

"I only thought of it recently in a moment of desperation. It has been hell for me. India is not like America or even Lebanon, you know. One man was all set to marry me, the horoscopes had been read, the dowry agreed upon, and the family was coming just to make it formal."

"What happened?"

"I poured hot boiling coffee over my legs and acted as if I had spilled it." She delicately lifted her sari to show him the scars.

"This put an end to everything, as I was in bed for a week."

"My God, Jhansi. Can't you just tell them you want to be a nun and that you don't want to marry? They will understand; they seem to be very understanding, and they are religious too, aren't they?"

"I've been telling them for two years now, but my father won't allow it. And, anyway, I can't be a nun now. Aren't nuns supposed to give their hearts to Jesus? I don't have my heart any longer; I've given it to you. It's yours, that's all. Besides, if I enter the convent, there will never be any chance of seeing you again."

He embraced her even tighter now and allowed his hands to explore her body. Her soft and sweet sighs not only pleased him but gave a deeper meaning to his existence.

"I have never stopped thinking about you, Jhansi. I miss your presence. I miss your smile most of all."

"Thinking only? And loving?"

Thomas just held her, but said nothing.

"You miss my smile, do you? Well, I no longer smile from my heart. Today I really smiled for the first time in two years. Can you believe this?"

Thomas didn't answer. He just kissed her gently on her cheek, and the rapture returned. He had never experienced such elation, not with his wife, nor with Juliet, nor with Shivani, nor with any of the two or three girls he had loved before getting married, and all from a simple embrace, a tender kiss on the cheek. The only thing he could compare it to was the joy and peace that came when embracing his children, but with Jhansi in his arms, he experienced ecstasy as well. All of this transpired in two or three minutes, but an entire lifetime was contained in those few minutes, as Thomas often reflected on once he returned home to find himself almost all alone.

"Will you be comfortable up there?" her father asked, when they entered back into the little apartment.

"Certainly, but I might have to come down in the middle of the night to use the washroom."

"No problem; we'll keep a key next to your cot."

Jhansi's mother came out of the kitchen announcing that the food was ready. They showed him to the washroom first and then all took turns washing, as the room was barely big enough for one. Everyone sat on the floor except Thomas and Jhansi's father, and the food was served. He'd noticed the delicious smells upon entering the house, but hadn't yet been able to fully take them in. Now as the food was served, he took his time with each of the seven small dishes placed before him. The aromas were nearly as satisfying as the food itself. He'd eaten at some very good Indian restaurants in America and the Middle East, but they all paled in comparison to what he was now smelling and tasting. A great variety of foods were contained in small white bowls and placed in a semi-circle on a large circular dish that had rice in the middle. Jhansi schooled him on what to taste first and on which combinations were the best. He was the only one with eating utensils. Everyone else simply poured the sauces on the rice in various combinations and ate with their hands after mixing the rice and sauces together. He was used to eating with his hands, but he had always used the medium of bread in good Middle Eastern style.

The custom of eating rice and vegetables soaked in rich curry sauces, without bread, directly with one's hands, was entirely new and at first a bit shocking. Jhansi made a joke when she noticed his surprise. She had anticipated it even before they sat down since she knew very well the eating habits he was accustomed to. In fact, she had learned his habits so well after nearly three years of serving him that she used to bring him things even before he asked. She knew presentation was important to him, so she did her best to make even the simplest dish, glass of juice, or cup of coffee appealing in its presentation.

"You eat with your eyes first, right?" he used to say to her.

Among the first things he tasted was the sambhar, a deliciously hot and spicy but light vegetable curry that was typically South Indian. Its color was nearly that of gold, and its flavor, which penetrated Thomas to the core, was just as valuable. He expected it to be heavy and rich judging from its scent and color, but it wasn't; it was simultaneously light and rich. Not only his mouth tasted the extremely spicy curry, but somehow his whole face took the flavor in as well. As his eyes watered ever so slightly, Jhansi's mother feared she had made it too spicy and asked her daughter in Tamil to attend to him.

"My mother fears it's too hot for you."

"No, not at all, it's superb; I'm just getting used to it. I've never tasted anything as tasty as this; its flavor is exquisite."

Jhansi and her mother were notably gratified by this compliment and assured him that the best was yet to come.

"Of course we are biased, but the best Indian food is prepared here in South India," volunteered her father.

"Not only the best food, Father, but the best of everything in India is found here," said the youngest daughter.

"And the worst too," said her father with some conviction.

"Well, for better or for worse, this is the most Indian part of India," stated a longtime friend of Jhansi's father, who had been invited to eat with them and who had a distinguished aura about him.

"Now, is that because South Indians have been in India the longest?" asked Thomas respectfully, sensing the man's learning.

"Yes. Precisely. The languages of South India—Tamil, Malyalam, Telegu, Kannada, and Kanarese—are Dravidian, not Indo-European languages. You see, we are the descendants, more or less, of the Pre-Aryan peoples that originally lived along the river Indus in what for the most part is now Pakistan."

"Yes. I'm somewhat familiar with the excavations of the ancient cities of Mohenjo-daro and Harappa, which show that a thriving urban civilization existed in that area over four thousand years ago."

"That's right," said the gentleman.

"And I believe this civilization spoke a non-Aryan language, perhaps a sort of proto-Dravidian, which is even older than Sanskrit."

"Many scholars argue this, that's right."

"And from what I know, this civilization was technologically and artistically quite advanced."

"Right again, Dr. Sleiman, I'm impressed," said their friend, who knew Indian history well. "That proto-Dravidian language spoken then, in fact, was probably a great-grandfather of our modern Tamil."

"Well, that makes a lot of sense," said Thomas, "since the Indo-Aryan tribes that came into the Indus Valley about fifteen hundred years before Christ drove the indigenous people due south."

"Wait a minute, who were these Indo-Aryan tribes?" asked one of Jhansi's sisters, just in her first year of high school.

"And if we Tamils are descendants of such a great civilization, why were these new invaders able to drive us out so easily?" added another similarly aged boy neighbor, who didn't like what he was hearing.

The teacher in Thomas could not be contained, and he said, "The Indo-Aryan tribes broke away from the Indo-Iranian wing of the once fairly cohesive Indo-European speaking tribes that lived between the Caspian and Black Seas and which underwent a great dispersion around 2000 BC. That dispersion led some tribes to Ireland and England, others to Germany, Greece, and Rome. Still others wound up in Iran, and from there some tribes eventually broke away and came down into the Indus Valley through Afghanistan's Khyber Pass. And with respect to your question, young man, you may take comfort in the fact that these Indo-Aryan tribes, much less advanced than the pre-Aryans, had the distinct advantage of entering into the Indus Valley shortly after cataclysmic floods and earthquakes had nearly devastated the area along with its remarkably advanced civilization. Your ancestors had already been defeated by nature; they had no other choice but to flee south for their lives."

"I didn't know your area of expertise was India, sir," said Meena.

"Oh, please, my dear, I have no area of expertise, not even in my own field."

"But you know things about India's history that I don't know or that I've forgotten."

"Well, I have come to love India, and especially South India," he said, glancing furtively in the direction of Jhansi. "Love sharpens the intellect and the memory." Only she got his meaning.

Jhansi was proud of him and his knowledge, and took comfort in the fact that he was her guest. Her parents too came to admire him during the meal. Thomas sensed their approval and reveled in their acceptance of him.

There was a lull in the conversation as everyone returned to the important task at hand: eating. Thomas enjoyed the meal nearly to the point of intoxication.

"I'm sure the Aryans didn't cook like this," he said, at which there was a general uproar of laughter.

CHAPTER NINE

A fter lunch, they insisted he take a shower and rest a bit. It didn't take him long to get used to showering with a little bucket, but the absence of a toilet and paper was quite an adjustment. Once he had finished, they brought him to a tiny little room right off the kitchen. The kitchen was immaculate, though small and cramped. It was then that he got a good look at the Hindu shrine. He immediately recognized Shiva and Vishnu, but wasn't sure who the other gods and goddesses were. One image of Vishnu incarnated caught his attention, and he wondered, in light of Christianity's one incarnation, how it was that Vishnu had had so many incarnations. All this flashed through his mind within seconds as he passed through the kitchen into the little room. Jhansi and her mother unpacked his suitcase while he rested on the one lone bed in the one lone room of the tiny apartment. Jhansi came in and out of the room freely to make sure he was comfortable and to arrange his things as they were unpacked.

"Please just give me the book in the side of that bag," he said to her. "I'll keep it by me."

The house gradually got very quiet. Everyone had either gone up to the roof, as the sun's rays had been diminished by some unexpected clouds, or had fallen asleep in the front room, which a few moments before had been a dining room. Jhansi came in again and stood close to him. There was just enough privacy for him to hold her hand. He remained lying on the bed with her standing right next to him. Though her eyes were full of happy expectation, they somehow reflected a penetrating dolor.

"Thank you for coming. I can't believe you're really here."

"Nor I . . . so what did you think of all the confessions I made to you in the numerous letters over the last two years? You never directly responded in your return letters. I thought you would hate me forever." Thomas looked at her, measuring her response.

"Hate you?" she exclaimed, her voice low. "For what? For wanting to be close to me while I was sleeping?"

"But I caressed and fondled you without your permission; that's why I felt I had to tell you."

"Will you stop worrying about it now? If it makes you feel any better, I wish I had awoken. Now forget about it once and for all."

"I'm sorry that I had to unload all those things on you, but my conscience was bothering me, and . . . and about . . . uh . . . your sister, Shivani . . . uh . . . ."

"Stop it, please."

That, very much unlike his confession of fondling her while she was asleep, which somehow amused her, had hurt her deeply, but she'd managed to get over it.

"You no longer think of her, right?"

"Of course not. First of all, she's married now, and I have trained my mind not to even think about married women. Secondly, all I ever wanted in her was you. I told you that in my letter."

"I know. And I believed you. Anyway, it's over. You have confessed it to me and to your priest; now just forget it and let it all go. No one holds anything over you, especially not me."

"Thank you, but . . . ."

"Oh, do you think God is angry? If I'm not, why would he be? Don't think about it. Excuse me for saying so, but didn't you learn anything from Ibsen?"

"From whom?" He was completely caught off guard by the name of Ibsen.

"Ibsen! Didn't you read all his plays one winter?"

"How did you know that?"

"Wasn't I your maid for three years?" she said playfully. "Maids know everything."

"But seriously, how did you know that?"

"First of all, you were constantly misplacing your books and forever asking me where they were. Secondly, you were eternally talking about *A Doll House* and *The Wild Duck* and *Hedda Gabler* to anyone in the house who was interested."

Thomas was shocked and began to recall what she was talking about.

"And of course, *The Master Builder*; you talked about that for weeks on end."

Dumbfounded, Thomas finally said, "How do you remember those?"

"I read them too."

"What? When?"

"When my work was done, when Sister left or was sleeping; when the kids were at school and you were at the university. I always wanted to talk to you about them, as you used to go around trying to discuss them with anyone who would listen, but I was always too shy, and I didn't want the others to know that I'd been reading rather than working."

Still amazed, Thomas said, "Well, what did you mean just now when you asked me whether I had learned anything from him?"

"Have you forgotten one of the most common topics in some of those plays?"

"Honestly, Jhansi, you surprise me. Of course I haven't forgotten." He searched his memory to recall exactly what she could be referring to.

"Don't trouble yourself now, my sweet; you've had a long trip. I'll tell you later."

"No. Tell me now."

"Later."

"Now!"

"Okay. Don't you remember how the dark, suppressed, and guilty secrets in the lives of Ibsen's characters caused so much havoc for them?"

"Yes, I do remember now. Poor little Nora. Wasn't she the main character in *A Doll House*? And what's-her-name in *The Wild Duck*, who hid her affair from her husband all those years."

"Yes, but the affair was over by the time she married. Gina was her name," she said, "and there was no need to reveal the affair; doing so ruined everything . . . and all for nothing."

"My, what a sharp memory you have! But I still really don't get your point. I'm not hiding anything from you. I want you to know everything about me, even the dark side. That's why I told you everything—about Shivani, about the fondling, and even about the times I ran off to confession because I had looked at pornography and masturbated."

"Okay, I know everything now, and it doesn't matter. I love you. I see your goodness; that's enough light to chase away all the darkness, which, after all, my king, is next to nothing."

Thomas was relieved to reveal all his secrets to her, and wanted also to reveal them to his wife.

"Thank you, Jhansi, thank you. I wonder if my wife would respond as you have if she knew everything."

"You mean you still don't understand, my great king? You can't expect her to. She's your wife; that's the point, and you must never breathe a word to her about Shivani or me or the fondling. That would dishonor her. Don't you love her?"

"Why of course I do . . . she is . . ."

"You cannot tell her everything; just tell me. And then hide me without guilt in your hair, like Lord Shiva hid Ganga. I won't disturb your marriage or your purity. I will just love you from above, so to speak. And stop thinking about the fondling and about your fleeting moments of sexual impurity, and about the fling with my sister, although," she said hesitatingly, "you really should speak to her on the telephone sometime before you leave."

"Does she know I'm here?"

"No, not yet. Rest now; you must be exhausted."

"Can you lay down next to me?"

"I wish," she said lovingly, "maybe later," and walked gently out of the room.

Thomas had difficulty sleeping at first. He reached for the book he'd placed on the nightstand. It was his latest Narayan novel, which he'd begun on the flight over. He was so struck by one particular passage that he resisted the sleep calling him and quickly committed it to memory. After two or three pages, he finally fell into a deep sleep and dreamt about secrets and wild ducks and dollhouses; he also dreamt he was a little boy in a delightfully foreign country looking at photographs of the people he loved. When he awoke, she was right next to him with a very serious look on her face. He reached out and took her hand to kiss it, but she quickly reached out and kissed his first.

"Why do you love me, Jhansi?"

She just kept smiling and kissed his hand again.

"Come on, let's go, if you wish, over to the house of my father's friend; his family wants to meet you."

"Sure, let's go."

They stepped out onto the street about an hour after sunset. Thomas had noticed the density of the jostling crowd when he arrived, but now it had thickened even more.

"What's going on tonight? Is there a festival or something?"

"There's a feast for the god Shiva," Jhansi's father replied.

"Oh, so that's why there are so many people, huh?"

"Perhaps a few more than usual, I suppose."

"You mean it's usually this crowded?"

"Oh yes, and more so, because sometimes two or three feasts are going on at the same time; there's always some sort of Hindu festival going on."

Thomas was amazed at the variety of colors, sounds, and smells. India was foreign—more foreign than any place he'd ever been to, and he'd been all around the world. The Indian sense of space was unique. At times, he literally had to step over a few people who'd decided to go to sleep, presumably for the night.

"Are they homeless?" he asked Jhansi.

"No, not necessarily, but it's hot tonight, and they'd rather sleep out."

"So they have homes?"

"Some do, some don't; who knows?" she said nonchalantly. "Why, are you afraid you'll be out here with them?" she said teasingly.

"Don't you wonder who they are and what their stories are?" he fired back, ignoring her little joke.

Jhansi got more serious.

"Some of them are Bhangis, some are Chamars."

"You mean untouchables?"

"Yes, different classes of untouchables, I guess."

"But I thought India's constitution abolished the practice of untouchability in all its forms."

"It did, in 1950, article seventeen to be exact," quipped Jhansi, who'd been one of the best students in her high school.

"Then why . . . ?"

"Be careful!" she screamed, as she pulled him out of the way of a bullock cart. "You're not untouchable; they'll run you over if you're not more careful."

For Thomas, the energy on the streets and in the fly-ridden shops was staggering. They turned left off of what he thought was the main street on to a street even more dense and alive. For a moment, he imagined himself in the middle of a major tourist section in some Italian city, throbbing with life, but this was grander because it was more real, with none of the artificiality one sees in the tourist sections of those cities. And there weren't any tourists. In fact, Thomas noticed he was the only non-Indian around.

"Now what were you asking me?" said Jhansi calmly.

"Well, I was just wondering why, after fifty years, the law hasn't been enforced. In my college days, I remember reading about the brilliant Dr. B. R. Ambedkar, an ex-untouchable, and Nehru's Minister of Law, who got a PhD from Columbia University. I thought his tenure marked the beginning of the end of the practice."

"You're right, he probably was India's greatest untouchable, but don't forget," said Jhansi's father, getting in on the subject now, "toward the end of his life, he was so discouraged with the way that so many upper-caste Hindus simply ignored article seventeen that he became a Buddhist."

"Anyway," said Jhansi, with a slight air of authority, "caste systems are everywhere, aren't they?"

"What do you mean?" Thomas questioned her.

"There are classes in every society, that's all. Ours may be more pronounced and caused by a different belief system, but it's impossible to escape class differences in any society, and anyway, what a boring world it would be without all the differences."

"So I see that it was not only the high-caste Hindus that drove the good minister to despair, but Catholics from Madras as well."

"On the contrary, I'm all for article seventeen."

Thomas accepted her words somewhat reluctantly since there was still so much to say on the subject, but he sensed something final in her comments preventing any more discussion.

"No reply, Dr. Sleiman," she said teasingly.

"No, Miss, except that I see you haven't changed your paradoxical way of speaking and thinking."

"I can't," she said laughingly. "I'm Indian."

Actually, he had wanted to ask her whether she thought it was intrinsic to man's nature to discriminate. He asked himself whether man ought to discriminate. He imagined himself organizing a high-level conference debate on the stratification of souls and the metaphysics of gradation, which would draw Pythagoras, Plato, Jesus Christ, Marx, Gandhi, and liberation theologians to a conference table. She took hold of his forearm with both of her hands as he reflected on the subject. He loved the way she held his arm.

Is the way she holds on to me Indian too? Her femininity is intoxicating, just like her mother's food. I wonder what caste she belongs to?

They finally arrived at their destination after passing a few small Hindu temples and numerous shrines. Each shrine brought with it different gods, different smells, different sounds, and different devotees. After a tour of the house, an unusually large one for the area, and after meeting all the inhabitants, they took their seats on a balcony that looked out over the jostling crowd below. When an old yellow water truck pulled up next to a Hindu shrine, it was instantly attacked by a horde of womenfolk. As honey attracts swarms of honeybees, dozens immediately stormed it with plastic water pails in one hand and pocket change in the other. The vast variety of India generated a unique energy that fiercely captivated him. As he threw a look at Jhansi sitting on the edge of the balcony, he realized it was the first time he was really beholding her in her native surroundings, and he was even more enamored of her. She possessed some strangely beautiful charm.

He remembered Sriram, one of the main characters in Narayan's astounding novel *Waiting for the Mahatma*, who was instantly cured of his infatuation with Northern European women when he first saw Bharati, a Southern Indian beauty to whom, after just one passing glimpse, he devoted his life.

"What are you thinking?" she said, noticing his momentary absence.

"About Sriram and Bharati."

"You have other Indian friends besides us?"

"Yes. In a way, I do feel they are friends."

"Why is your speech so cryptic?"

"They are characters in a Narayan novel."

"I see. What's it about?"

"Well, it starts out with the displeasure of a young boy upon seeing the framed photograph of his mother, who died delivering him."

"Displeasure? Why?"

"He wanted her to look like the woman in the portrait that hung in his neighbor's little shop."

"And whose portrait hung in the shop?"

"Oh, it was the portrait of some European queen with red cheeks. His enthrallment with it led him into Kanni's shop each day where he sat and stared at it for hours. He wanted to buy the portrait, but Kanni wouldn't part with it. And then one day, without warning, he laid his eyes on Bharati, and everything changed. I've memorized the passage just today if you would like to hear it."

"Of course I would; go ahead, please quote it if you really can."

"All right, here it is: 'As he approached the Market Fountain a pretty girl came up and stopped him. 'Your contribution?' she asked, shaking a sealed tin collecting box. Sriram's throat went dry and no sound came. He had never been spoken to by any girl before; she was slender and young, with eyes that sparkled with happiness. He wanted to ask, How old are you? What caste are you? Where is your horoscope? Are you free to marry me? She looked so different from the beauty in Kanni's shop; his critical faculties were at once alert, and he realized how shallow was the other beauty, the European queen, and wondered that he had ever given her a thought. He wouldn't look at the picture again even if Kanni should give it to him free.'"

"I like it," Jhansi said with a gracious smile.

"I knew you would; that's why I bothered to memorize it."

But there was another reason, of course: it spoke to him about himself, and this he would not share with Jhansi, at least not yet. Whereas just the day before, his thoughts were full of the fair-skinned Juliet, everything had changed once he saw Jhansi again, everything, and all in an instant. Juliet was not a queen, of course, but at times she acted as if she were. Like the time she slapped Thomas right across the face when he told her, once he returned from India, that he couldn't continue with her anymore. She sensed it had to do with Jhansi, and of course it did, but Thomas couldn't bring himself to tell her directly. He was stunned by that slap, as it'd been the first time anyone had ever slapped him like that. Not even his mother or father, as he told her a few moments later, had ever slapped him across the face. When he was tempted to go back to her, all he had to do was to think of that episode, and the desire to see her would pass. Only once, after he got back from India, would he ever hold Juliet again. The other thought, of course, that made his desire to see her dissipate quickly, was of Jhansi, that South Indian beauty whose eyes, like Bharati's, sparkled with a sad sort of happiness that wasn't totally of this world.

"I like the name Bharati, don't you?" Thomas asked her on their way back home.

"Yes, I do. Do you know what it means?"

"Sure. It means India."

"You're a very good student, Dr. Sleiman," she said, and they went on teasing one another in playful exchanges about little nothings.

The crowd had not dwindled at all. Jhansi's father was ahead of them conversing deeply with his friend about politics, as if they were ministers of high repute and their thoughts really mattered. Jhansi suddenly yelled out to a friend whom she spotted on the other side of the street. Thomas wondered how she'd been able to pick her out in the sea of humanity that flooded the soiled streets. Her friend came running over embracing Jhansi as if she'd not seen her for some time. She kept peeking at Thomas every few seconds as they talked on a mile a minute in Tamil.

He finally asked them blankly, "Are you talking about me?"

Neither of them answered, but they giggled like teenagers.

"She's my best friend; her name is Sita. You may speak to her in English; her English is even better than mine."

"Very pleased to meet you, Sita. My name is Thomas."

"I know your name, sir. I have heard it often."

Jhansi gave a little nudge to her friend, and the two were giggling again. Sita's face, a bit darker than Jhansi's, shone with a refreshing innocence. Thomas could see in her expression the depth of her affection for his Jhansi.

"We used to work together at the studio; we were both receptionists."

Thomas just nodded politely.

"Please, Sita," Jhansi pleaded, "come over soon. I miss you."

"I will come soon. I miss you too, my dear. I don't look forward to going to work anymore now that you have left me all alone there."

"Is he married now?" Jhansi asked in spite of herself, and they both switched immediately to Tamil, continuing the conversation for a few seconds more.

"We must catch up with my father. Come over."

"Of course, I'll come see you soon."

She politely and warmly took leave of Thomas by bringing her hands together as if to pray, and was off.

"Is who married now?" Thomas asked once they began walking again.

"I'll tell you later."

"Why not now?"

"Why are you so curious?"

"I'm not really so curious; I'm just asking, that's all."

Jhansi was quiet for a while and then finally said, "I left my work because the manager wanted to marry me."

"Was he rich?"

"Very much so."

"Handsome?"

She smiled shyly.

"I see that's a definite yes."

"No, it isn't. I mean . . . he was handsome, but I didn't notice."

Thomas looked at her over the top of his glasses in a way that made her realize how contradictory her reply was.

"I mean, yes he was, but I didn't care. I don't care. I quit so he would stop pursuing me. I refused to tell him anything about myself."

"That's the only reason you quit?"

"Yes, and I made sure he knew that too so as to show him how dead set against him I really was."

"Why? What did he do to you?"

"Nothing, but I can't even think of another man in my life. Never! Never! I shall die first."

"Never say never, my dear."

"I shall forever say never, and you shall see," she said with firmness while searching for his hand. She held it tightly all the rest of the way home, where they found her father waiting for them.

"He's probably hungry, Jhansi. Go up and get something ready for him," Thomas ordered once they came near her father. Jhansi went up ahead of them, leaving them to converse about the weather and other such things. She appeared twenty minutes later announcing that their food was ready. After a light meal, they all got ready for bed and went up to the roof together. It was a full moon. Jhansi had fixed a cot for him, while everyone else just slept on the cement with a bit of padding underneath. When she came over to say goodnight to him, he asked, "So is he married now?"

"Yes. Yes. Thank God. He is. And I no longer have to worry about him coming after me as he told Sita he would."

"Wouldn't you have any say in it?"

"No. I told you. This is South India. It is still more traditional than other parts of India, and if he'd put enough pressure on my parents, they would have finally forced me to marry him, I think. I'm twenty-four, you know. My relatives are already asking why I'm not married. And I can't keep pulling the coffee stunt. Anyway . . . it hurts," she whispered softly as a tear welled up in her eye.

He wanted badly to thrust his arms around her tiny little waist and pull her down next to him and kiss her all over, including the scars on her legs.

"Goodnight . . . thank you for coming all this way to see me."

"Thank you, my angel, for receiving me."

She left him and took her place next to her sister a few yards away. When he glanced in her direction before finally giving in to the sleep forcefully calling him to surrender, he noticed in the moonlight that she had begun her holy hour, kneeling on the cement, rosary in hand, praying to the Virgin, as had been her custom since the time she'd made her first Holy Communion at age seven.

CHAPTER TEN

He awoke very early the next morning to the sound of crows. Everyone was still sleeping. He sat up and entered the morning silence after situating himself so that he could see her. His thoughts went back immediately to the previous evening. He recited quietly the passage he had memorized so as not to forget it. The word caste kept coming to mind, and he speculated on what it had to do with the ideas of perfection and evolution, two ideas occupying his mind ever since his lengthy discussion with a woman in Iran who was writing a dissertation on the concept of spiritual perfection in Islam and Christianity. She argued that many Christian and Islamic mystics had similar beliefs when it came to the topic of spiritual perfection and its attainment. She liked Thomas's paper and asked him to help supervise her work; he readily agreed.

"Perfection, gradation, caste, evolution, stratification," he repeated to himself. "What would be my theme," he wondered, as he now seriously entertained the idea of organizing a conference on the metaphysics of gradation and the stratification of souls. "I suppose I could link it to a cultural day at the university and invite the Indian ambassador to give a talk on the richness of Indian culture. He would introduce the idea of caste in Indian history and then brag about how article seventeen of the constitution banned it. At this point, I would mischievously ask why the ban had never been implemented." H e began to take delight in the imaginary conference, and asked himself what his precise contribution would be.

"I think I will speak about the Christian Doctrine of Deification," he concluded, and began mentally to put together the outline of his paper. "I will begin with a quote from St. Athanasius; this will positively shock my audience into really listening. They'll need this, especially if I'm not the first or second speaker since they're usually brain dead after the first two presentations. Then again, I could be the first presenter. But this won't look good if I'm the organizer. Anyway, whether I'm first or last, I'll get their attention with the quote from Athanasius: 'God became man so that man might become God.' His mind raced on; he wished he had a pencil and notepad to jot down the outline. "I must first put the doctrine into its historical context," he reasoned. "But how will it all relate to an Indian cultural day? Perhaps we should keep the two events separate."

He then remembered the key that Jhansi's mother had left near his cot. He got up quietly, descended the stairs, and entered the house. In a few minutes, he was back on his cot with pencil and notepad in hand, staring at the lovely young woman who was his inspiration, still fast asleep. Before he penned the following words, he had decided that the two events should be separate.

"'The Catholic Church had to defend its age-old Doctrine of Deification at the time of the Reformation since Luther had claimed that human nature was completely corrupted by Adam's sin. Notice, the Church had always held it, but only felt the need to officially teach and defend it when Luther challenged it. Luther thought that justification was essentially a juridical act, an *actus forensis* by which God declared the sinner to be justified, although the sinner remained intrinsically unjust and sinful. According to this Lutheran view, then, one's sins were merely covered up, not really taken away. The Council of Trent in the sixteenth century attacked this view and defined justification, rather, in the light of St. Paul's letter to the Colossians, chapter one, verse thirteen, as '*translatio ab eo statu, in quo homo nascitur filius primi Adam, in statum gratiae et adoptionis filiorum Dei per secundum Adam Jesus Christum Salvatorem nostrum.*'"

He paused at this point to look at one of the huge brave crows that had crept up beside him. Glancing over what he had written, he said to himself, "But perhaps it's supercilious these days to force the audience to wrestle with the Latin." The crow inched closer. "Or maybe not; they should know enough Latin to understand this much," he argued with himself. "If they don't, they have no business attending the conference. Then again, I've forgotten most of the little Latin I ever knew. Yes, but they won't know that. If I just quote the Latin without bothering to translate it, those who don't understand will be instantly cowed. Thank God our professors made us memorize this passage in order to pass our comps. No. I won't translate it. This will serve them right; give them some humility, perhaps, and it might even help to save their souls since most of those damned academicians are bubbling over with intellectual pride and self-importance anyway. Get a hold of yourself, for heaven's sake, Thomas; aren't you one of those damned academicians? You want them to understand, don't you? Is your purpose to cow them? No. Of course not. Okay, I'll provide the translation. Now let me see if I can still translate it."

He went on talking to himself like this for another five minutes and then spent the next ten minutes translating the Latin into readable English. He finally wrote, "Translation from the condition in which man is born as the son of the first Adam into the state of grace and adoption among the children of God through the second Adam, Jesus Christ, Our Saviour."

He then wrote the following: "This meant that a true eradication of sin is achieved through the saving works of Christ, and that through supernatural sanctifying grace the inner man is completely and radically renewed or born again, and is made to actually participate in the divine nature."

He paused to read all that he had written and was extremely pleased with it. "The entire first chapter of St. Peter's letter, in fact, has always been a preferred reference for deification theologians," he said to himself. "I must be able to recall the relevant biblical references since I ask my students to do so on their exams. Well, let's see . . . there is 1 Peter 1:4, and I'm sure the Greek fathers liked to quote from Psalm 81:6, 1 John1:12, and Titus 3:5."

The rest of the scriptures came to him without thinking, and he quickly jotted on his notepad James 1:18, 1 Peter 1:23, and John 10:34.

He paused to watch the brave crow peck at what seemed to be a bone of some sort underneath his cot. After ruminating for some minutes, he wrote the following: "The term deification, which means to become like God, was used by many of the Fathers of the Church in both ancient and medieval times, including great saints and sages such as St. Athanasius, whom I have already referred to above, St. Augustine of Hippo, Hippolytus of Rome, Maximos the Confessor, St. Bonaventure, St. Thomas Aquinas, and others. The Council of Trent drew from this rich tradition of deification theology as well as the many liturgical expressions of deification to attack and destroy the position of the Reformers. From the Latin-Rite liturgy, the Council pointed to the offertory of the Holy Mass, which says, 'Grant that by the mystery of this water and wine, we may be made partakers of His Divinity who vouchsafed to become partaker of our humanity.' The Syro-Maronite Liturgy has something very similar in its Communion Rite of its divine liturgy: 'You have united, O Lord, your divinity with our humanity and our humanity with your divinity; your life with our mortality and our mortality with your life. You have assumed what is ours and you have given us what is yours, for the life and salvation of our souls. To you be glory, O Lord, forever.' This is a very ancient prayer going all the way back to the first Christians who were Jews. Thus the original is in Syriac, a dialect of the Aramaic language spoken by the Jews at the time of Christ."

Thomas happened to know quite a bit about this ancient form of Semitic Christianity because he belonged to an Eastern Rite of the Roman Catholic Church, which still used Syriac in its liturgies and whose origins went back to the earliest Jewish-Christian communities. He debated at this point whether to go deeper into the early Jewish-Christian concept of deification and perfection. He could write pages and pages on the Syriac tradition and even include a section on the Syriac tradition of Christianity in India, since most of the thirty million Christians in India traced their origins to St. Thomas the Apostle and the Syriac tradition of Christianity. He thought he could somehow tie the existence of these Malayalam-speaking Christians, living mostly in the South Indian state of Kerala, into his overall theme since he vaguely remembered that the famous Indian writer, Arundhati Roy, had referred to their special caste status in her award-winning novel, *The God of Small Things*. That reference stayed with him because of her powerful description of how the Paravans (yet another group of untouchables) had to crawl backward while sweeping away their footprints with a broom so that high-caste Syriac Christians and Brahmins wouldn't defile themselves by stepping in them.

He gave it much thought, then decided it would distract from the main theme: the teaching of divinization or deification in Christianity. After arguing with himself for the better half of fifteen minutes, he finally wrote the following: "In its teaching on deification, the Catholic Church is cognizant of two extremes that have tended to emerge among the so-called deification theologians, and which has led (and still leads) them down wrong paths. Both may be called gnostic forms of deification thought, as self-gnosis is pivotal in each form."

He hesitated again and put down his pencil; the bold black crow had gotten what it wanted but was still loitering around the cot. "Should I define gnosticism for them?" he asked the crow, who cocked his head and peered at him with a beady eye. Taking that skeptical look as an answer, Thomas murmured, "No. Not necessary," and picked up the pen again:

"The main characteristic of the first form, which has many variations, is the conviction that man, by nature, is already a god. Thus, one deifies oneself through self-knowledge since one is a god who does not yet know who or what he is. By discovering the right gnosis, then, one is propelled along the path of a kind of spiritual evolution wherein the divine being in him from birth emerges and develops. The path of deification here is first and foremost a path of knowledge, that is, a gnosis whereby man simply discovers who he already is. In 1835, the great German scholar, F. C. Baur, in his monumental work, *Die Christliche Gnosis*, claimed that this gnostic element of deification was present in the philosophy of Hegel. And L. Kolakowski, in his three-volume work *Hauptstrmungen des Marxismus*, maintained that something similar to this could be found in the philosophy of Marx."

Should I translate the German titles into English? he wondered, and then decided to leave them as they were. He continued writing, shifting to the first person: "I am no expert on the thought of either Hegel or Marx, but such elements are quite easily discernible by even a non-expert in these philosophies and are generally recognized in the Catholic intellectual tradition as new and improved forms of the heretical deification theology found in ancient Gnosticism. The Church rejects it precisely because the one who seeks deification in this way does so not through the sanctifying grace of Christ's death and resurrection, but through one's own efforts and decisions with respect to self-knowledge. In addition to this, such forms of deification theology claim, quite arrogantly, according to the Church, that the one deified receives for himself, through self-discovery, everything that God possesses including the identity of substance. The Church taught (teaches), rather, that one is deified first and foremost by sanctifying grace through which he receives (man's relation to God is first receptive) for himself everything that God possesses except the identity of substance."

He now took a longer break to look it over from the very beginning and was pleasantly surprised that he'd been able to produce so much verbiage off the top of his head.

I wonder if she'll understand any of this, he thought. "Well, I'm not writing it for her anyway," he told the crow, who seemed to have become his companion for the morning. "But, then again, she is my inspiration, so it is for her in a way. She inspires me in that she thinks well of me. No. It's more than that; she loves me. She has deified me."

This last thought gave him great energy and joy, which must have affected the crow, who took to his wings and flew off for new adventures.

"In fact, she makes me want to become better than I am, to evolve spiritually and intellectually, to become perfect. Now what's wrong with that? In taking me as her hero she has in effect become my heroine."

He didn't see the small smile on the lips of his muse, who feigned sleep hoping to hear more.

He reflected on the whole idea of hero worship again, and his writing went off on a long but related tangent. When he went back to read what he had written, it was hardly intelligible. He had been so taken by his subject that he had failed to notice that Jhansi was awake.

She startled him by asking, "Have you long been awake?"

"Oh, good morning, Jhansi. How did you sleep? Pleasant dreams? Look what I've been doing. Would you like to read it? Or would you like me to read it to you?"

"Which question should I answer first? You've asked four."

"I'm sorry, I got all worked up while writing down a few thoughts this morning," he said, showing her his notes.

"You call these a few thoughts?" she said as she glanced at the better part of eleven pages.

"Yes, you may read it if you wish, although it's boringly academic."

"Why do you write if it's boring, but more than that, how does something so boring get you so worked up and excited?"

"Oh, the topic is not boring at all. It's of extreme importance. In fact, there is nothing more important. It's all about who we are and where we're going and why and how we're going there. But I mean the academic manner may put you off a bit, although it's really not that scholarly either, because I'm not really a scholar, you know. It's related to our brief discussion of the caste system last night."

She just smiled. "I knew you wanted to pursue that topic."

"Then why did you cut me off?"

"I didn't; you stopped, remember?"

All but ignoring her last statement, he said, "Jhansi, haven't you ever asked yourself who you are?"

"I know who I am," she said with great confidence and simplicity.

"You do?"

"Of course I do. I am the slave of my great king."

"Stop it, Jhansi."

"Stop what? You think I'm kidding?"

"And who were you before you knew your great king," he asked, convinced that he'd stumped her.

"I wasn't."

"You weren't what?"

"I wasn't. I was born when I started loving and serving him," she said without a trace of affectation or romanticism.

Thomas was startled.

"Why do you look so perplexed? I've told you this much time and again in my letters."

"But I always thought it was some sort of literary hyperbole or something. I didn't know it was . . . true."

She stared at him blankly as if unable to comprehend what he'd said. "You mean you thought I was lying?"

"No. I didn't think you were lying, but . . ."

"But what?"

"I thought that perhaps your emotions had gotten the best of you. After all, you did tell me that I was your first love."

"And my last," she asserted with conviction.

"When and where did you learn this word love, Jhansi?"

"I learnt it growing up. Doesn't every language have this word?"

"Yes, but it means so many different things depending on the era and the place. And to add to the confusion, we say in English, I love apple pie, I love horses, I love horse races, I love history, and I love you, as when I declare that I want to marry you."

"Well, in Tamil we have different words for different kinds of loves."

Thomas sat up amazed, and said with all attention, "Please tell me."

"Well, first there is *anbhu*, which is the love of parents and family. Then we have *natpu*, which is the love of friends and relatives. And then there is *khadhal*, which is the love of lovers, and, hopefully, the love between husband and wife."

"Will you teach me the proper spellings and pronunciations of those words? I think I'll include them in my magnum opus on love."

"In your what?" she asked unwittingly.

"In my great book on love; I think I was born to write it, but I just can't seem to get started."

"So you're like Nagaraj in Narayan's *The World of Nagaraj*, are you?"

"Yes, I suppose, but unlike him, who was simply writing the definitive work on the life and times of the great Indian sage Narada, 'who for all his brilliance and accomplishments carried a curse on his back that unless he spread a gossip a day, his skull would burst,' I am writing something more profound and comprehensive."

"So what's your purpose in writing this great book?"

Thomas was speechless. "My purpose?"

"Yes. Nagaraj wanted to write about the life of Narada because, as he said, 'lives of great men remind us that we could make ours sublime.'"

"Uh . . . well . . . I guess my purpose is somehow commensurate with that."

Although her English vocabulary was quite good due to the thorough Indian education she had received, the word commensurate was new to her. While wondering what it meant, she said, "Now, about what you've written this morning—who we are and where we're going and why and how we're going there—what does that have to do with your great book on love? You said it was our discussion on caste that got you started."

"It was. You see, I went from caste, to stratification, to gradation, to perfection, to deification, to identity, to eternal destiny, to love, where it all began; for if I didn't love humanity, I wouldn't have asked you about those untouchables in the first place."

"I'm confused," she said. "I know what it means to love a human being, but I'm not sure what it means to love humanity."

Thomas again fell silent, pondering the interesting philosophical question she had unknowingly raised about both the nature of universals and the nature of love.

"That question, Jhansi, pretty much embodies the whole of medieval philosophy." He almost forgot that he was not in his classroom.

"Really? How so?"

"Well, I can't just explain it like that. You need some background first. You need to study the history of philosophy wherein one finds a particular unity. There's a great book by a famous French scholar titled *The Unity of Philosophical Experience*, which I highly recommend." He said this instinctively as if giving her an assignment.

"Yes, sir, Master Teacher, I shall find it tomorrow and begin it immediately," she said, poking fun at his tone of voice.

He laughed at himself and again grew quiet. By this time, Meena had awoken and joined them. She had gotten in on the tail end of the conversation on love. Their mother had gotten up as well and was already done preparing coffee, which she was now serving them.

"Why haven't you helped our mother, Meena?" asked Jhansi, wishing she could have Thomas to herself a while longer.

"I tried to, but she declined my help and told me to join you."

The four of them drank their coffee quietly; the others were still sleeping. Their mother asked Thomas if he'd slept well and how long he'd been up. Jhansi told her a bit about what he'd been doing all morning. This led them into a conversation about the untouchables. Jhansi's mother assured them that even she remembered seeing the Paravans with their brooms.

"Thank God those days are over," said Meena, embarrassed for her country.

"Don't kid yourself, my child; those days are not at all over."

Once everyone had gotten up, they planned their day during breakfast and finally agreed on a trip to a Hindu shrine, a poet's memorial monument, a museum, and the university. It was decided that only Jhansi and Meena were to accompany Thomas. On the way to the poet's monument, Meena returned to the subject of love after first asking her sister's permission to address Thomas with a question.

"Sir, do you think the word love is real, or have we merely learnt it from romantic novels and films?"

"Could you elaborate a bit, my dear," said Thomas enthusiastically, delighted by the question.

"Our history teacher believes that romanticism is a creation of Western society and that the very word love lacks substance. Do you agree?"

"I do agree in a way, but should we reduce love to romanticism? You probably haven't read Gustave Flaubert's *Madame Bovary*, have you?"

"No sir."

"I didn't think so, since you study primarily English and Tamil literature at the university, right?"

"That's right, but I have a pen pal from Pondicherry, and she tells me that they read a lot of French literature there."

"Anyway, it has been translated into English. If you can get a hold of it, I suggest you read it. The translation by Mildred Marmur is good, although the one by Eleanor Marx Aveling is pretty good too, at least that's what one of my students recently told me."

"Tell me about it, sir, if you please."

"Yes. Well, it's a powerful statement on the futility of romanticism created by some romantic literature. The story is about a young woman who ruins herself and her husband because of the silly and senseless notions of love she has learnt from sentimental novels. So I think your teacher has an important point to make. However, I think there's an authentic romantic literature that fosters genuine sentiment as opposed to sentimentality. If you're really interested, I would recommend you read Marie Corelli's *Love and the Philosopher*; it's a masterpiece! At any rate, to ignore the importance of such literature for the proper shaping of the intellect and the emotions is just as unwise as to indulge in the bad stuff."

"But how do you know the difference?"

"That's the job of the teacher of literature. Hopefully, the teacher possesses the cardinal virtues of prudence, justice, fortitude, and temperance. Or, in the worst-case scenario, is striving to possess them, and can therefore point out the proper paths to follow."

"I think Narayan takes up this whole romantic issue in his novel *The Painter of Signs*," Jhansi added, finally getting in on the conversation.

"Remind me; I've forgotten," said Thomas.

"Don't you remember the dialogue between Raman and Daisy sitting under the stars on the granite steps with their feet in the cold and refreshing water?"

"Vaguely, but remind me," said Thomas, delighted by her comment, which made her seem more beautiful to him than he had ever seen her before.

"I think it's best to listen to Narayan himself. I've got the book at home; we'll read it together when we get back."

When they arrived at the impressive monument, they argued a bit with the motor-rick driver over the high fare, and made their way toward the monument as the two girls eagerly told Thomas all about the love poems written by the great poet, many of which were carved in the stone monument.

After a long day and a delicious supper, they made their way up to the roof. They brought with them a small lantern so that Jhansi would have enough light to read some passages from *The Painter of Signs*:

They sat on the last step with their feet in water. It was cold and refreshing. The stars shone, the darkness was welcome, cool breeze, cold water lapping the feet, the voices and sounds of the living town far away muffled and soft; habitual loungers on the river-bank passing across the sands homeward softly like flitting shadows. The air had become charged with rich possibilities. He threw a look at her, and felt drawn to her. He edged a few inches nearer involuntarily. She did not move away, but said, "Don't try to get into trouble again."

Meena interrupted. "What did she mean by 'get into trouble again'?"

Recalling the storyline, Thomas answered. "Raman approached Daisy one night from underneath a jutka carriage while she was sleeping in it above him. Anticipating his intentions, she left her sleeping quarters just in time, escaping to a nearby tree where she spent the night."

"Why were they sleeping there?"

"We can't retell the entire story now, Meena. Read the book if you wish, but let me continue this passage without interruption."

"Very well, go ahead, sister."

"But she should know, Jhansi," said Thomas softly, counteracting Jhansi's harsh tone. "This was the first time Raman had seen Daisy for many weeks." He was surprised at how quickly the details of the story returned to him.

"Yes," admitted Jhansi, sensing that she had been too harsh, "because Daisy had left him without even saying goodbye after the carriage episode; poor Raman thought she'd turned him in to the police."

"You can imagine his joy in seeing her and learning that she had not only not turned him in to the police, but that she had allowed him back into her favor," said Thomas, recalling his earlier confession to Jhansi about his own moment of weakness.

To Meena, Jhansi said, "Okay, dear, that should put you into the picture. Now let's see, where was I?" Glancing at the passage she had been reading, she said, "Oh yes, Daisy was telling Raman not to get into trouble again, and Raman merely said, 'I like you. I feel lost without you.'" From this point on, Jhansi read the passage uninterrupted:

"Better than getting lost along with me," she mumbled on. "I love you, I like you, are words which can hardly be real. You have learnt them from novels and Hollywood films perhaps. When a man says 'I love you' and the woman repeats 'I love you'—it sounds so mechanical and unconvincing. Perhaps credible in Western society, but sounds silly in ours. People really in love would be struck dumb, I imagine."

"Love is the same in any society," he said, after all venturing to utter the term love. If she was going to push him into the river for it, well, he'd face it.

He said, "I agree with you. I don't believe in the romanticism created by the literary man. It has conditioned people's thinking and idiom and made people prattle like imbeciles in real life too."

She laughed at his observation, and he felt pleased that he had after all made some mark. No further speech for a little while. Then his hand seemed to move by itself and find hers, which felt cold and soft.

She did not reject his touch, but just laughed and said, "You are an incurable romantic in spite of what you say!"

"Who wouldn't be with you so near?" He wanted to say many things to her which would express his innermost feelings, with all the intensity, muddle, and turbulence. He wanted to place his whole life before her in a proper perspective so that she might take him seriously. He rambled on in a reminiscent manner. He did not know where to begin or how to continue. He wished to express to her that meeting with her had been a landmark in his existence—how much he owed her; wanted to speak of his philosophy of life; wanted to justify himself as a sign-board painter.

"Superb isn't it," asserted Thomas, always impressed with Narayan's simple and fresh mastery of the English language.

"So where do you think Narayan stands on the question of love?" asked Meena.

"Well, I think he makes you feel more with Raman than with Daisy," said Thomas. "At least I was more sympathetic with Raman throughout," he added, as if the passage had been some sort of redemption for him.

"What about you, Jhansi?" he asked.

"I think Narayan was an incurable romantic, but his romanticism was free from any sentimentality. Maybe it was like what Robert Louis Stevenson described in one of his poems as a rare and fair romantic strain."

"Interesting. I'm very impressed, Jhansi," he said sincerely. "What's the title of the poem?"

"You don't know, Dr. Sleiman?"

"No. I don't."

"It's called 'Come My Beloved Hear From Me.'"

"Can you recite it, Jhansi?" Meena asked, surprised, since she had not heard her sister speak of it before, and was duly impressed with her sister's quick and witty conversation.

"Sure," Jhansi said, but she hesitated.

"Recite it for us, please," they both asked in chorus.

"Not now; maybe later."

"When later?"

"We shall see." Changing the subject, Jhansi said, "Come on, Meena, let's leave Dr. Sleiman to continue the work he began this morning. He has mentioned twice now that he hopes he will find time to work a bit while he's here."

The girls excused themselves to bring up a small table, pencil, and paper for Thomas, and a cup of tea.

Thomas got right to work on presenting to his imaginary audience the broad outlines of another major theological error, which gnostic theologians had historically been guilty of. He wrote: "The other extreme is likewise quite ancient, and also appears in the clothing of modern philosophy, especially in the thought of the great German philosopher Martin Heidegger. Important Catholic theologians such as Hans Urs von Balthasar (arguably the most important Catholic intellectual of the century—as well as one of the only 'universal scholars' in the world in the twentieth century) describe this form as a 'deification of contingency' whereby the path is also knowledge of self, but a knowledge that ends in making 'absolute' man's 'radical finitude'—that is to say, by 'deifying' his absolute and radical limitedness, man thereby posits himself as 'unconditionally autonomous.' But to posit 'unconditional autonomy' is to claim for oneself that which traditionally can only belong to one being, namely God."

After about an hour of rereading and adjusting what he had written, he put his pencil down. The moon, not quite full, was shining brightly, its light penetrating the darkness. As he got up to go downstairs, Jhansi met him in their previously discovered private space just inside the stairwell at the top of the stairs. They instantly embraced, and she whispered in his ear a poem:

Come, my beloved, hear from me
Tales of the woods or open sea.
Let our aspiring fancy rise
A wren's flight higher toward the skies;
Or far from cities brown and bare,
Play at the least in open air. . .
Love, and the love of life—act
Dance, live and sing through all our furrowed tract;
Till the great God enamoured gives
To him who reads, to him who lives,
That rare and fair romantic strain
That whoso hears must hear again.

PART FOUR

AND TIME THAT GAVE DOTH
NOW HIS GIFT CONFOUND

CHAPTER ELEVEN

T he next day brought them to St. Thomas Mount, a well-known Christian shrine in Chennai where tradition says Thomas, one of the twelve apostles of Christ, suffered martyrdom. It was called Peria Malai in the local language. Today they were alone. Thomas cherished the fact that they would be alone the whole day, and wondered aloud why her parents had suggested they go alone.

"Do you think they suspect anything?" he asked.

"Oh no, not between you and me. But they think there may be something between me and your brother."

This reminded Thomas of the talk he must have with her parents, but he didn't want to think of it right then since he had no idea what he was going to say.

They journeyed in an auto-rick with just room enough for three: two in the covered backseat, and one, the driver, in front. The rough-riding, noisy machine was transmuted into a heavenly carriage of sorts whenever their legs or shoulders touched. His right arm eventually found its way around her in a manner that was not at all obvious. When his hand rhythmically touched her bare shoulder, she closed her eyes softly to revel in the peace it gave her. He was practically gaping at her for the better part of the half-hour journey; she looked straight ahead. It was too noisy to talk, and they really didn't need to. Their communion was authentic and extreme. Without haggling over the fare, they got down from the cycle as if descending from a royal coach and climbed the steep steps up to the mount while reading the various biblical passages written in Tamil and English posted along the path. There were also several warnings posted threatening to haul off to jail anyone who disrespected the serenity of the holy space, and some of the scriptural verses mentioned the word sin.

The combined effect of these posted messages forced Thomas to question whether he was violating the holiness of the place by walking hand in hand with a woman who was not his wife.

It's a contradiction, damn it, to come here together in this way, he preached inwardly to himself.

Unable to discover the cause of his apprehension, which she noticed instantly, Jhansi too began to experience some uneasiness. The more they ascended, the harsher the messages became; the word sin seemed to be in every other passage. The mood grew heavier, and the lightness they'd been enjoying began to disintegrate. At the crest sat a man officiously dressed. Thomas imagined an incredulous stare in the man's eyes and prepared himself for arrest. He was all but ready to turn himself in like a worn-out fugitive when Jhansi suggested they say a little prayer; the heaviness vanished directly.

We love each other, he asserted silently. *What on earth is wrong with that, for heaven's sake?* He made a mental note that he had used the word love.

It was the tenth of May. A cool breeze and some sweet mango juice refreshed them as they sat near a jasmine vine on a wooden bench, protected from the scorching sun. They were looking at a little book they'd bought from a small library near the main church, which documented the history of the shrine. Flipping through the pages together, they noticed a picture of the place where they were sitting, ostensibly very near the actual site where St. Thomas was martyred. Under the picture was the following caption: "There is no greater love than this: to lay down one's life for one's friends. It was here at this place that St. Thomas laid down his life for Christ, his greatest and most intimate friend."

There's that word again, Thomas pondered. *I must find the auspicious time to begin the book.* The beginning moment was so important, but he mustn't fall into the same trap that Narayan's Nagaraj did, so obsessed with finding the right time to begin that he first sought the right time to decide upon the right time to begin. Paralyzed in an infinite regress, he finally began, but a little too late; he died before finishing.

Preoccupied by these reflections, Jhansi too grew melancholy.

"What is it, Jhansi?"

She didn't answer.

"Jhansi, what is it?"

"Thomas," she said, calling him by his name for the first time in the nearly five years she'd known him, "if death is the greatest proof of love, then I want to die. My heart is telling me that once you leave India in a few days, I might never see you again. If I'm right, then next year on this very date, May tenth, I want to die."

She spoke as if in a trance uttering some sort of eerie prophecy. The tone and content of her speech disconcerted him deeply.

"Stop it, Jhansi; what are you saying?"

"I'm saying what I've said for two years now; it's not a mere passing emotion."

"What is that?"

"That I cannot live without your love."

Her combination of the words *your* and *love* confounded him. Not only was the word love a great mystery, but now she had qualified it by your, an even greater enigma.

My love? What is meant by me? Who am I? he ruminated. *And what on earth is love? I need at least two chapters on the relation between love and personal identity,* he concluded, revising instantly his earlier plan to accomplish it in one.

She sat silently gazing eastward, as if contemplating some great eschatological mystery.

"Jhansi, this is nonsense. You've lived nearly twenty years without my love. You didn't even know me," he said, and added secretly, *whoever I am (or was) twenty years ago.*

"No. I wasn't really alive then. Why won't you believe that I was born again on that cold winter's night when you showed me how to massage your feet by massaging mine; I will never be the same. I'll never forget it. It was my left foot."

"Listen, Jhansi. We shall continue to write, and whenever I can, I will come to India. Either this or . . . you must forget me . . . or . . ."

"No. You can arrange a secret place for me near you," she interrupted abruptly. "I'll devote my life to you. I won't be a burden, you'll see. I'll take care of you and give myself to you. I'll demand nothing except to be near you. You'll hide me in your hair like the god Shiva who supports the River Ganga on his entangled locks. Sister will never know." She still referred to his wife as sister, just as she'd done for the three years she had served her.

Thomas remained quiet, so she continued.

"Shiva's spouse, Parvati, never knew about the goddess's wild and raging affection for Shiva, even though she was so near. It detracted not from his affection for his wife. In fact, Ganga's divine love enabled Shiva to perform his godly duties more perfectly; it made him more divine."

"You mean it deified him?"

"Yes, something like that."

"Wow! I must incorporate this into my presentation somehow," he said, trying to lighten the mood.

"Forget about your presentation," she said firmly, forcing him to take her seriously. "First get it into your life, and then you'll really be able to talk about it."

Thomas began to entertain the idea as a real possibility.

There is some logic in it; after all, Shiva had always to be straight to support Ganga on his head. He had to be more disciplined, more noble. Perhaps she's right. I'll become pure next to her purity. I'll become more . . . .

"Wait a minute. What's wrong with me?" he uttered under his breath as he checked himself. "What's wrong with me? And what's wrong with you, Jhansi?

It's not fair to Rita. It's dishonest. I have promised before God and my family and hers to love her until death."

"Then love her. Do you imagine I want anything else? If you even think of leaving her, I will leave you first."

"What?" he said incredulously. "The thought has never even crossed my mind. She's my wife, for God's sake, and the mother of my children; I love her deeply."

"I know you do; that's why I love you. She and the children are part of the you I love. I love the way you love them, especially how you relate to your children. I'll help you love them; that's all. You'll have more love to give them. Just let me love you."

Thomas was not used to this logic. He had never encountered anyone like her before.

"Put yourself in Rita's place, Jhansi."

This was too much for her, and she grew quiet; a moment later, she whispered despondently, "Then there's no other option."

Composing herself, she managed to say, "Keeping in touch through letters and a stormy trip once every few years will never work. It's not enough for me, and, besides, my parents will force me to marry, which will certainly end in some awful disaster. And as for forgetting you, it's impossible. Can you forget me?"

He was caught off guard by her question, and mumbled something unintelligible.

"If I die," she said confidently, "then you'll forget me. I think this is the best solution."

"I've never seen this theatrical side of you, Jhansi." He was relatively unaffected by what he mistook for mere drama.

"I'm not acting, my dear."

"Then what are you saying?" he asked authoritatively, and not without some indignation. "Are you threatening to kill yourself unless I bring you with me?"

"Not at all; true love is incapable of such manipulation."

"Jhansi," he said, with some fury, "suicide is a grave sin against God and against man. If you're going to speak about true love, never even allude to it again, or else I'll—"

"You'll what?" she challenged. "Is it your turn to threaten now? I didn't mention suicide, sweetheart, you did. But now that you have, is it all that different from what St. Thomas did right over there?"

"Of course it's different, Jhansi. What's the matter with you? He was killed by others because he loved and worshipped Christ."

"Well, we've just read that he knew he was going to die up here on this mount, but he came up anyway. All I'm saying is that if it's better for you and your family that I die, I am ready."

Thomas was beside himself with amazement. She was serious. The way she had addressed him by his first name added considerably to his bewilderment. Not even in her letters did she ever address him as Thomas. It was always my *kadhala*, or sweetheart, or my spirit, or my grace and paradise, or *habeebe*, or my dream, or my great king, or my prayer, and, sometimes, my Jesus, my savior, but never as Thomas.

"Do you really think it could work, Jhansi? I am not a god like Shiva. I'm a man. And I'm a Christian man who believes and teaches that monogamous marriage is a sacrament, a great mystery wherein Christ's own relationship to the Church is embodied, proclaimed, and passed on. You should know this. You're a Christian too. Man is an image of Christ, and woman an image of the Church. And just as Christ gave himself to the One Church and died to redeem her, so I am called to give myself completely and totally to my one wife."

"So continue to give yourself to her, and sacrifice your life for her. I will not distract you from this; I'll help you. We'll live in complete continence if you wish; our relationship shall be, what do you philosophers say, purely platonic or something like that. I'll sacrifice this much just to be near you once in a while. I'll stay hidden in your matted locks, my Shiva. I won't dare trespass into the territory of Parvati-Rita. I know I have no right there. Not only as a Christian do I know this, but as a woman I know it as well. Do you think I've forgotten that I was once your maid? But please let me be near you. Kiss me from time to time on my forehead and cheeks. We'll live noble lives; you'll see. I'll work and help my family and send money each month to my father, who has worked so hard for so long, and who is now at the end of his rope. He's starting to give up, Thomas.

This is my first and last request of you; please talk to my father before you leave. Tell him that you will send for me in a few months and that you will arrange my future and my marriage."

Thomas was stupefied and defeated by her strength and beauty and sincerity. He had a great desire to reach out and hold her tightly, but they were in public. His hand found hers, and they sat in silence for a long time, enjoying the breeze, the shade, the smell of the jasmine, and the warmth of each other's hands.

On the way down the mount, Thomas had a great urge to look toward the southwest at some open fields with much greenery interspersed in between. He couldn't get a clear view of what he knew he wanted to see. Once he got to the right position, the view finally opened up, and he saw some boys playing cricket far below them. The characters of Narayan's famous novel *Swami and Friends* unexpectedly came to life. But much more than that, he too became a little boy again. He could faintly hear their young voices, so full of life, so full of hope, so real. Sudden flashbacks of his own childhood playing baseball with his brothers and dad after school came rushing in. Bright spring days flooded his memory with their promise of an approaching summer carrying pledges of delicious freedom from school and buses and homework and bells and books. The pure voices penetrated him deeply and without complication. Innocence, life, love, loneliness, communion—they all blended together.

An overwhelming gratitude at being part of the great mystery of life and death gripped him tightly and would not let go. He knew somehow that he had been there before. In spite of all the uncertainty that their conversation had just created in him, he was fiercely happy and somehow peacefully sad simultaneously.

They returned in the early evening and found everyone waiting for them, anxious to learn all about their day. They did manage to make it to the University of Madras where Thomas met some officials with whom he discussed a number of affiliation possibilities.

"They seemed genuinely interested, didn't they, Jhansi?" Thomas said over dinner.

"Yes. You have a way of making almost anything interesting," she said, half-joking with him.

"Thank you, my dear."

Jhansi's mother noticed the ease with which they conversed and detected the affection in her daughter's voice.

They took turns describing the events of the day and gave a detailed account of their visit to St. Thomas Mount. As they relaxed after dinner, Jhansi's father suggested that if they wanted to go to Bangalore, they should plan on going at night on the bus so as not to waste a day traveling. They decided to catch the bus that night.

The ride was a memorable one. Jhansi's mother sat in front of them, and they sat together directly behind her. Jhansi fell asleep on his shoulder with both arms wrapped around his arm. Thomas didn't sleep: he was excited to be in India and was ardently animated by the turquoise blue sari she had donned for the journey, not to mention that he was considering what exactly he would say to her father.

The morning found them in Bangalore—much cooler and cleaner than Madras. They rented a room for the day, ordered some food, took turns showering, and settled in for a little nap. Upon waking, Jhansi's mom went to visit her mother and her brothers and sisters, all of whom lived in Bangalore, where she too had grown up. Jhansi went also, leaving Thomas to relax privately for a while, as he'd requested. But he urged them not to be too long.

She obeyed. Within forty minutes, she was back, and she came back alone.

"Where's your mom?" he asked, surprised at this sudden intimacy.

"I told her I was worried about you all alone here, and she told me to go back after I'd paid respects to my grandmother and my aunts and uncles. So that's what I did. Here I am," she said, bolting the door behind her.

They sat on the edge of the bed gazing eastward out the window. It began to rain. They went together to the window and opened it enough to breathe in the clean air without getting wet. His hand met hers, and they watched the rain penetrate and feed the hungry soil like a man making love to a woman.

Is the word rain masculine in her language? he wondered.

Spontaneously, they conceived and gave birth to a poem together. It was as natural as the feminine soil receiving the rain and giving birth to a flower—a flower made of rain and soil and sunshine. Jhansi began:

I noticed how you rushed on down
To give relief to dry, bare ground
I heard your thunder crash and toil
I saw the gratitude of soil

I smelled the scent of soft hard rain
And felt myself a child again
The flowers began a hymn of praise
For what had been denied for days

Thomas continued:

What is this freshness that you bring?
Throughout the summer, fall and spring
I wonder where your origin lies
Beneath the seas, beyond the skies

Announced by light and swaying trees
Your force did force me to my knees
And when at last you did appear
Your friend within became a tear

"Oh, what shall we name it?" she asked him, as if still a little girl.

"Why, 'The Rain,' of course; what else?" Thomas declared confidently. She looked directly into his eyes and desired him more than ever before.

"I wonder what's in my mother's mind," she asked aloud.

"I'm surprised she allowed me to return here so soon, especially since my uncle was there."

"Is this the uncle you told me about in your letters—the one who wants to marry you?"

"Yes. His pursuit has been relentless, though gentle."

"Does your mother know you don't want him?"

"Of course, I told her directly."

"Did she take personal offense? After all, he is her favorite brother, right?"

"She was hurt, but she has continued delicately to encourage it, until today."

"And your father?"

"My dad loves him; he's all for it, especially since he knows my uncle would never ask for a dowry."

"Do you like him, Jhansi?"

"Yes. He's very kind and good, but I've never looked at him in that way."

"How old is he?"

"He's your age."

"Does he have a good job?"

"Quite good, yes."

Thomas quietly considered how right the match would be, although the idea of a girl marrying her mother's brother slightly offended his semi-Western sensibilities.

"Why do you ask so many questions?"

"Why not," he retorted rather abruptly.

A tense mood ensued. He retreated into himself and swiftly decided to encourage her to marry her uncle, although he was absolutely jealous.

She sensed it in a flash and said unwaveringly, "I have but one great king; I will never have or serve another."

As before, he grew apprehensive at this solid declaration, for he was acutely aware of the risk and responsibility it entailed. Nevertheless, this time, instead of arguing, he surrendered instantly. He immediately enfolded her within his arms, and for the next hour they experienced the incarnation of their poem.

CHAPTER TWELVE

T heir time in Bangalore passed rapidly. He met her relatives, went on a tour of the city, and purchased some gifts for family and friends back home. Before long, they were back under the ferocity of the early morning Madras sun. Meena was the first to greet them.

"It seems like you've been gone for ages. Madras is miserable without you."

They hadn't much to say in return. They were worn out by the night's bus ride—the return not being nearly as smooth or exhilarating as the departure. With their strength regained after some dhal and a short nap, they began to communicate normally again. After the usual explanations demanded by such trips, Meena related the exchange between her and her professor of literature at the university.

"When the right opportunity arose, I asked what he thought of Gustave Flaubert's *Madame Bovary*, and I summarized Dr. Sleiman's reading of it. He generally agreed. He got so excited that he got off on a tangent and explained in detail Flaubert's famous statement: 'Madame Bovary is me.' His conclusion was that Flaubert loathed himself, since it was impossible to find even one redeeming quality in Bovary's character. I then asked if he thought there was such a thing as authentic romantic literature that fosters genuine sentiment as opposed to sentimentality. He encouraged me to elaborate. I referred to the authors Dr. Sleiman mentioned, who dealt with romantic themes in such a way as to form the intellect and the emotions upon the patterns of virtue rather than vice. I named Greene, Hardy, Austen, Pasternak, James, and Narayan. He was thoroughly impressed and compelled the other students to follow my lead by reading widely and outside the recommended authors in class, just as I had done."

"But you haven't read those authors, Meena," Jhansi said accusingly.

"I know. I went up after class and told him he had unduly praised me, but he just laughed it off, thinking I was being modest."

"So did you clear it up?"

"No. I've just decided that I will go ahead and read everything they wrote."

"Then you'd better get busy," warned Thomas. "They were all tremendously productive. The stamina of great writers never ceases to astound me, you know. I'm hoping just to finish one book. And I'm sure I could finish it if I could just start it."

"You mean you haven't even begun?" asked Meena.

"Not really. Oh, I've been able to outline certain themes, and I even submitted to a friend of mine a rough draft of what I think will be the first chapter, but I've not been able to begin writing. Do you know what I mean?" he asked her, not giving her a chance to answer. "I need one monumental event to give me the needed impetus. Once this comes, everything else will flow naturally."

"What kind of book will it be?" Meena asked.

"That's another problem," he said, revealing his consternation. "If I am to follow the basic writing principle of writing what you know, then I must write an autobiography of sorts, since unlike the great writers of fiction, I'm not able so far to write out very effectively the material of my life in rigorous rearrangement and creative disguise."

"Why not?"

"Because I am neither a great writer nor a writer of fiction. I don't live to write nor do I write to live. I am an assistant professor, professing mostly my ignorance of things that most everyone else thinks are obvious. For some mysterious reason, I have been compelled lately to write a book, which I want people to read."

"You've written books before, haven't you?"

"Yes, but not for real people to read. I wrote them to committees, or to other academicians in order to get promoted, or to earn the title of Doctor."

He chuckled at the sound of it, and amusingly thought of how his students, some of his colleagues, and all of his Egyptian worker friends loyally called him by that lofty title, something hardly anyone ever did in the States.

"So do you see my problem? I want to write a book that ordinary people will read, but so far I'm only able to write in an autobiographical way."

"What's the problem with that?"

"No one cares about my autobiography, and not only that, but I haven't earned the right to write an autobiography."

"I think you have," said Jhansi.

"I care," Meena joined in enthusiastically. "I will read it. And your mother and father, and brothers and sisters, and wife and children, and friends, and even some of your colleagues and students and relatives will all want to read it. And surely they think you've earned the right to write it."

"Well, this is another problem. I don't know if I want all the people I love and all those who love me to read it."

"Why not?" they protested in unison.

"Precisely because I am writing about love. Do you see how esoteric this thing we call love is? But I have energy only to write about it; there I go again referring to love as it, when it really isn't an it at all, but rather a who, a person, and not just one person, but many. You see, this has something to do with how, although there is something consistent and constant about me, the I in me changes depending on whom I'm with. I seem to be many different persons to different people. There's this interesting relation between what is one and what is many within me that's mysteriously connected to love. Anyway, every time I get close to seeing precisely what the relation is, it eludes me."

"What do you mean you are many persons?"

"Well, I'm the person/son to my father and mother, and the person/ father to my sons and daughter, and the person/husband to my wife, and the person/teacher to my student, and the person/student to my teacher. And now I'm becoming a new person, I think, the person/writer to whomever it is, unlucky soul, who reads what I write. And I am the person/uncle to my nieces and nephews and the person/brother to my sisters and brothers and the person/son-in-law to my wife's parents and the person/brother-in-law to my wife's sister, and to the spouses of my brothers and sisters, and the person/lover to . . . uh . . . well, this is particularly mysterious, and much of the book must address this. Anyway, at the center of all these relations is love, the unifying force that gives all these relations meaning. If this force isn't present, then none of these relations are very real; they're only names of things that were perhaps once real. If love is present, the relations become more and more real; if love is lacking, those relations are less real, for love is the unifying reality behind, beneath, on top of, surrounding, and at the very heart of reality itself, which is all about relation. Every single real thing is only real in relation to something else."

He glanced around the room for a suitable example. "That little stool you're sitting on," he said, pausing as they all looked at the stool, "is only what it is in relation to you, the sitter. And even within itself, the individual pieces of wood only get their meaning in that they are connected to other pieces, all connected or related in such a way as to give the stool reality. Food is only really food because it is eaten. In other words, the experience of eating food is the same as being in communion with another in love."

"Could you say that again?" asked Meena challengingly. Thomas continued without answering.

"This is at the center of Shakespeare's great metaphysical question, to be or not to be. He asks this in the context of a profound meditation on love, doesn't he? If I could add to it, I would say to be or not to be in loving communion with another—that is the question of questions. As far as I'm concerned, if it doesn't somehow concern love, which necessarily must bring in relation to the other, then it isn't."

"It isn't what?" Meena asked, totally overwhelmed by his rambling discourse.

"It is not. I mean it isn't something; it's rather the lack of something, just as darkness is not something in the same way that light is something; it is the absence of light. Non-reality is the lack of love. The less love there is, the more non-reality."

Jhansi understood perfectly what he meant since she had heard it so often, but Meena remained perplexed. Noticing the quandary he had created for her, he smiled and said, "Don't fret, Meena. If you think I've created problems for you, consider the ones I've created for myself. I have to write a book on love, and I don't know what I am or what love is. And to make things worse, I don't know why I am compelled to write it, and I can't seem to really start it since I am waiting for the compelling moment, a moment, mind you, that I have no control over. It must come by way of an event that suddenly inspires me to write, an auspicious moment. In the meantime, everything I write and read and do needs to fit into the main theme of this book, a theme, again, which eludes me each time I try to pin it down. Aren't you glad you're not in my shoes, whoever I am?"

Jhansi, who had been listening patiently and not without amusement, said to herself, *I'm glad I know who I am. It is quite simple: I am his lover, and he is my lord; that's that.*

She reminded Meena of the preparations they needed to make before his departure and left him alone on the roof for a while. In the ensuing moments, he got what he thought was a brilliant idea.

"I shall write a preface to warn the readers, supposing there are any, of what they're getting into. This will make things clearer for everyone involved, including, and most especially, me."

He grabbed the pencil and pad he'd brought up to the roof earlier and scribbled down the following:

Dear Reader,

Unlike great writers of fiction who rigorously write the material of their lives in imaginative rearrangement and creative disguise, I have written the material of mine in an autobiography of sorts. It is a kind of confession in which I've been able to free myself, though not totally, from the oppressive shackles of my personal life, but I've managed to do a bit of imaginative rearranging and creative disguising of my own. This has served to break some of the fetters and has consequently worked wonders for my peace of soul. You, the reader, will have to be the judge of just how imaginative and creative it really is. I beg you not to be too harsh in your criticisms. I implore you to bear in mind the difficulty of my subject. I've been deeply troubled over how to classify it. It's not pure fiction, but it's not a pure autobiography either, and it breaks all the rules. And I can assure you that I've not broken the rules on purpose for the sake of novelty or for reasons of vanity. In fact, I don't even know all the rules. I stumbled upon the first one when a friend of mine read a rough draft of the first chapter and told me I was guilty of authorial intrusion.

That sounded serious, and I found myself in a panic. But he assured me that it was a common mistake made by all novice writers of fiction, and he encouraged me to continue writing. I told him I wasn't writing pure fiction, and he told me that I shouldn't have called it a novel then. I suppose I called it a novel because the whole experience has been so novel to me, and because, as I have mentioned, imaginative rearrangement and creative disguise are indeed to be found here in some measure. Finally, I want to thank you in advance for taking the time to read this; without you, I, as author, do not exist. It is a story about those I love. And it has brought me closer to the impenetrable mystery of personal identity and the unfathomable mystery of love. And though I am certain of the deepest connection between the meaning of I and the meaning of love, their ultimate meaning still eludes me. But I'm grateful for this ambiguity since life is not a puzzle to be pieced together, but a veritable mystery to be lived.

T. S.

CHAPTER THIRTEEN

Before long, time's scythe had ruthlessly mowed away all but twelve of the one hundred and twenty hours it had so generously given to Thomas and Jhansi. It was ten at night; Thomas's plane was scheduled to leave at ten the next morning. He was back down in the tiny bedroom lounging on the bed, directing the little packing that remained. Jhansi went in and out gloomily; his misery was also apparent.

"Isn't there a way to stop it, or at least slow it down?" she asked.

"No. 'Like as the waves make toward the pebbled shore, so do our minutes hasten to their end, each changing place with that which goes before; in sequent toil all forward do contend.'"

"Don't tell me; Shakespeare, right?"

"Of course; who else? Do you know it?"

"It sounds like one of his sonnets, but I can't be sure."

"You're right, number sixty. 'Nativity, once in the main of light, crawls to maturity wherewith being crowned, crooked eclipses gainst his glory fight and time that gave doth now his gift confound. Time doth transfix the glory set on youth and delves the parallels in beauty's brow, feeds on the rarity of nature's truth, and nothing stands but for his scythe to mow. And yet to Time in hope my verse shall stand, praising thy worth despite his cruel hand.'"

Jhansi sat down and pondered this for several quiet moments. Thomas finally broke the silence.

"Yes, it's a two-edged sword, isn't it?" he declared. "It's too long for those who mourn and take life and themselves too seriously, and too short for those who are forever frivolous, but at least in this life, we can't get away from it."

"Perhaps in the next, Janma, there won't be time," she speculated.

"Oh, so I see you have adopted some of the Hindu beliefs in regard to the next life," he challenged. "Can you square this belief with the Christian teaching on the afterlife?"

"I'm not sure. What exactly is the Christian teaching on the afterlife?"

"Do you want an entire course on eschatology now? There's not enough time. Anyway, I suspect that in the next world, or, if you prefer, in the next Janma, there won't be any time. You know I am planning to devote a good amount of space to time in my book," he said with confidence. "I've done the outline already."

"Can't wait to see what this space devoted to time is all about; and why not spend some time on space too," she said wittily, enjoying the banter, and added, "I hope I'll be able to find some comfortable space to read this book of all books sometime."

"You're quite a clever creature, aren't you?" His eyes twinkled at the delight he felt in poking fun back at her; he didn't want to break the lightened mood that she had created with her smile.

"Anyway, the main point I make is that, for those who love, time is eternity."

"Sounds too idealistic to me," she complained.

"You need to understand it in context," he asserted.

"In which context?"

"I deal with time in the context of how divine love—*agape* love—orders and perfects all other loves, or, if you will, how it creates the proper space for all the other loves."

"And what exactly do you mean by divine?"

"The Holy Trinity, of course, the community of three persons who love one another perfectly and completely."

"If they are three, how can they be one?"

"Jhansi," he said, his surprise evident, "I thought you, of all people, understood this."

"I'm not a theologian, Dr. Sleiman."

"You don't need to be a theologian, just a lover," he said in a low voice.

"How so?" she whispered.

"The eternal exchange of knowledge and love is so alive and instantaneous that the persons somehow get lost in one another. Their exchange can't be measured; it's outside of time. It's eternal. Did you forget what you wrote in one of your letters?"

"Which one?"

"The one where you said you wanted to become me. And I wrote back to say I would let you become me only if you allowed me to become you."

Jhansi blushed at the mention of this, as if suddenly recalling a primordial truth which she had forgotten.

"Is this what you meant in that letter when you told me to read Narayan's *The English Teacher*?" She remembered how that book had considerable influence on her when she read it.

"Yes. Precisely," Thomas whispered enthusiastically. "Narayan understood this perfectly. But it took the agonizing sting of losing his wife to typhoid fever before he could really plumb its depths. So you did get the book when I asked you to?"

"Of course I did; it's right up there." She pointed to a wooden shelf that served as a small library.

"Bring it down, please; I want to read something for you."

He hurriedly found the passage he had in mind and read aloud: "We stood at the window, gazing on a slender, red streak over the eastern rim of the earth. A cool breeze lapped our faces. The boundaries of our personalities suddenly dissolved. It was a moment of rare, immutable joy—a moment for which one feels grateful to Life and Death."

As he was reading, she again felt the force of what was perhaps Narayan's greatest novel and repeated quietly, "Yes, personalities suddenly dissolve."

Meena had been near the door listening. She'd heard all but the latter part of the conversation since they'd been whispering. She now gently butted in.

"You will send me a signed copy of your book, won't you?"

"To be sure I will," he said, though his eyes and thoughts were still full of Jhansi and the conversation they'd been having. Meena reminded him that he'd not addressed the topic of secularism as he had promised to do on the first day he arrived.

"You assured us, Jhansi, remember, that there would be plenty of time for it, but here we are, and time has run out," she said accusingly. Jhansi stared at her without comprehending.

"Are you dreaming, Jhansi?" her sister said in a raised voice.

Thomas came to her rescue. "No need to worry, my dear, you'll read all about secularism in my book, provided I ever write it. At any rate, I can always refer you to some good reading on the topic."

"Thank you. I'd like that."

"But your teachers here will also be of great help, I'm sure."

"Yes. We have some excellent professors, but very few of them show connections between one branch of learning and another in the way you try to do."

"Try is the operative word, my dear. I don't know how successful I am. My students often complain because we end up talking about theology when we start out talking about logic. You're right, though. I try to show them connections between philosophy, theology, economics, history, poetry, literature, and science, but usually I lose them, or I get lost. It's really frustrating for them and quite embarrassing for me."

Their laughter lightened the mood a bit. Meena then questioned him about the term eschatology.

"I overheard you use this term, sir; what exactly does it mean?"

"Were you eavesdropping on us?" asked Jhansi, suddenly returning to the conversation as if waking from a dream.

"No, but I just. . ."

Thomas interrupted her to ease the tension between the sisters. "It's a branch of theology that refers to a study of events that take place at the end of key moments in the human experience. In Catholic eschatology, it refers to nine categories: Death, Particular Judgment, Heaven, Purgatory, Hell, Second Coming of Christ, Resurrection of the Body, General Judgment, and the End of the World."

"Do you teach this course at the university?"

"We don't have an entire course on it, unfortunately, but I give them a mini-course tucked into a broader introduction to general theology."

"The nuns at school taught us that Purgatory is a very painful place," said Meena.

"And did they say why it was painful?" he asked.

"Yes," said Jhansi quickly, before her sister could answer, and added slowly and thoughtfully, "they said it's like being separated from someone you love."

"Yes. This is what the Church teaches," he said approvingly.

"Our teachers said it was a horrible place where you are punished by hot red fire for your sins," challenged Meena.

"Yes. The Church teaches this as well," he said, as if incognizant of any contradiction between the two statements.

Meena protested. "It sounds as if we were taught two different things."

"Not really. If you imagine God as an infinitely hot and bright all-consuming fire of love, then the flames of purgatory, or hell for that matter, are simply the hot white flames of his love. If you have not gotten used to the divine fire of love while on earth, then the hot red and blue flames of his love will scorch and burn you in the next life. For those already on fire with love, the flames amount to a heaven of ecstasy. Those who are imperfect in love are purified until they become love. This is purgatory. You see, one must become fire in order to approach fire; one must become love in order to have communion with love. So I suppose it's a painful state that is permeated with joy. I once gave a public lecture titled The Joy of Purgatory: Reinterpreting Catholic Eschatology. My largely Protestant audience was expecting me to back away from the traditional doctrine based on the title of the paper. I did this purposely to entice them to attend the lecture since Protestants have long rejected the doctrine as a Catholic superstition or worse."

"Why so?" inquired Jhansi.

"Well, the Reformers were rightly concerned with the fact that the doctrine was expressed in terms that could be interpreted as a belief in salvation by works, since it sounded as if both the penance done on earth for the souls in purgatory and the sufferings endured by those who were there earned them entrance into heaven. On reading many traditional Roman Catholic explanations of the doctrine, it does at times sound as if purgatory is a second chance to merit salvation by paying for our sins via so many good deeds to gain entrance into heaven. This bothered the Reformers, who claimed rightly that traditional Christianity was not about earning one's way into heaven, but about being saved by God's grace through faith in Christ's death and resurrection."

"You mean our Church taught something false?" asked Meena in a panic.

"No. This was never taught officially by the Church. Even a cursory glance at the formal doctrines of the Church and the commentary on these doctrines in the writings of many of the saints clearly show that such explanations are neither official nor adequate. First of all, the all-important Christian truth stressed so intensely by the Reformers that we are saved by God's grace through our faith in Christ, and not through any works of our own, is a truth that the Catholic Church has taught down through the ages. We see this in the works of St. Augustine against Pelagius, and the most recent Catechism of the Catholic Church emphatically states, 'Since without faith it is impossible to please God and to attain to the fellowship of his sons, then without faith no one has ever attained justification, nor will anyone obtain eternal life.' So the claim that we can save ourselves through our own good works is rejected by the Catholic Church as well. The Catechism also teaches emphatically that 'salvation comes from God alone.'

"Likewise, it is virtually impossible to find in the writings of the saints any traces whatsoever of over-confidence in one's own works and deeds for the purpose of justification and salvation."

Thomas went on and on as if he were delivering a public lecture, incognizant of the fact that both Jhansi and her sister were finding it difficult to follow him.

"On the contrary, the saints stress, and at times seemed to be obsessed with, their own sins and the deficiency of their own works as compared to God's immense mercy and goodness. And as the realization of the indescribable goodness of God increases, they think less and less about themselves, whether their own virtues or vices, as they get lost in the unfathomable glory of God."

Thomas forgot about the packing and began to give examples. "For instance, in her treatise on purgatory, the fifteenth-century mystic and stigmatist, St. Catherine of Genoa, says that the souls in purgatory, having come closer to the divine fire, see nothing 'but the operation of the divine goodness which is so manifestly bringing them to God that they can reflect neither on their own profit nor on their hurt. Could they do so, they would not be in pure charity. They see not that they suffer their pains in consequence of their sins, nor can they for a moment entertain that thought, for should they do so, it would be an active imperfection, and that cannot exist in a state where there is no longer the possibility of sin. At the moment of leaving this life in the particular judgment, they see why they are sent to purgatory, but never again after that; otherwise, they would still retain something private, which has no place there. Being established in charity, they can never deviate from there by any defect, and have no will or desire, save the pure will of pure love, and can swerve from it in nothing. They can neither commit sin, nor merit by refraining from it.'"

"Why weren't we ever told about this mystic in our Catholic schools?" Meena complained.

"She sounds like a fascinating woman," Jhansi added. "We'd like to know more about her."

"She was indeed," confirmed Thomas. "She also speaks about the joy in purgatory."

"Tell us!"

"Well, she proposes that the pains of purgatory are remarkably more seductive and desirable than the most rapturous pleasures on earth, and suggests that this painful joy comes not from doing anything but from seeing everything, from receiving the knowledge of the truth about ourselves, our lives, others, sin, and God. Purgatory is a kind of spiritual education wherein 'sin is purged away as we are allowed to see in an instant the meaning and effects of all our sins on others as well as on ourselves, both directly and indirectly, through chains of influence presently invisible, chains so long and effectual that we would be overwhelmed with responsibility if we saw them now.' The saints, you see, understand that the 'web of human causality is at least as brimming with articulated efficacy as the web of physical causality, where every event in the universe occurs within a common field and makes some difference, however tiny, to every other event.' Only a few can endure the insight of the saints expressed so well by Fyodor Dostoyevsky in his famous Russian novel *The Brothers Karamazov*, wherein he states that 'we are each responsible for all.' To say that sin is purged away is not the same as saying that sin is paid for. The paying for sin was completed once and for all by the death of Christ on Calvary."

Thomas paused to see if they were listening.

"The Christian can stand confident that the sin he committed yesterday is forgiven totally and perfectly by the blood of Christ, but it may take him years to realize the meaning and consequences of his sin. For it is only after we remember our sin that we can forget it; it is only after taking our sin seriously through the tears of painful repentance that we can laugh at it in the pleasures of God's divine laughter. If on earth we have not remembered it or taken it seriously, God, in his infinite mercy, gives us the temporal state of purgatory to do this. This painful realization, whether on earth or in purgatory, purifies the soul as the sinner moves closer to the pure fire of divine love and is able to see with greater clarity the vileness of his sinful action as compared to the brightness and purity of love itself. This, of course, is the meaning of repentance—to turn away from our sins and move closer to God. The closer we get to the divine fire of love, the purer we become. If we turn to him in faith before we die, we are saved, but if the state or condition of our spiritual soul, though justified through faith, is still in need of sanctification and spiritual maturity, then we must be purged and educated through the ecstatic pleasure of temporal punishment as he brings us closer to the fire of love. For as the book of Revelation, chapter twenty-one verse twenty-seven, says, 'Nothing unclean may enter into the heavenly Jerusalem.'"

"This is such an eye-opener for me," said Meena. "It's really important to be taught these things about our Christian faith."

"Yes it is. St. Catherine of Genoa was a remarkable woman. She also spoke of this state as a peaceful one, and said 'there is no peace to be compared with that of the souls in purgatory, save that of the saints in the fullness of paradise.' She claimed that this peace is augmented by the inflowing of God into these souls, which increases in proportion as the impediments to it are removed."

"I don't get it," said Jhansi.

"Maybe this will help. Look, she teaches that 'the rust of sin is the impediment, which the divine fire continually consumes, so that the soul in this state is continually being opened to admit the divine communication. As a covered surface can never reflect the sun, not through any defect in that orb, but simply from the resistance offered by the covering, so, if the covering be gradually removed, the surface will be opened, little by little, to the sun and will more and more reflect his light. So it is with the rust of sin, which is the covering of the soul. In purgatory, the flames incessantly consume it, and as it disappears, the soul reflects more and more perfectly the true sun who is God. Its contentment and joy increases as this rust wears away and the soul is laid bare to the divine ray, and thus one increases and the other decreases until the time is accomplished. The pain never diminishes, although the time does, but as to the will, so united is it to God by pure charity, and so satisfied to be under his divine appointment, that these souls can never say their pains are pains.' While alive, we can choose to repent, but when we are dead, we cannot act for ourselves. This is why those who love us can still do penance for us; that is, as they choose to turn more and more perfectly to the saving acts of Christ, those on earth can unite their love for God to the souls of their dead loved ones and help bring those souls closer and closer to pure love itself through chains of influence that are invisible to us."

"So what was the reaction of your Protestant audience?" they asked.

"It was mixed, but I ended the presentation with a quote from one of my favorite Christian authors, C. S. Lewis, which almost everyone there received well."

"Do you remember it?"

"Sure. Lewis wrote, 'Our souls demand purgatory, don't they? Would it not break the heart if God said to us as we were about to enter heaven, "It is true, my son, that your breath smells and your rags drip with mud and slime, but we are charitable here, and no one will upbraid you with these things, nor draw away from you. Enter into the joy." Should not we reply, "With submission, Sir, and if there is no objection, I'd rather be cleansed first."

"It may hurt, you know."

"Even so, Sir."

Jhansi and her sister were captivated by the subject. "And what about hell?" Jhansi asked. Thomas needed no encouragement.

"Well, for those who have never loved, these fires of love are unbearable blazes of pain and torment. It's hard to imagine someone who has never loved, but I suppose it's possible."

"I have a professor at the university who not only does not believe in anything after life, but thinks that such belief prevents us from living well in the present. He doesn't think there is really an essential difference between our form of life and animal and plant forms. 'For all we know,' he says, 'we might simply become part of the soil and air when we die.'"

"Might is the key word here," said Thomas. "And I bet he'd change his mind if he ever saw a ghost or communicated with the dead."

"Speaking of which," interjected Jhansi, "when you were talking about purgatory and praying for the dead, I began to think about how central such communication was in Narayan's *The English Teacher.*"

"That's right," Thomas agreed enthusiastically, somewhat surprised at the connection she had made so quickly. "You know, besides the setting of that novel, there is little fiction in it. It is largely autobiographical. He dedicated it to his wife who, as Jhansi may remember," he added with a quick glance to Meena, "caught typhoid fever at a young age and died, leaving him with a little girl to raise. He was deeply in love with her and was completely devastated by her death; he was convinced he'd never write again. I think he even contemplated suicide, but for the sake of his little girl, he couldn't bring himself to do it. As far as I can tell, the only thing that saved him was his surprising discovery that he could communicate with his dead wife. At first he needed the help of a medium but later was able to do it alone."

"Both our parish priest and the Protestant minister who leads our Bible study say that communication with the dead is a sin," declared Meena, rather alarmed to hear Thomas mentioning it approvingly.

"It all depends," rejoined Thomas.

"On what?" she retorted.

"On whom you're contacting, and why."

"Wait a minute," said Meena. "I've never formally studied Christian theology, but the Scriptures are clear enough, aren't they?" She grabbed a Bible from its usual place on the bedside table and turned directly to the book of Leviticus in the Old Testament where she read passages pointed out to her just a week earlier at a Protestant Bible study she'd recently joined.

"'Do not have recourse to the spirits of the dead or to magicians; they will defile you.' That's from Leviticus, chapter nineteen verse thirty-one. And also from chapter twenty, verse six," she continued with great confidence, "'if a man has recourse to the spirits of the dead or to magicians, to prostitute himself by following after them, I shall set my face against that man and outlaw him from his people.'"

Meena paused in satisfaction, taking delight in apparent victory, until he broke the silence with, "I'm impressed. Glad to see you're studying our Holy Scriptures."

"Well," she said, undeterred by his flattery, and confidently awaiting his riposte.

"I think you've missed the most important one. Verse twenty-seven also says that 'any man or woman who conjures up the spirits of the dead must be put to death by stoning; their blood shall be on their own heads.'"

The sisters were awed by his accuracy, and Meena was intimidated. *Not only does he already know about these prohibitions, but he's pointed out one I didn't know. Yet he's apparently unmoved by their directness*, she thought.

He sensed her unease, and assuring her, said, "Don't worry; I'm not doubting the Holy Scriptures. It's just that one needs to understand them properly. You see, dear, what our religion forbids is the communication with the dead for the purpose of magically revealing the future or influencing negatively the course of events. Notice that the injunctions always mention magic alongside of communication with the dead. After all, weren't you just telling me that St. Catherine of Genoa must have been a remarkable woman, and that you'd like to get to know more about her? Well, she's dead, isn't she? Aren't all of the saints we venerate dead? Yet we have devotions to them. We speak to them; we ask them to intercede for us before the awesome throne of God."

"That's different, sir; they're saints."

"Right. That's why I said it depends on whom you're contacting and why. You've heard of St. Therese of the Child Jesus, haven't you?"

"Of course I have; she's a very popular saint here in India, even among some of the Hindus. I think I have her autobiography."

"Not only is she very popular, but Pope Pius the Tenth, himself a canonized saint, called her the greatest saint of modern times."

"So what about her? Did she advocate communication with the dead?" Jhansi said sarcastically.

"Meena, do you have that book handy?" he asked, ignoring Jhansi's question.

Meena jumped up to search for it on the little lonely bookshelf.

"Let me guess," said Jhansi, again with a touch of playful mockery in her voice. "You're going to quote something for us. How is it that you can remember all these references?"

"Well, this one stuck since I'm planning to use it in my book in a section I'm going to call Love after Death."

"I found it," Meena exclaimed excitedly. Thomas opened to the end of chapter four and read aloud the following passage:

I had always been the most tenderly loved by my sisters, and if they themselves had remained on earth they would have given me a similar love. That they were in heaven seemed no reason why they should forget me. On the contrary: they could draw on the divine treasury and obtain peace for me from it and thus show me that in heaven one still knew how to love! I hadn't to wait long for an answer. Waves of delicious peace soon flooded my soul. From that moment my love for my little brothers and sisters in heaven grew, and I loved to talk with them about the sorrows of exile and of my longing to join them soon in heaven.

"That's incredible," cried Meena. "Now I see the point. We should try it, Jhansi. Maybe our deceased relatives and friends could help us out of this fix we're in."

Thomas was amused at just how fast she had changed her mind, and wondered what fix she could possibly be referring to. He then added in a serious tone, "But be careful, especially if you find you need the help of a medium due to the weakness of your faith."

This scared them a bit, and they waited for him to continue.

"It's dangerous to get too dependent on a medium when you're contacting the dead, even if the medium is well meaning and a good person. I think this is one of the many profound messages in Narayan's *The English Teacher*, which is based on his real-life experience."

"How's that?" asked Jhansi.

"Narayan admits in his autobiography that sometimes the thoughts of the medium interfered with the messages the medium was receiving; this often led to errors in what his wife was telling him. Eventually, he was able to communicate with her directly, and was finally healed of his great wound when he came to know with certainty that she was alive in another and better state of existence. All thoughts of suicide vanished, and he was inspired to live and write again. In fact, his first novel after his wife's death was *The English Teacher* originally published in the United States under the title *Grateful to Life and Death*."

Their conversation ended abruptly when their mother summoned the girls to speak with their sister on the phone.

"My mother has called Shivani now," said Jhansi, rather flustered. "I think you should at least say hello."

"Yes. I'd like to."

"Very well, then, and after this, I think you should talk to my father. He'll be in the right frame of mind after speaking with Shivani."

"What do you mean?"

"Well, after speaking to one daughter who's happily settled, thanks to you of course, his thoughts will naturally shift to another one who is not. He'll bring it up with my mom, and together they will fret about the impropriety of having their younger daughter settled in marriage while their older daughter is not."

The conversation between Thomas and Shivani was brief but meaningful.

"So you've finally made it to India?"

"Yes. Your India is a vastly wonderful country, and I'm very happy to be here and to meet your family. I understand you are with child?"

"Yes I am. Guess when the baby is due."

"Your sister told me sometime in June."

"The doctor has set June seventeenth as the due date."

"June seventeenth," he repeated, hardly able to believe his ears. "Uh . . . do you have any names picked out?"

"Of course we do. If it's a boy, his name will be Thomas; if it's a girl, her name will be . . . ."

Thomas didn't hear the girl's name as that old familiar pain came rushing back. Jhansi noticed and motioned him to give her the phone, which he did. Jhansi spoke coldly but politely with her sister and said "glad that's over" as she hung up the phone.

"I think it's a good time now to talk to my parents. They are just beginning to vex themselves. Are you ready?"

"No. How does one ever get ready to lie?"

"No one's asking you to lie. Just tell them that you'll be arranging my future, and that by November you'll be sending for me."

"And what if they ask for details?"

"I'll help you; don't worry. They like you and trust you."

"Exactly. I'd like to honor that trust."

"You are. You're taking care of their daughter, aren't you? Please?"

Thomas went into the sitting room and began awkwardly with, "Uh . . . I would like to take your permission, sir, to . . . uh . . .with your permission, of course, to . . . uh . . . arrange for Jhansi's future."

"What exactly do you mean, Dr. Sleiman?"

"Well, I know that lately you and your wife have been anxious over Jhansi's future, and that all attempts to arrange her marriage have failed in some way or another."

"Yes," he said gravely, glancing at Jhansi.

"Well, I think I might be able to help in this regard."

"Oh yes. We've heard all about your family. Jhansi loves your mother dearly, and I understand you've an older brother who's not yet married, and lives all alone in a great big, newly built house."

"Yes. That's right, sir."

"And we understand that they've met?"

"That's right too."

"Do you think he likes her?"

"Yes. I know he does."

"Well, you have our permission then; when will you send for her?"

"I hope by late November, sir."

"Wonderful. We can all relax a bit then. We'll be praying that it works out." He looked briefly at his wife for a formal approval, which she gave with a slight nod of the head. At that, he got up and made a gesture with his hand that amounted to a handshake.

Thomas was astonished at how quickly and smoothly it went. He didn't have to lie after all. He simply answered the questions; Jhansi's father did the rest. Jhansi was beside herself with relief and joy.

"I will be able to endure anything for the next five or six months just knowing that I shall see you again," she said as they returned to the bedroom alone to finish the packing.

"But then what?" he asked, trying to hide his excitement, which was as keen as hers.

"We shall see," she said. "I don't think I'll live much longer than a few years anyway, and then you'll need not worry about me anymore. But all I know now is that I will not be forced to marry someone I don't love, and I shall see you again in five months or so. Thank you, my love. Thank you."

"You're welcome, I think," he said as he considered arranging her papers, finances, and living quarters, not to mention the problem of concealing the whole thing from any other living soul.

The matter-of-fact reference she'd made to her own death bothered him. He wondered if it was merely perfunctory or some sort of profound, prophetic premonition of her future; he feared it was the latter. She did have a deep inner life, so evident every time she closed her eyes in prayer. At such times, he found her most appealing, nearly seductive. That night as she performed her holy hour, engrossed in prayer, he secretly watched her. By the time she'd finished, everyone else had fallen fast asleep. He went back down to the apartment hoping she would follow him, which she did.

Their embrace that night might be compared to the one that created the Himalayas nearly sixty million years ago, when a colossal granite rock broke away from East Africa and collided with the rim of southern Asia's coastal region. At that encounter, not only did the southern edge of Tibet emerge from its sunken state below the sea to wed itself to what then became South India, but the world's youngest and tallest mountains erupted ecstatically hundreds of miles north of the point of penetration.

PART FIVE

THAT WHOSO HEARS
MUST HEAR AGAIN

CHAPTER FOURTEEN

O n their way to the airport the next morning, their impending separation of five or six months seemed like an eternity. A lot could change in that time. The goodbye was bitter, laced as it was with so much uncertainty. The only comfort for him was the beauty she radiated in her bright blue and gold sari. He loved the way she tied it leaving much of her tiny waist exposed, which highlighted her feminine and perfectly proportioned hips. Her shoulders showed straight and firm. Her long black hair, blown about by the drive to the airport, wildly adorned her shoulders and brushed against her waist now and then. The softness of her breasts seemed to yearn for his mouth. Her eyes, like turtledoves, sparkled playfully every time they came to rest on his. Her soothing scent filled the car like incense, and Thomas imagined that she might be a goddess after all.

But the magic disappeared, and all the comfort faded as soon as the plane departed. The familiar melancholy returned immediately and was only abated a bit when, upon his return, he saw how much his wife and children had missed him. When he took his children in his arms, he also realized how much he'd missed them. He'd missed Rita too. But their embrace was different. He loved her and she loved him, but on his side, he now loved her more as a sister than a spouse. For him this didn't mean anything superficial or merely obligatory; it meant rather something genuinely profound, as his love and affection for his own sisters and brothers were defining marks of who he was. His relationships with all of them were excellent, and the love between the siblings had grown over the years rather than diminished. He very rarely forgot a birthday, an anniversary, or an important event, even though he was oceans away from them.

Exactly when this change in his affections for Rita occurred, he couldn't remember. His confessor said the change resulted from the very first kiss of disloyalty with Jhansi, the first betrayal in his married life, and therefore he was to blame. He was convinced the kiss was the effect, not the cause. After giving it much thought, he finally came to believe that figuring out the proper cause-and-effect relationship really didn't matter much. The facts were the facts. Eventually it came out. They knew each other too well to have any real secrets between them, and anyway, he was a bad liar. Her intuition enabled her to ask him point-blank one day, after he'd returned from India, whether he'd slept with Juliet or Jhansi.

"Of course not," was his answer, but he went on to tell her about the intense and unusual loneliness he'd been experiencing for the last few years. She understood immediately.

"I know it's been difficult for you. But you're usually so strong that I often forget you might be having a hard time. I'm partly to blame, I know."

"No, don't blame yourself for anything, honey," he said, "but sometimes I feel like I'm going to . . ."

"To what, honey," she said with some panic in her voice as his voice quivered and tears welled up in his eyes.

"I feel like . . ."

"Don't be afraid to talk to me, sweetheart; just say it."

"I feel at times like I'm . . . starving to death," he said as a tear forced its way out.

"Don't cry, *elbee*. Please don't cry. I can't bear it," she cried out as she held him tightly. "I don't give you what you need sometimes, I know, but you know how hectic it has been the last four years."

He didn't blame her, and he loved her for saying that. He felt as if she really understood him. He admired her for not accusing him of any evil intention as she had done before, which had caused an ugly scene. She had called him a big liar and threatened him with divorce when she first discovered that he was seeing Juliet. She'd suspected it for some time.

"But we haven't really done anything," he argued.

"Just seeing her outside the university is enough," she screamed, "or talking to her on the phone; you're both liars!"

"Is my whole life a lie now because I didn't tell you I was seeing Juliet? I swear before God and on the life of our children that I have not made love to her. What do you want me to do, write down our conversations, tell you when we're going to meet? I didn't want to hurt you."

At this, she had exploded.

"And you were going to be a priest. Some priest you would have been. You're a hypocrite. I hate you. If you don't want to hurt me, then why are you seeing her?" She was nearly hysterical.

Thomas didn't have an answer. He just stared at her. Again, she screeched the question.

"My God, Rita, get a hold of yourself. The children will hear." His words only made her more irate as she yelled the question again. One of the children began to cry, and he pleaded with her to stop yelling, but all in vain.

"Some priest you would have been," she said again.

At this, he finally snapped. He picked up a chair and threw it in her direction. The rage blinded him as he picked up a glass table and smashed it on the floor. This was enough to force her to come back to her senses, but now Thomas was out of his mind with rage and stormed out of the house. He came back late into the night and avoided Rita, who was in their bed trying to sleep. He stole into the children's room and found his eldest son still awake and whimpering.

"What is it, my love?" he asked his son.

"Daddy?"

"What, *elbee*?"

"Promise me you'll never do that again."

The words struck him to the core of his being, and tears of contrition welled up in Thomas's eyes. They rolled softly down his cheeks and dropped onto the lifeless stuffed teddy bears and Barbie dolls lying abandoned on the floor. The children had deserted their toys and taken for cover in their beds when all of the horrible screaming and violence began. They weren't used to it. Normally, the house was full of laughter and tenderness.

But this time was completely different. There was no blame in Rita's voice, only compassion and understanding. He admired her for taking some of the blame. He wished with all his heart that she could satiate his emotional, spiritual, intellectual, and physical thirst. As she held him tightly, he vowed never to even look at another woman, but a few weeks later, the hunger returned. He struggled wildly over whether to call Jhansi, and even thought of calling Juliet, but he resisted both ideas courageously.

"It'll pass; everything passes, even hunger and thirst," he told himself. But another voice responded with *Yes, but only after you eat and drink.*

A few days after he returned from India, he went to the office. While going through a mound of mail, grown larger during his absence, Mr. Morrison stopped by to hear about his trip. Their exchange was lively but brief. As usual, his first day back after one of his trips was quite hectic.

"I'll let you get back to work, Dr. Sleiman. I can see that you're extremely busy. Just wanted to welcome you back." Dr. Morrison started out, and then he turned around and remarked loudly in his distinct British accent, "By the way, did you know Narayan died?"

"No! What? I didn't! When? Where?"

"In Madras, I think, or I suppose they say Chennai these days, don't they?"

"Who told you? How old was he? At what time? Where exactly was he?" continued the assistant professor, shocked and bewildered by the news.

Thomas retired to his favorite chair in the corner of the office and took a deep breath. He stared out at the mountains, which seemed more majestic than usual; the monasteries that crowned the peaks seemed to exude more holiness and purpose than ever before. The shades of blue in the soft sky were gently interrupted by the slow moving downy shapes that people called clouds, their distinct white brilliance defying description.

"He's dead," he whispered.

The auspicious moment had arrived.

Later that evening, Thomas sat down with a long yellow pencil and a lined yellow notepad, and began the book.

In memory of R. K. Narayan who died in Madras in the wee hours of the morning on May 13, 2001, he wrote at the very beginning, dedicating the work, of course, to Jhansi. He wrote a letter to her and told her he'd begun; he churned out ten thousand words a week for a solid month, and then began to share parts of the book with a few very close friends. For the most part, he told his own story, rearranging and disguising only when the muses decided to aid him. The death of the great Narayan had awakened something in him; writing was effortless.

Around this time, Thomas handed the opening lines of the book to Mr. Morrison: "Reluctantly rising from its pacific repose, the moon melted the darkness."

"What do you think? Is there too much alliteration? Is it too affected?"

"Perhaps a bit, but on the whole, I was rather moved by the introduction."

Mr. Morrison offered some constructive criticism and encouraged Thomas to continue writing. After a few months of almost effortless writing, Thomas came up against a wall. While he was explaining the book to Jhansi one evening during a long-distance phone call, she suddenly asked him, "So how's it going to end?"

He'd never thought about the conclusion until that moment.

"The ending?" he repeated foolishly.

"Yes, Dr. Sleiman—you know, the conclusion."

"Oh, yes, the conclusion—certainly. Well . . . uh . . . well . . . the ending is . . . uh . . . quite sad, I think, but happy too. Well, uh, that is to say that . . . uh . . . to say that at least it ends in a . . . you know, dates are important . . . uh, well, January twelfth is a critical date in the ending, but not exactly, as you will see. Uh . . . look, Jhansi, my dear, I've got to hang up. This is costing me a fortune. You'll see soon enough. I'll be sending it to you. I want to publish it in India. Can you help me?"

After that conversation, writing was nearly impossible. The passing of several months produced only a few pages. A severe struggle went on inside him. It centered around one simple question: whether to bring Jhansi from India or not. It became the perennial problem of his life. He even coined a phrase: "to bring or not to bring; that is the question."

Confusion dominated his life. Where would she stay?

Perhaps she could stay with the nuns at the convent near the university; she could work there, and they could both be safe. Besides, he could see it from his office. This would bring some consolation. But how would he ever see her alone? But then again, perhaps it was better not to see her alone.

Bewilderment besieged him.

"It's not fair to Rita," was the overwhelming solution he reached one day, only to be overturned with "it's not fair to Jhansi, either; doesn't she have some rights in all of this?"

On other days, he asked, "What about me?"

The perplexity persisted and intensified with each passing day.

"But my duty toward Jhansi surely mustn't be compared to my duty toward my wife, for God's sake."

His thoughts went back and forth like this when duty was foremost in his mind.

"Duty is important, but it's so hazy at times. There's no question that we should always do what we ought to do, but the problem is, what ought I to do? I know. I ought to do the right thing, that's all," he would say to himself, satisfied that he'd finally made a firm decision.

But a few hours later it was, "But what really is the right thing? Am I doomed to drown in a sea of relativism, something that I've taught against all my life? Are there no absolute standards of right and wrong?"

He took a strong position against relativism in his Ethics class.

"Relativism is a dead end no matter which way you go with it," he told his students with conviction.

"If you say there is no absolute standard for determining which actions are right and which are wrong, then you're involved in a contradiction because you're maintaining that the position you're taking is right."

His confessor assured him that bringing Jhansi to Lebanon would definitely be the wrong thing to do, as did a good Christian friend of his, who urged him to give Jhansi up altogether.

"Try not to think of her at all, my friend, and don't even pray for her, at least not until your mind and heart have settled down somewhat."

"Don't even pray for her?" he asked in disbelief.

"No, this only agitates the situation; you'll never get over her unless you hang on the cross for a while. I know this is hard to hear, but I say it out of Christian charity. It'll cost you some pain, but afterward, you'll enter more deeply into Christ's glory. Don't forget, Thomas, even Christ, who was a divine person, was afraid to do the will of his father. He understands your suffering; he suffered too. Contemplate his agony in the Garden. He endured it for you, Thomas; he loves you."

It all sounded right to Thomas, and his friend's paramount sincerity was unquestionable.

Is God speaking to me through him? he wondered.

His first inclination was to think yes. Thus, he made a firm resolution to obey the divine will rather than his own. But his consternation was colossal. He was impatient at home and work. He enjoyed neither eating nor drinking. He played "tiger" less with the children, all of whom noticed that something was wrong with Dad. He trained himself to denounce thoughts of her as wicked temptations from the demons themselves. When this didn't work, he modified his strategy for dealing with the evil forces by denouncing not thoughts of her, but just the thought of her and him living near each other. The words of his friend rang in his ears for weeks on end:

"Jhansi can never be what Rita already is. Rita is an image of the Church, and you are an image of Christ. You must love her just as Christ has loved his Church. He gave up his very life for the Church. And you, Thomas, as a Christian, must do the same. Forget about Jhansi; it's the right thing to do. It'll pass; I assure you. You're a victim of the same thing that caused so much havoc in my life before my conversion: sentimentality. If you could see yourself when you talk about her, you would know that you've fallen prey to the structural sin of romanticism. You'll be able to see it if you look long enough. I'd suggest you read Flaubert's *Madame Bovary*. Do you know it?"

"Yes, of course! I've not only read it . . ." He was about to say that he had mastered it and taught it. He decided to remain silent.

"Am I speaking the truth, Thomas? You know, don't you, what's the right thing to do?"

"Wait a minute," he said aloud, unable to restrain himself this time. A slightly tense mood prevailed.

"My sentiments are genuine. They're not based on some sort of romantic ideology, but on something infinitely more enduring."

"Like what, Thomas?"

"They are based on a person—a real, flesh-and-blood human being, a woman."

"Fine, let's say this love is rooted in something more enduring, and that it's not just a passing infatuation born and bred on the reality-distorting Hollywood movies and romantic novels of your youth. Let's say further that there has never been a more genuine and authentic love in all of this great wide world than the one that you two have. Even so, Thomas, you are married to Rita. You must sacrifice this love for your wife's sake. You must deny yourself. Our Lord has made it perfectly clear: 'He who loves me will deny himself, take up his cross, and follow me.'"

With great conviction and determination, Thomas strove to forget all about her. He abandoned the approach of attributing all thoughts of her, and her and him together, to the demons, and simply attributed his illicit desire for her to his own human weakness.

"I must strengthen my will," he concluded. "I'll do the right thing; that's all."

In spite of his courageous efforts, it didn't work. He simply couldn't convince himself that the right thing to do was to forget about her. "If I were certain of the right thing to do," he told his confessor after they'd left the confessional one morning, "I would do it, but I'm not certain. In fact, I believe our relationship is a good thing that somehow makes us more noble and pure. I know it sounds crazy, Father, but I'm convinced of it. I love the me who emerges when I'm in her presence. Do you know, Father, we pray together."

"Let's go get a cup of coffee and talk more about this, Thomas."

As they were drinking their coffee in a little café not far from the rectory, his confessor and friend brought up the subject again. "I don't deny that a man and a woman who aren't married to each other could have a purely platonic and even holy relationship. And I'm not saying that every extramarital relationship is sinful. St. Francis and St. Clare were madly in love, I suppose. Perhaps their love even helped them to become holy."

Thomas was elated to hear him speak in this fashion.

"Yes, yes, Father, and did you know that John Stuart Mill sustained a platonic relationship with Mrs. Harriet Taylor, a married woman, for twenty years? Three years after her husband died, they finally got married. Most of the motivation and substance of his writings he ascribed to her. Do you know that when she died, he bought a house near her grave?"

The priest cut him off with, "Well, it sounds a bit too romantic for me, Thomas."

"But it's true, Father; have you read anything by Mill? He wasn't a mushy-minded romantic."

"I don't know. What about Mr. Taylor? How do you think he felt? Was it just to him?"

"Yes. She remained faithful."

"Yes, but only in her body. Don't you think she was committing emotional adultery all those years before her husband died?"

Thomas listened carefully as he'd never heard the expression emotional adultery before.

"Thomas, I know you're not going to like this, but I think you're guilty of emotional adultery too. By thinking of Jhansi, calling her, and writing to her, you're committing a sin."

After a moment's reflection, Thomas asked confidently,

"Is not lust the essence of adultery, Father?"

"Why sure it is. Christ himself said that anyone who looked lustfully at a woman had already committed adultery in his heart."

"And is not lust the flipside of murder in that both actions tear one's soul from one's body?"

"Well, I suppose so, yes. Perhaps this is why the sixth commandment, thou shalt not commit adultery, comes right after the fifth, thou shalt not kill. But what's your point, Thomas?"

"My point is that if lust is the malicious and selfish separation of the value of one's person from the value of that person's body, then a man could lust after his own wife."

"Certainly! I know many women who suffer just such abuse at the hands of their husbands. And if I'm not mistaken, I think the Pope said something like this publicly a few years ago. He took a lot of criticism for saying it, even from some Catholic theologians."

"Okay, then, if the essence of adultery is lust, and a man can lust after his own wife, then a man ostensibly could be guilty of committing adultery with his own wife, right?"

"This is a funny way of putting it, though I see your logic. But what are you really driving at, Thomas?"

"I'm saying that if a man made love to a woman without a trace of lust or selfishness, it could not be called adultery, even if she weren't his wife."

"What? Are you trying to get me to say that it would be just fine for you to make love to Jhansi?"

"Not exactly . . . no . . . I'm just trying to get you to admit that if I were to make love to her, I wouldn't be guilty of adultery."

"Fine. I'll go for that. But it would still be sinful."

"Yes, I know, but which sin would I be committing? You see, adultery just sounds too serious to me. It's too close to murder, and besides, she's not married."

"But you are."

"Okay, Father, then which sin would we be committing if we were to live in total continence, avoiding sexual intercourse, or all sexual orgasms altogether? Would we still be committing emotional adultery? If there's no lust, then there's no adultery, emotional or otherwise. I don't think Mrs. Harriet Taylor did anything wrong at all. She remained faithful to her husband and only married Mill three years after her husband died. In fact, I think they both lived heroic lives."

"Just like the one you're planning to live, I suppose."

"Why not?"

"Because it's dangerous, Thomas, that's why not."

"Well, this way I shall never become complacent or mediocre. I shall be forced to live a very balanced life. I must be careful and strong, like Shiva, in order to love another woman besides my wife."

"You know what, Thomas?"

"What?"

"They didn't teach us in the seminary how to deal with men like you."

"Is that a compliment?"

"I'm not sure, but I think you must watch out for spiritual pride; it is the worst kind. Lucifer fell because of spiritual pride. And on that note, I'll see you next Friday for your weekly confession."

"Certainly, Father."

In between his classes and duties at the university, Thomas investigated ways of bringing Jhansi from India. It was more complicated than he'd thought. But rather than distracting from his teaching responsibilities, these activities enhanced his lectures. For when he had to commit time or money to these investigations, the tremendous reality and responsibility of what he was doing caused him to go through the moral struggle all over again. This did wonders for his lectures on moral philosophy.

"What was Nietzsche really getting at by calling his book *Beyond Good and Evil*?" asked one very bright student just as Thomas had started his introductory lecture on Nietzsche's ethics during the fall semester.

"Good question, Ziad. Have you finished it yet?"

"Yes, but it's nothing like the other stuff we've read on ethics. He seems to glorify evil."

"Very well put. That's exactly what he does."

"But you've taught us that, according to the classical works on ethics, good and evil are absolute, not relative categories. Nietzsche seems to be worlds apart from Plato and Aristotle when it comes to ethics."

"And he's blatantly anti-Christian, sir," said another student after two long weeks of nothing but Nietzsche. "Why are we spending so much time with him?"

Thomas worked hard to help them see that aspects of Nietzsche's moral philosophy somehow supported traditional ethics, and that in some ways Nietzsche was in the Christian ethics camp.

"We don't get it, sir," most of them complained.

"If you ask me," volunteered one young man, thoroughly steeped in a branch of Protestant fundamentalism, "Christ had people like Nietzsche in mind when he said 'woe to those who call good evil and evil good.' He turns everything upside down."

"On the surface you're right, but go deeper, Paul."

"If we go any deeper, we'll drown," another protested.

"Splendid. That's what I want."

"But you always maintain that the teacher should help the student swim and survive. Why are you giving us contradictory messages?"

"They aren't contradictory, just paradoxical."

"Please sir, speak plainly to us. What are you up to with this Nietzsche stuff?"

"Look, my dear students, I want you to drown in the waters of your moral misconceptions so that you may be resurrected upon more solid and pure ground. Allow Nietzsche to strip away the connotations that stubbornly cling to your limited notions of good and evil so that more noble and innocent notions may reign instead. Loosen up with respect to what your myopic vision of good and evil is so that a more decent and tighter vision may transport you beyond the heavens toward the infinite and vast throne of God himself."

"But Nietzsche wasn't even a theist sir; he didn't believe in God."

"But he believed in some sort of . . . uh . . . I don't know, what shall we call it . . . summit of evaporation, perhaps, wherein all worldly things are judged against the foundation of an absolute and immutable pole of mystery, for which he could find no other image except the wind."

"Why the wind?" asked one girl, who had never before said anything in class.

"Because we can't get hold of it, it's hidden, it's powerful, and it's real. It moves all things, but we can't move it; it's a reference point for good and evil beyond our inadequate judgments of good and evil. So you see, Ziad, although Nietzsche's ethics aren't reducible to any kind of objectively graspable norm, they are nonetheless rooted in something we may call divine and eternal. Now I don't have any proof of it, but I like to think that one of my favorite poets, Robert Louis Stevenson, had Nietzsche in mind when he wrote his poem, 'The Wind.'"

"Let's hear it, sir," they said, always excited to get him off on one of his poetry recital tangents.

Thomas was all too willing and delivered it with great feeling:

"'The Wind,' by Robert Louis Stevenson," he said, unable to recite that particular poem without the formal introduction with which he had first memorized it, a tradition he stringently continued when he taught it to his own children. And then he launched forward:

I saw you toss the kites on high
And blow the birds about the sky
And all around I heard you pass
Like ladies' skirts across the grass
O wind a-blowing all day long
O wind that sings so loud a song

I saw the different things you did
But always you yourself you hid
I felt you push I heard you call
I could not see yourself at all
O wind a-blowing all day long
O wind that sings so loud a song
O you that are so strong and cold
O blower are you young or old?
Are you a beast of field and tree
Or just a stronger child than me?
O wind a-blowing all day long
O wind that sings so loud a song

The class loved it, all but the fundamentalist, who shouted out, "But what about the Ten Commandments, sir? Aren't they objectively graspable? What could be clearer than 'thou shalt not kill' or 'thou shalt not bear false witness' or 'thou shalt not steal?' I'm sorry, but I don't see how Nietzsche's obscurity can be interpreted as anything remotely Christian. Why do we need him when we have the clear norms of the commandments? When Holy Scripture says 'thou shalt not commit adultery,' there's no gray area; everyone knows exactly what it means."

"Except me," Thomas mumbled to himself. "Look here, Paul. I believe Nietzsche was attacking a certain form of Protestant Christianity, and in doing so he unwittingly brought attention to the importance of the most genuine Christian virtues."

"I don't see it," Paul protested.

"I'm not surprised," Thomas muttered under his breath. "Look. If nothing else, just include in your exam essay that, according to some interpretations, Nietzsche stressed the importance of a virtue-centered ethics over a rule-centered ethics. There are even some readings of Nietzsche that consistently maintain commensurability between his ethics and the ethics of Christianity."

"Fine. But out of principle, sir, I will write in parentheses that I don't buy it."

"That'll be just fine, Paul. Out of principle, you must do that, I suppose."

When he saw that Dr. Sleiman was about to move on, Paul coughed up another complaint.

"You must not have read Nietzsche's *Thus Spake Zarathustra*, sir?"

"Of course I have."

"With all due respect, sir, you must not have read it carefully then."

His disrespectful manner made many of the students uncomfortable, and not a few of them wondered why Dr. Sleiman so calmly tolerated Paul's arrogance.

"Would you care to explain?" the assistant professor asked politely. The student pulled out a piece of paper containing quotes from what his Protestant pastor had told him were anti-Christian philosophers, and read out with great confidence: "The way does not exist."

"Could you elaborate, Paul?"

"This is Nietzsche speaking, sir, through the mouth of Zarathustra. Don't you get it? It is the devil himself speaking. He flatly contradicts Jesus, who said 'I am the way, the truth, and the life.' The Bible says Jesus is the way, and

Nietzsche says that the way does not exist. This is why our pastor is so critical of university education and modern philosophy. He says that it leads us away from Christ."

"Well, I too am critical of modern university education and modern philosophy, Paul. But I think you're misinterpreting Nietzsche and taking him out of context. The passage you've just quoted is from part three, chapter fifty-five, 'Of the Spirit of Gravity,' isn't it?"

Paul remained silent, as he had no idea where it had come from.

"Isn't that where you're quoting from, Paul?"

"It doesn't matter where it's from, sir. What matters is what it means."

"But if you don't know what comes before or after, how can you really understand what it means in the proper context?"

Paul was quiet now, and most of the class enjoyed the way the assistant professor was gently tearing apart Paul's flimsy hypothesis. Dr. Sleiman quoted from *The Genealogy of Morals* and *The Birth of Tragedy*, and showed how the major themes in those works complemented the insights in other works such as *Ecce Home* and *Beyond Good and Evil*. He kept circling, and suddenly he swooped down hard and fast by coming back to the passage Paul had so naively quoted in order to show him what it really meant. When the assistant professor was finished, Paul was so thoroughly beaten that his appearance evoked empathy from the very ones initially irritated by his arrogance.

The assistant professor quickly took advantage of the teaching moment, a moment that he had created by nearly forcing Paul into a state of humility. He gently lifted him up again by saying, "You're right, Paul, many have read Nietzsche much closer than I have. I'm no expert, but I do know, as I have just shown, that there is a fundamental similarity between Christ's admonition to become like little children and Nietzsche's emphasis on innocence and purity. This is no small point since Christ clearly says that 'unless you become like little children, you shall not enter into the kingdom of God.' Moreover, in Nietzsche, just as in Christianity, it is precisely in the weakness of our innocence and purity that we are strong and noble. Do you understand?"

"Yes, sir," Paul said meekly, and with the utmost respect.

The class was spellbound by Dr. Sleiman's teaching, and no one dared to break the silence until the same shy girl who had spoken up earlier, genuinely interested in what was meant by the allusion to the wind, pointed out something about the poem that even Thomas had never thought about.

"Sir," she said, with a confidence that surprised the class, as it was so out of character for her, "do you think when Stevenson says 'or just a stronger child than me,' he could have had this point in mind?"

"Which point, Aline?"

"The one about being strong when weak, noble when innocent, courageous when pure, divine when a child. I mean, we don't usually think of children as being strong, much less stronger. And he identifies this apparently very strong child with the wind."

Thomas was astonished not only by her perceptiveness, but wondered why she had been so silent before.

"I appreciate very much your remarks, Aline. I think you might be on to something there. This would support my theory, wouldn't it, that he did have Nietzsche's wind in mind when he penned that particular poem."

"Yes it would, sir. And one more thing, could you tell us exactly what you mean by the term secularism? You've mentioned it many times now, and it seems that sometimes you mean one thing and at other times another."

He instantly thought of Meena and of ways to include a section on secularism in his book on love.

I've promised her my thoughts on this subject, not to mention a signed copy of the book. I must get back to the book, he mused inwardly as he launched into a scathing but highly nuanced critique of secularism, which he directed mostly to Aline.

The class atmosphere was different when it met a few days later; most everyone was convinced that something indisputably important and relevant could be learned in his class. Many met outside class to discuss ethics and the meaning of virtue. Thomas had gotten them to see that virtue was necessary for happiness. They all agreed they wanted happiness; the problems emerged when they had to define virtue.

"Is the good life relative, simply a matter of taste?" he asked, challenging them, "or is what makes my life good basically the same thing that makes your life good? Is the virtue of chastity, for instance, good for saints and nuns, or is it good for everyone?"

Thomas knew the very mention of chastity would increase their interest.

"Before we answer, sir, could you give us an etymology of the term like you usually do? This helps tremendously."

"We haven't time for a thorough etymology now. I read somewhere that the Russian word for chastity has to do with being whole or balanced, which is also somehow related to being clean."

"Not surprising," volunteered one student politely. "I remember being taught in Catholic grade school that sex was dirty."

"I highly doubt whether you were taught this, Bashir. I think you probably misunderstood."

"I may have, sir, but this was the general impression I got. And not only me, but many of my friends."

"Look, let me try to clear this up, and in doing so I'll try to relate it to the question concerning the nature of virtue. The ancients identified four cardinal virtues: prudence, fortitude, justice, and temperance. These main virtues were subdivided into other virtues. Now, although these virtues were given objective definitions, they weren't understood as static things. In other words, the ancient philosophers claimed that since these virtues were qualities of the human soul, they inevitably had a kind of elasticity and subjectivity due to the individual nature of the people possessing these qualities. Chastity, as part of the virtue of temperance, was said to be the virtue that moderated sex. In a word, a sexual act was considered unchaste if totally separated from the ultimate purpose of sex."

"Fine, sir, but what did they consider the ultimate purpose?"

"Isn't it clear?"

"You mean the procreation of children, right?"

"Yes, of course; isn't that obvious? The primary purpose of sexual intercourse is to have children."

"But aren't there other purposes, sir?" asked another student who rarely spoke up in class.

"Well, that's been a point of debate over the ages. Christian ethicists, building upon the insights of Aristotle and others, agreed that the primary purpose was procreation, but they also were cognizant of another purpose, namely, the reunification of man and woman."

"Why reunification?" asked one very vigilant student.

"Because of the biblical teaching regarding the original unity of man and woman. You see, when the Bible says that 'a man shall leave his father and mother and cling to his wife, and the two shall become one,' what it really means is that the two shall become one again."

"If God wanted them one, why did he divide them in the first place?"

"Look, if you really want the Christian answer to that question, you'll need to take my course in theology, because it all must be understood in light of the diversity and unity of the Trinity."

"Sir, why do you always bring everything back to the Trinity?"

"Because if the Trinity is existence itself, or better yet, being itself and more than being, then everything that exists somehow shares in this reality."

"What about evil, sir? Does it share in the reality of the Trinity?"

"We are really getting off track now, but the short answer is that evil isn't so much something that exists as much as the lack of existence, a kind of disordered being-less moving toward non-being. But let's get back to virtue. I brought up chastity as a virtue, a concept that has had a fairly consistent definition throughout history, and I'm claiming that since virtue is the key to happiness, and chastity is a virtue, then we must be chaste in order to be happy."

"Most of my friends are happy, sir, precisely because they are not chaste. When they aren't sexually involved with a girl, they are quite sad and depressed, not to mention moody," shouted one student, as many in the class burst out laughing.

"That's right," chimed in one of his friends.

"And the last thing they have on their mind is the procreation of children."

Thomas didn't know where to start. There was so much to say and so many misconceptions to overcome. There were so many profound and beautiful things he wanted to tell them about chastity. He wanted to show them how the mystery of man knowing woman in sexual intercourse was a holy and sacred participation in the very act of the Father eternally knowing the Son. He wanted to show them how and why virtue was necessary for happiness. He wanted to show them that chastity was more erotic and pleasing than lust. He wanted to teach them the difference between virginal chastity and marital chastity, and prove to them, in the light of the Son's eternal procession from the Father, that virginity was a higher state. He wanted to show them how the two states were complementary, not contradictory. He wanted to show them how Christian ethics didn't destroy pagan ethics, but perfected it. He wanted to show them that the life of virtue was exciting, not boring. He wanted to show them that becoming virtuous meant nothing more than becoming like little children and that to become a child again meant, paradoxically, to become a god.

He wanted to share the twenty-page paper he had written supporting and elucidating, against the backdrop of Catholic Trinitarian theology, what Narayan said in his autobiography about sex. But there was so little time, and there were so many distractions. He jumped from one subject to another so quickly that he ruined what had been a teachable moment, disposed as they were that day to really listen to what he had to say. He tried to give them so much that he ended up giving them very little, and when he dismissed them, he knew it.

"I genuinely apologize if I have totally confused many of you. I'll be in my office quite late today if any of you would like to stop by."

To his surprise, a few students did show up later and questioned him about two things in particular.

"We didn't quite catch the point about the connection between the Father eternally generating the Son, on one hand, and the act of sexual intercourse, on the other. And also, you kept talking about the autobiography of your favorite novelist, sir. We sort of lost you there. Could you explain what you were getting at?"

"Gladly—yes, gladly," Thomas said with all sincerity, realizing he'd been given another chance to do his duty.

"Let me start with the second point first, and this will inevitably lead us to the first point. You see, I wrote a long commentary on a paragraph that my favorite author, R. K. Narayan, wrote on the topic of sex in his autobiography. I agreed with it, of course, but tried to show how, in light of the mystery of the Blessed Trinity, we could also say that included in the ultimate purpose of sex, having children, there is another complementary purpose, which is also ultimate, in a way. I did this by plumbing the depths of that most mysterious book in all of sacred Scripture, The Song of Songs."

"Isn't that book about a wild love affair between a man and a woman?" asked one student who had read widely and deeply.

"Yes, it is. But it's really about how the Divine Lover playfully and masterfully pursues the individual soul. Interestingly enough, there is no mention of children, just a profound meditation and celebration of *eros*."

"Could we see your paper, sir?"

"Why of course," he said enthusiastically as he searched for it beneath a pile of books and other papers scattered wildly on the desk before him.

"Here it is," he declared triumphantly, and he handed it to them. "You see, I start by simply quoting Narayan, and then I begin the commentary. Why don't you read the first two pages out loud?" Thomas suggested, always willing to hear someone read what he'd written.

One student took it in hand and read: "'Why So Much Fuss About Sex?' by Dr. Thomas Sleiman. Somehow, for the working out of some destiny, birth in the physical world seems to be important; all sexual impulses and the apparatus of sexual functions seem relevant only as a means to an end—all the dynamism, power, and beauty of sex have a meaning only in relation to its purpose. This may not sound an appropriate philosophy in modern culture where sex is a fetish in the literal sense, to be propitiated, worshipped, and meditated on as an end in itself; where it is exploited in all its variations and deviations by movie makers, dramatists, and writers, while they attempt to provide continuous titillation, leading to a continuous pursuit of sexual pleasure—which, somehow, Nature has designed to be short-lived, for all the fuss made—so that one is driven to seek further titillation and sexual activity in a futile never-ending cycle.'"

"Yes. That's the end of the quote," Thomas interrupted. "Next, I begin my commentary. By the way, I like the way you read. Please go on."

The first two pages turned into nine, as Thomas would not let the poor student leave off reading. At the beginning of page ten, the student tried politely to stop, but Thomas compelled him to go on by insisting that the answer to their first question was approaching.

Approaching, in fact, was the key word because by page twelve the answer still had not come, although the necessary background knowledge had been masterfully presented. Thomas reluctantly noticed that it was just too much for them to grasp all at once, and suggested they continue another time. The students readily agreed and left the office. Two days later, they were back and ready for more.

"Where did we leave off?" he asked them.

"Well, we've understood so far, sir, that the Son's eternal procession or eternal birth from the Father is an eternal movement of knowledge wherein the Father is the eternal knower or speaker, while the Son is the eternal known or spoken word."

"Yes. Very good."

"We've also understood, sir, that the Son or Word going out from the Father is a word spoken eternally in love. And in speaking this one Word, the Father says everything that can be said. In this, the Father is truly a man of few words. In fact, sir, as you've explained, the Father knows himself as Father in his Son, and in knowing his Son, he knows all things."

"Fine, go on."

"We've also come to see, sir, that the Holy Spirit's eternal procession from the Father, through the Son, is like an eternal return of the Son in loving thanksgiving back to the Father. Thus, there is an eternal going out in knowledge and love and an eternal return in love and knowledge. Or to put it another way, the Father is the Singer who eternally sings one Song in the melody of Love—three divine persons eternally and infinitely giving and receiving knowledge and love, that is to say, giving and receiving one another."

"Yes. Now you realize, of course, don't you, that all affirmative language about God is merely analogical? The only time our language about God is univocal is when we are denying him."

"No, sir, we didn't quite get that point."

"It's quite simple. When I say God is beautiful and Jhansi is beautiful, the term beautiful is an analogy since created beauty is only like uncreated beauty. But when I say that God is not vindictive and human beings are vindictive, the term vindictive is univocal, that is, it means exactly the same thing in both statements. This means that the terms we use to describe what God is not are more accurate for us than the terms we use to describe what God is. Now do you understand?"

"Yes, we think so."

"Good. Go on then."

"Okay. We've also understood that these two eternal movements of knowledge and love, these two processions, if you will, can be spoken of in terms of four relations. The first relation of the Father to the Son is an eternal active generation, whereas the second relation of the Son to the Father is an eternal receptive generation. Both of these relations are associated with the first procession of the Son from the Father by way of eternal generation."

At this, they paused to look at their notes to make sure they had gotten everything right.

"We've also understood, sir, that the second procession, wherein the Holy Spirit proceeds from the Father through the Son by way of an eternal spiration, can likewise be spoken of in terms of two more relations. These are the relation of the Father and the Son to the Holy Spirit, which is an eternal active spiration, and the relation of the Holy Spirit to the Father and the Son, which is an eternal receptive spiration."

"That's correct. Go on."

"But we didn't understand what spiration means, sir."

"Literally it refers to breathing, and here it's a kind of twisting and turning, a bending and breath-buckling, a kind of stretching and straining in love, but don't worry too much about it. Remember, all affirmative language is merely analogical anyway."

"Yes, sir, we'll keep this in mind. Now, from what we've understood, man is more properly appropriated to the Son while woman is more properly appropriated to the Holy Spirit. Right? And this is based on sacred Scripture, which speaks of woman proceeding from God through man, whereas man proceeds directly."

"Exactly; very good."

"Now we gather from what you've written, sir, that when man knows woman in the marital act of sexual intercourse, he steps into the place of the Father, who is the knower. Woman, on the other hand, when known by man, steps into the place of the Son, who is the known. Man's participation in the Trinitarian dynamic then is Son-Father; woman's participation is Spirit-Son. Each child that proceeds from this union of the man and woman, whether male or female, enters first into the reality of the Son, since every child is first and foremost a receptive generation. And since the Holy Spirit proceeds from the Father through the Son, each child participates in the reality of the Spirit since each child comes from the Father-man through the Son-woman. Is that right, sir?"

"Yes. Good, good. Please continue."

"We gather from all of this that each act of sexual intercourse must be open to the conception of a child if it is to be an act that truly promotes unity between man and woman—precisely because the child is the embodiment of the unity of man and woman. This is the meaning of the biblical saying 'the two shall become one flesh.' The child is the one flesh of both man and woman, similar to how the Holy Spirit is the one common love between the Father and the Son."

"Good. But does this mean that each act must result in the conception of a child in order to be a good act?"

"No, sir. If this were the case, there would be far too many children," one replied, chuckling.

"What does it mean, then?"

"It means, as we have understood you, that each act must be open to this unity."

"Right. Very good! So we can say then that the unity of man and woman in the marital act is an end in itself only if it is also open to a mysterious unity that allows for the conception of a child, even if no actual conception takes place."

When they returned to his paper, and one of them began reading aloud again, Thomas reflected on what all of this might mean for his relationship with Jhansi. They had both agreed that it would be purely platonic. In that moment, he realized that his union with her could be good and holy only to the degree that they were open to life. Since this couldn't mean openness to life in a child, as they were to abstain from sexual intercourse, it had to mean openness to life in another way, in a spiritual dimension. What this dimension was, he couldn't say.

"I'll just have to wait and see," he said to himself. No longer listening to his student's reading of his own text, his mind wandered. Given his natural propensity for the dramatic, Alexander Pope's great poem "Eloisa to Abelard" came gently and gradually to mind.

"Perhaps our destiny will be similar," he reflected. "She will go off to a convent like Eloisa did, and I, like Abelard, will become a priest. Our children will be spiritual children. We'll consecrate our lives to Jesus and to his holy Church. Our passion will be transformed into passion for Christ and for the salvation of his people." He wondered if Rita would allow him to become a priest, since in their particular rite of the Roman Catholic Church, married men could be ordained as priests. When he focused his attention on listening again, the student had come to the part in the paper where he'd presented a kind of theology of the body, not only the body of man and woman, but the body of the entire cosmos.

"Thus," his student read, "the very rise and fall of water in what we call rain, the ebb of the ocean's tide, the very expansion and contraction of the cosmos and of each human muscle every time we move, every inhalation and exhalation of breath is a participation in the mystery of the Son going out from the Father and returning to Him in knowledge and love. The very body of woman is receptive in that she receives the body of man. She receives in a giving sort of way, but man gives his body to woman in a receiving sort of way. And woman, in receiving man, then gives back the child to all mankind. Just as the Holy Spirit is the common love of the Father and the Son, so too woman is the common person in humanity since both man and woman come through her. A mother's love is common; this may be why a woman has the common chromosome. And to say that woman is common is not to say that she is ordinary in the sense of unimportant. On the contrary, the level of any civilization is the level of its womanhood."

Thomas suggested they stop so he could answer their questions, but neither of them could formulate any.

"I thought you would have had all kinds of questions at this point."

"We need time to digest it all, sir."

"Of course, of course. Have you had enough for today?"

"Maybe we'll just finish this section on the natural goods of marriage from the Catholic point of view."

"Fine. Read on."

"As I see it, the natural goods of marriage, which are universal and not specifically or exclusively Christian, are perfected by the supernatural Christian good of marriage—the wedding feast of Christ, the Lamb—the subject of the last book of the Bible. That is to say that both the pro-creation of children and the unity of the spouses are ends in themselves only on the natural level, but are ultimately for a higher and greater purpose as a means to the eternal wedding feast of Christ, the Lamb, where, as the groom, he will mean everything to everyone. Christian marriage, due to the grace of the sacrament, points toward and embodies this loving union between Christ and the Church. Again, this is only through the grace of sacrament, which must be continually renewed by the reception of the grace of the other sacraments, primarily the Eucharist."

The student took a break at this point to clear his throat.

"This is the reason for the strict indissolubility and monogamy of marriage since the union between Christ and his church lasts eternally, and Christ is forever loyal to, and always for, his spouse and only his spouse. This spouse, then, is the Church, the chosen bride, the body and soul of which is 'made up' of all those who truly love him, and indeed of the entire cosmos—all according to a sacred order. Every human being without exception potentially constitutes one cell in this living body of the bride. On the individual personal level, every human being is preparing for his or her wedding in heaven. Women are naturally chosen for this reality as they are already 'bridal' by nature, but men, who symbolize the groom, are also called to be brides of Christ. Here we embark on a great mystery: the relationship between one's body and soul, and between man and woman. Men can only become brides to the degree that they recapture the original unity between man and woman. In other words, a man can only become a bride of Christ through a woman. The only way for a man to touch the mystery of being a bride is through union with a woman, who is flesh of his flesh and bone of his bone. Man's heart, as it were, is incomplete without woman, who was taken from his side, his rib, from the center of his being—from his heart, one could say. Only by touching her can he become full again, and only when he is one with her can he become 'bride.' Then, and only then, can he become fully himself in order to enter into unity with God, his origin and spousal end. The celibate man is called to this as much, and indeed even more deeply and directly, than the married man. In other words, virginal chastity is higher than marital chastity since the latter is only an image and a promise of the former. All of creation, angel, man, woman, animal, plant, mineral, rock, gas, and literally the entire cosmos, is called to enter into a bridal union with the Holy Trinity."

"Sir, if you don't mind now, we need to go."

"I know. I know. We'll finish it another day. Maybe you regret coming to my office."

"Not at all, sir, but it's nearly ten, the night guards are out, most of the doors are locked, and our parents might start worrying about us."

"Is it that late? I hadn't noticed the time; my goodness. All right. Goodbye. Goodnight."

Thomas called his wife to tell her he'd be late, as he had to begin a paper on metaphysics, which he'd been asked to deliver at an important conference in Rome.

"What's metaphysics?" she asked sincerely. "And what is the point of all these papers you give?"

Thomas wasn't quite sure how to answer. All he was able to say was, "The topic is too complicated to get into right now. I must begin this paper tonight because it's due next month, and I haven't written a word yet. You remember that Spanish mystic I told you about; well, he writes a lot about metaphysics too. You know I'm the keynote speaker, don't you?"

When he hung up, he took out a print of Raphael's *The School of Athens*, which he kept handy in his desk drawer, and placed it in front of him for inspiration.

"I can't very well write about the problem of universals without gazing from time to time at Raphael's masterpiece," he murmured.

In this state of mind, he picked up his pen (he still stubbornly refused to use a computer when composing the first draft of a paper) and wrote the following without hesitation:

Someone once portrayed the whole history of medieval philosophy as a long debate over the nature of universals. Granting the merit of this insight, I would go even further and suggest that the whole history of philosophy, from Thales to the present, is one magnificent metaphysical drama wherein the most genuine human sages and indeed the entire human race are caught up in a fierce and ferocious intellectual battle that almost completely transcends them, even though they occupy center stage in the conflict.

These lofty intellectual hostilities are ardently associated with an ancient and bitter spiritual dispute over the nature of universals—a dispute that began, perhaps, long before the appearance of humankind. Glimpses of this struggle are seen only occasionally and only by the most attentive and astute philosophers. This sublime discord, to which all authentic intellectuals are drawn, is what defines metaphysics. Such metaphysical speculation, far from a pedantic ivory-tower form of pondering, set in the historical context of a so-called myopic scholasticism, is at once the most basic and most exalted speculation possible—a reflection in which, to varying degrees, all people of all times, whether wittingly or not, are involved.

For though this ancient feud took place before and above man, the essence of the dispute revolves around the very meaning and destiny of the universal man. Thus, this metaphysical drama is the key to a proper understanding of history itself, for the question ends ultimately in demanding human persons to choose sides and to daily align themselves, as they "write" history, with either the violent and deceptive spiritual powers of iniquity and corruption that are passing away, or with the gentle and true sacred forces of goodness and beauty that last forever. In a word, the dynamic discourse of universals is the most universal discourse of all.

After the advent of Nominalism and even after Cartesianism had attempted to radically reduce philosophy to mere epistemology, metaphysics stubbornly refused to give up its historical role of defining the very essence of the philosophical enterprise. One part of this Cartesian reduction consisted in removing the universal ideas from the mind of God, where Augustine, in his attempt to modify Plato's exaggerated realism, had so masterfully placed them.

Once Descartes disassociated the universal ideas from the divine, his methodological decency compelled him to find the orphaned universal concepts a proper home. His devotion to this daring procedure finally ended when, with a masterful stroke of surgical precision, he delicately undertook to place the universal concepts into the very mind of man. But a surgical error went unnoticed during this grandiose epistemological experiment. And, such an imprisonment could not last.

The metaphysical debate emerged again and again in the most unlikely of places, much to the dismay of those who thought the controversy (associated as it was with theology at best and with religious superstition at worst) had disappeared forever. In the last century, for instance, when Willard Quine asked what mathematics was really all about, it quickly became evident that the three supplied answers, Logicism, Formalism, and Intuitionism, clearly corresponded to the traditional philosophical positions in regard to the question of universals, with Logicism corresponding to Realism, Formalism to Nominalism, and Intuitionism to Conceptualism.

In the words of Quine, "Classical mathematics . . . is up to its neck in commitments to an ontology of abstract entities. Thus it is that the great medieval controversy over universals has flared up anew in the modern philosophy of mathematics." To his credit, Quine himself came down on the side of Logicism, thereby committing himself to a variety of realism. To be sure, neither modernity nor the arrival of post-modernity lessen the importance of the debate over universal truth; in fact, they intensify it.

Modern science and technology testify to both the significance of the debate and to the weighty consequence of coming down on the right side of it. In the case of modern science and technology, of course, there is no contention over which side is the right one. If universals did not really exist, how could we ever refer to laws, for instance, which cause all specific electromagnetic spheres or fields to act in certain expected ways? If modern technology did not presuppose the genuine existence of universals, would we ever have confidence to stake our lives on the reliability of our cars and airplanes?

Those who think that postmodernity's deconstructionism has toppled the Western metaphysical tradition have understood neither deconstructionism nor the universals' quandary at the heart of the metaphysical tradition. The former is primarily a response to, not simply a rejection of, the phenomenology of Edmund Husserl, and thus counts as another contribution to metaphysics. Surely, both Husserl and Derrida strongly resisted certain systems of metaphysical programming, but only the superficial would claim that philosophers of such magnitude weren't engaged in metaphysics. John Paul II, in fact, recently described phenomenology as "first of all a style of thought, an intellectual relation with reality, whose essential and constitutive traits one hopes to gather, avoiding prejudices and schematism." If this is an accurate characterization of phenomenology, which I think it is, who could imagine Derrida disagreeing with it, and who could fail to see its important metaphysical implications? Besides, it is appropriate to call to mind here the famous statement of E. A. Burtt in his monumental work, The Metaphysical Foundations of Modern Physical Science, who wrote in the early part of the last century, "The only way to avoid becoming a metaphysician is to say nothing."

At any rate, I trust this brief overture constitutes a suitable setting in which to address briefly the complex dynamic of relations and interactions in and among metaphysics, the doctrines of deification and the incarnation, and eschatology. To be more precise, I shall assert that although the orthodox Christian doctrine of deification has been all but abandoned today in the West (a process that began as early as the Reformation), the doctrine is absolutely central to the orthodox Christian creed. In light of this assertion, I shall attempt to sketch out in a general and brief way how the new metaphysics of Fernando Rielo sheds abundant light on the relation between the universals debate and the doctrine of deification. Such light, while synthesizing anthropology, eschatology, and incarnational theology in novel and exhilarating ways, gives new life and energy to both metaphysics and to the doctrine of deification as well.

Thomas looked approvingly at what he had written. He sat back, lit up his pipe, and stared contentedly at Raphael's philosophical masterpiece with Plato pointing up and Aristotle pointing down. In spite of his severe critique of Raphael's chubby angels, he admired exceedingly this particular painting. Something bordering on happiness emerged within him. Jolting him out of his reverie, the telephone's obnoxious wake-up call startled him, and as soon as he said hello, he heard his wife lambasting him for staying in the office until two in the morning.

CHAPTER FIFTEEN

Sometime during the fall semester, Thomas came to a decision. He secured her visa and found a place for her to stay. He couldn't wait to give her the news; the delicious sound of her voice over the telephone was indescribable.

"You mean in six weeks, everything will be ready?"

"I mean in about six weeks, you should be here."

"Oh my God, are you sure? Can it be true? I can't believe it. Thank you. Thank you. Thank you, my love. I love you. I can't wait to be in your arms."

"I'm dreaming about you, Jhansi, most every night."

"Tell me."

"Most of the time we're just looking at each other; sometimes our faces are touching. I can't wait to see you. I need you. I'll always need you. I want you."

"You have me. I am yours. I am you. I knew you would manage somehow. I knew it."

"Well, you can't believe how many things had to fall into place at the right time; it seemed impossible at times."

"Is it possible that God has helped us, Thomas?"

"Why not? Have you forgotten already?"

"What?"

"Your favorite poem, of course:

Love, and the love of life,
Act Dance, Live and Sing
Through all our furrowed tract;
Till the great God enamored gives,
To him who reads,
To him who lives,
That rare and fair Romantic Strain
That whoso hears must hear again."

His writing became easier and more productive once he'd made the decision. His friends instantly noticed his changed mood.

"Seem to be a bit more relaxed these days," said Mr. Morrison one crisp cool morning during one of the regular visitations.

"Ah, yes, things have fallen into place nicely as of late."

"Glad to hear it, my friend."

"By the way, Mr. Morrison, it seems you're a kind of prophet."

"Why's that?"

"Didn't you hear that V. S. Naipaul won the Nobel Prize for literature this year?"

"Oh yes! I told you that an Indian was going to get it one of these days."

"That's what I meant. Although he wasn't really an Indian, was he? He was from Trinidad."

"Well, yes, but anyone who has ever read his book *India: A Wounded Civilization* knows that the soul of his writing is Indian from beginning to end."

"I haven't read that yet."

"Oh, it's tragically delightful," he said, taking a puff of his pipe.

"Sounds charmingly harsh. I'm thrilled he got the award. Is that the book he got it for?"

"No. I believe it was for his *A House for Mr. Biswas*, an outstanding novel. Have you read it, Thomas?"

"Not yet, but it's on my top-twenty list. I've heard good things about it. And as it was published in the same year I was born, I'm sure it will have special significance for me."

Mr. Morrison just smiled and thought to himself how naive and almost superstitious Thomas was at times.

"But I have read his *An Area of Darkness*; it's a favorite of mine. Do you know that one?"

"No, I can't say I do; would you recommend it?"

"By all means; not only is it a superb piece of travel-writing, but his account of what happened to him in India gave voice to what I felt while there. I had so many experiences in India that I'd wanted to put into words but could not. Great writers never cease to amaze me. Powers of observation are one thing, but capturing those observations in words is quite another."

"Oh, I know, I know," agreed Mr. Morrison. "He certainly deserved the award."

"You knew that Narayan was nominated for a Nobel Prize . . ."

"Is that right? I didn't know that."

"Oh yes. Many great writers were quite surprised that he didn't get it. Graham Greene once stated that after Evelyn Waugh, Narayan was the novelist he admired most in the English language."

"Well, I've not read everything he has written like you have, but based on the little I've read, I think he certainly deserved it."

"Beyond a doubt, Mr. Morrison; sometimes those awards are highly political."

"Yes, I know. At any rate, it's nice when someone like Naipaul, who really deserves it, gets it," he mumbled through the corner of his mouth, enjoying his pipe.

"Sure is," agreed Thomas as he took in the rich and soothing aroma of the Englishman's pipe tobacco. The aroma of the pipe prompted Thomas to ponder what Mr. Morrison had meant by 'Indian from beginning to end.'

Would Naipaul himself agree with that statement? he mused inwardly.

"You look puzzled, Thomas."

"Well, you've taken me back to *An Area of Darkness*."

"Come again," Mr. Morrison quipped, entering into the puzzlement.

"Naipaul's book, *An Area of Darkness*."

"What about it?"

"I don't know," he said, and then added after a moment of silence, "on which basis do you so easily say that his writing is Indian? What counts for Indian writing?"

"Look," said Mr. Morrison with authority and confidence, "Naipaul himself says that his 'Indian memories . . . are like,' uh, what does he say? Oh yes, like 'trapdoors into a bottomless pit,' thereby admitting that although he was a stranger in India, he came to understand just how Indian he really was."

"I see," said Thomas thoughtfully. "But when it comes to the novel and to fiction, where does the Indian stand?"

Waiting for an answer that never came, Thomas answered his own question.

"If I'm not mistaken, Naipaul dwells on how much confusion is revealed in the awkward efforts of Indians to write novels, claiming, as he does, that the impetus in such writing is a 'peculiarly Western curiosity concerning the human state,' whereas the Indian intellectual's 'basic hunger' is for the 'unseen,' a hunger that is not really satiated by this Western 'concern for the condition of men.' But from beginning to end, as I perceived it, *An Area of Darkness* is nothing if not a profound meditation on the condition of men."

"Now I see the source of your perplexity," said Mr. Morrison. "Well, in this light, then, would you claim that he's not really an Indian intellectual at all?"

"He's exactly what he is: a Western intellectual of Indian descent. His basic curiosity concerns the human state, but he has an ancient, ancestral hunger for the unseen as well. And I think he is perfectly aware of this; it comes through loud and clear in *An Area of Darkness*."

Thoroughly enjoying the conversation, Mr. Morrison asked enthusiastically, "So in this context, then, what did he think of the novels of Narayan?"

"Ah, ha. It's funny you ask. I've been thinking a lot about that lately. Naipaul himself tells us exactly what he thinks of Narayan."

"Is that right?" exclaimed Mr. Morrison. "Where?"

"Where else? In *An Area of Darkness.*"

"Well, what does he say?"

While Thomas paused to remember the precise words, Mr. Morrison became a bit impatient and began talking authoritatively about *A House for Mr. Biswas.* Thomas reluctantly withdrew his attention from the effort of trying to remember exactly how Naipaul had characterized Narayan's writing, as he was forced to pay attention to Mr. Morrison's mini-lecture. Thomas didn't mind, as many of his colleagues did, Mr. Morrison's pontificating manner. In fact, Thomas rather enjoyed it, since Mr. Morrison was usually right. Besides this, Thomas always felt that his pontification sprang somehow from humility and love; there was something innocent about it.

"Now that's an extraordinary book, though a bit depressing, I must say. What I was so impressed with, besides the accurate descriptions of the day-to-day life of early Indian emigrant communities in Trinidad, was the insight he offered into the awesome spirit of perseverance possessed by most Indians. I was impressed by the way that Mr. Biswas, the main character, who is actually based on Naipaul's father, I'm sure, kept rising out of his despair against all odds. At times, you think things have completely fallen apart between Biswas and his son, or between Biswas and his wife, and yet the relationships continue to grow and deepen. Wounds heal."

Thomas had no comment as he hadn't read it, but vaguely remembered Naipaul saying somewhere in *An Area of Darkness* that India's greatest strength was her power to endure. As soon as his friend finished, his thoughts turned again to answering the Englishman's question.

"Ah, yes," he said triumphantly, "now I'm starting to remember what Naipaul said."

"I'm listening."

"Well, he claims there's a contradiction between Narayan's style and his mindset, or what I think Naipaul says is between his form and his attitude."

"How so," said Mr. Morrison, demanding an explanation.

"Naipaul thinks Narayan's mindset is part of an older India, which was or is, I suppose, if that older India still exists in pockets, incapable of self-evaluation. In this he would describe Narayan's attitude as negative."

"So where's the contradiction?"

"I'm getting to it, but I'm trying to recall the precise way in which Naipaul so cleverly captures it. Let me think for a moment."

"Take your time; I'm in no hurry this morning," said Mr. Morrison. "All my editing work for the journal is done, thank goodness," he added as he searched his pockets for more tobacco.

Thomas began slowly. "Yes . . . so his attitude is negative in that he denies concern, but his style and form forever imply it."

"But need this be described as a contradiction? Why not simply an intended and mysterious paradox?"

"Right. Excellent! Well, I think Naipaul actually refers to it as a calm contradiction in which is embodied a sort of magic. If you have just a moment, let me find the passage. I'm pretty sure it comes toward the end of the book. I can find it quickly," he said, and he dashed off to his bookcase.

Settling in his chair, he said, "I've got it. Listen to this. 'The virtues of R. K. Narayan are Indian failings magically transmuted . . . . [He] seems forever headed for that aimlessness of Indian fiction—which comes from a profound doubt about the purpose and value of fiction—but he is forever rescued by his honesty, his sense of humour, and above all by his attitude of total acceptance . . . . [It] has this result: the India of Narayan's novels is not the India the visitor sees. He tells an Indian truth. Too much that is overwhelming has been left out; too much has been taken for granted. There is a contradiction in Narayan, between his form, which implies concern, and his attitude, which denies it; and in this calm contradiction lies his magic, which some have called Chekhovian.'"

Thomas paused at this point to mention that Graham Greene had often compared Narayan's greatness to that of Chekhov's.

"Interesting," said Mr. Morrison. "It's all very fascinating. So, do you agree with Naipaul, Thomas? Is the India of Narayan's novels the India the visitor sees, or not?"

"I suppose it depends on the visitor, doesn't it?"

"You're avoiding the question; you know what I mean. You've read every one of Narayan's novels over and over, right? And you've visited India. Which India did you see?"

I saw her India, he thought, *"failings magically transmuted."*

"That's a big question, Mr. Morrison. It demands an extensive answer."

"Very well. Shall I wait for your critical essay on the subject? I'll publish it in the journal, if you'd like."

"That'd be fine. I'd love to publish something like that, but before that, I'd like to see all the other essays published. I'm still waiting for the ones on Uganda and South Mexico and Thailand and Sweden, that you promised to publish."

"Yes, yes, they're coming, they're coming." Mr. Morrison said defensively.

"With all due respect," Thomas said chuckling, "they've been coming for quite a few months now."

Mr. Morrison chuckled too.

"So what else does Naipaul say?"

"Let me finish reading the passage. 'He (Narayan) is inimitable, and it cannot be supposed that his is the synthesis at which Indian writing will arrive. The younger writers in English have moved far away from Narayan. In those novels which tell of the difficulties of the Europe-returned student, they are still only expressing a personal bewilderment; the novels themselves are documents of the Indian confusion.'"

"Fascinating," whispered Mr. Morrison reflectively, in between the perfect smoke rings that appeared magically from his mouth and which softly filled the little room with an intoxicating aroma. "And did Narayan ever say anything about Naipaul's work?"

"Oh yes, but not much. It appears in a short story he wrote titled 'Second Opinion.' And if I'm right in assuming that Narayan presents his own view through the mouth of the protagonist there—I think the hero's name was Sambu—then he somewhat approved of Naipaul's view of India as a wounded civilization."

"That's peculiar."

"How so?"

"Well, you must be familiar with the biting criticism of Naipaul's work by the great Palestinian intellectual Edward Said?"

"Of course I am; I've done some work on Said's thought. But what does that have to do with Narayan," he asked innocently.

"Don't you see the problem?"

As Thomas was puzzling over just precisely what Mr. Morrison was getting at, Mr. Morrison added, "So in which context did you write about Said?"

"It was in the context of a review I did on Hillare Belloc's essay on Islam."

"Oh I love Belloc. Could you send it to me?"

"Sure; I'll send you at least the short preface just as soon as I get back from class this afternoon." He looked at his watch. "Oh, God! Excuse me, Mr. Morrison. My students are waiting for me in class. I hope they haven't left yet. I'll be in trouble with the chairman again."

He darted off to class, leaving his friend sitting all alone in the office.

"Shall I close the door?" Mr. Morrison called after him, but Thomas had already vanished.

Failings magically transmuted, thought Mr. Morrison as he made no hurry to get up and leave, and finished another bowl of tobacco.

There was no sign of Mr. Morrison when Thomas returned, although a comforting aroma lingered, reminding him of the fine conversation they'd had earlier. The thought soothed him, as he had just endured a truly miserable hour with students who, for some reason, just weren't receptive this day. Recalling his promise to send the preface to the piece on Belloc, he stormed his computer and pulled up the desired piece, which read as follows:

> First, let me say that I like very much and agree with Belloc's approach to history. He strives for a philosophy of history that is free from the categories of progress that dominated historical narration at his time. He also stays clear of any secularization of historical narration. As a Catholic, I applaud this. I like very much and agree with the way he develops this philosophy of history, namely, toward a theology of history whose hermeneutical key is the struggle between the powers of darkness and the forces of light and goodness.
>
> What I cannot agree with, however, is the way he so easily and confidently applies this to the extremely complex and mysterious histories of both Christianity and Islam, or in his words, to Christendom and Mohammedanism. In fact, by insisting on the term Mohammedanism,

which Muslims staunchly reject as the name of their religion, he underscores his point about Islam being a heresy, since all ancient heresies took the name of their founders, but he also makes his most important point for his theology of history: the battle is between Christ and Satan, seemingly to imply that Satan's false prophet is Mohammed. Of course, he doesn't explicitly say this, but this seems to be the natural implication in this theology of history. He also assumes that Christ is always on the side of Christendom, which isn't at all clear to me in my reading of history, and he constantly uses the terms "them" and "us" as if everyone automatically knows what the antecedents of those pronouns are. I don't think Belloc ever really appropriated, at least here, the lesson learned by Augustine, which is there in *The City of God*, namely, that the Eusbeian way of writing Church history was somehow naive because it assumed too quickly and too confidentially to know all the details and patterns of the workings of divine providence in history.

Belloc's view of history, at least as I read it in this particular essay, is strikingly close to Augustine's immature view, which he held while in his thirties. He believes that the period from Constantine to Theodosius was the beginning of an unending and universal political order that would go under the name of the Christian Roman Empire, and which was not only the work of divine providence but a clear expression of the divine will. Case closed; no room for qualification.

But as Augustine matured, he eventually saw that all history, including the history of the Church and Christendom, is an extremely complicated mixed bag of good and evil forces that cannot be sorted out in a definitive or meaningful way until the Last Day during the Final Judgment. This, in my reading, is the brilliance of Augustine's *City of God*: he changed his mind about history and church history. As we know, there are devils in the Church and in Christendom, as well as saints, and likewise, there are "saints" in Islam as well as devils.

I do agree (how could one not) with Belloc's implied point about the military nature of the origin of Islam as compared to the peaceful and "sheep among wolves" beginnings of Christianity. I always point this out to my students, as it is so powerful (I use Newman here), but I also point out how soon things changed in Christianity once poor and weak sinful men got their hands on worldly power.

I realize the essay is about Islam and not about Christianity, and I think Belloc's presuppositions in his theology of history make for a reading of Islamic history that is very interesting and meaningful, but not quite right. His narration of the history of Islam is accurate in many ways: his description of its historical origin, the recording of the dates of its progress and the stages of its original success; his description of its consolidation; and his explanation of its increasing power. The only thing I would take exception to is his explanation of Islam as an exclusively Christian heresy. I agree with everything he says about its belief system and the fundamental commensurability it has with Christianity's belief system, but he does not take into account the influence of Judaism on Islam. In many ways, Islam is as much of a Jewish heresy as a Christian heresy.

At any rate, I can agree with much (if not all) of what he says about the nature of Islam, but, again, when he makes statements such as, "It [Islam] very nearly destroyed us," he assumes that "us" and "Christendom" are singular things, which everyone should understand immediately. The problem, however, is that Islam is not monolithic, and neither is Christendom. When he says "the threat which it remained to our civilization," he assumes that we, whoever we are, are civilized, and Islam is barbarous. Now perhaps at certain times and in certain places this was true, but at other times, it has been quite the opposite. Or when he says, "Missionary effort had no appreciable effect on [Islam] . . . [but] the Mohammedan never becomes a Catholic," he is simply repeating old stereotypes of Islam and Muslims that are demonstrably false. In the case of Lebanon alone, major conversions of Muslim families to Catholicism in the late Middle Ages are notorious and form the very fabric of Lebanese history. Even today, many conversions are happening throughout the Middle East. I have just now spent an evening with an entire family who converted from Islam to Catholicism; the father has adapted Islamic Koranic chant to the Psalms. The other night he gave a public performance, claiming, as he did, that Koranic chant has its origin in Christian and Jewish chant.

Belloc, as important and brilliant as he is, has this blind spot: he has fallen prey to what the great Palestinian Catholic writer, philosopher, and intellectual Edward Said spent his life describing: "Orientalism." Said's masterpiece, *Orientalism: Western Conceptions of the Orient*, shows definitively how the idea of the Orient derives in great part from the "impulse not simply to describe, but also to dominate and somehow defend against." He shows this especially to be the case with respect to portraying "Islam as a particularly dangerous embodiment of the Orient." Said writes, "Orient and Occident correspond to no stable reality that exists as a natural fact. Moreover, all such geographical designations are an odd combination of the empirical and imaginative." Although some Muslim fundamentalists have tried to turn Said's work into a systematic defense of Islam and the Arabs, Said expressly denies that this is what he is doing. The work is well worth reading as an amazing piece of scholarship, but in terms of the task you have set for me, assessing Belloc's essay, it is invaluable, because Belloc is a prime example of how powerful Orientalism can be and has been in Britain on many British intellectuals, including the great Arthur James Balfour, who in a public lecture to the House of Commons on June 13, 1910, described the Orient as containing a class of people who "belong to a wholly different category."

Such prejudice was not always present in the West. One needs only to look at the work of Chaucer, a man who predated the notion of Orientalism as a tool for dominance and control, who wrote so splendidly in *The Canterbury Tales* about the great Muslim scientists: "Well knew he the olde Esculpius and Deyscorides, and eek rufus Olde Ypocras, Haly and Galyen, Serpion, Razis and Avicen, Avverrois, Damascien and Constantyn, Bernard and Gatesden and Gilbertyn."

Chaucer named fifteen authorities in that quote: five Greeks, one Frenchman, two Englishmen, and seven Muslims. About a century later, as Said masterfully shows, such high praise of Muslim scientists and philosophers had disappeared. This was characteristic of a gradual French then British and now American intellectual academic movement, which created the notion of the Orient (Islam being just one part of it) dominated by political motives. In other words, a new kind of sophistry developed wherein intellectuals sold their souls to politicians with grandiose political agendas, and some of the Oriental scholars jumped on the bandwagon to divide the spoils. The case of India is a stunning example of Orientalism at its best.

Finally, although I do think Belloc ought to be read today, primarily because of his valuable approach to history, which is both courageous and brilliant, I don't think his work is very helpful for the present task that the Church in her infallible Magisterium has laid before us: missionary work. I don't think it was an accident that Our Lady, the Virgin Mary, chose Fatima as the place to appear to the children and to speak to the world. Fatima and Mary are the two most reverenced women in Islam. I think she was expressing her wish for their "full" conversion to her Son, whom they also reverence and respect, but not "fully." The Catechism, following Vatican II, clearly says that "Christians and Muslims worship the same God." This means that we who know the Trinity must help, by our example and by our prayers and witness, even to the point of shedding our blood, to show the Muslim the fullness of the truth about God, and thus about man. Essays such as Belloc's, as important as they are to a certain degree, seem to create serious obstacles to that mission. I also think that many Christians living in first-world, affluent Western societies can learn a lot about their faith from Muslims, including things that they (we) have forgotten about God, such as his justice; his promise to reward and punish (heaven and hell); his insistence that the first commandment is really the first. The Muslim tendency not to separate church and state, its refusal to bow to secularism, are all things that Christians and even Catholics in the West can relearn about their own faith from Muslims.

Mr. Morrison called Thomas the following day, and they picked up their conversation about Naipaul, Narayan, and Said. Forty-five minutes into their conversation, the telephone rang.

"It's long distance, Mr. Morrison, from America; can we continue later?"

"Sure, I'll ring you up tomorrow."

The voice at the other end offered warm congratulations to Thomas for winning a poetry contest and inquired as to where and how the award money should be sent. Thomas had forgotten all about it. He'd gone to the United States earlier in the year where he met some Neo-Cons who were impressed with a paper he had given at an Ethics conference. They told him about a publishing house that specialized in poetry dedicated to the unborn, and that held annual competitions. Thomas submitted a poem titled "But I'm a Woman," which he now learned had won first prize. Thomas much admired the sincerity of the people there who had dedicated their lives to ending the legalization of abortion, but marveled at how some of them, while speaking courageously on behalf of the unborn, nevertheless were avid supporters of the sanctions and war in Iraq, both of which were brutally claiming the lives of countless innocents while tearing up the Middle East—a region of the world that he now identified as his home. After Thomas hung up the phone, he sat in his favorite chair and slowly recited in a whisper the poem he had submitted:

A woman's right, they say, once you pay, and pay, and pay
A woman's right, he said, so what if someone's dead; it's a woman's right
But I'm a woman, though in the womb, or I would have been—well, soon
But now I'm just a girl, a very little one
Look, I have toes and fingers—count them, one by one
A woman's right, they say, once you pay, and pay, and pay

And I have a heart, and a mouth too, and a nose, and eyes
Can't anyone stop these vicious lies?
Don't I have rights, though not a voice?
Just a death sentence
In the name of Choice

A woman's right, they say, about six thousand now, every day, and every day
they pay and pay

Count them now one by one,
Make sure nothing's left
The womb must be clean
Ignore the silent scream—if you can
And count them one by one
We've got to get them all—don't stall
That's our job you know, fingers, toes, and all

A woman's right, they say, once of course you pay, and pay, and pay

But doc, she's alive, and look there's blood
No, it's just mud, just think of it as mud
That's what I used to do
When I was like you
When it was all still so new

I had nightmares in those days
To kill in so many different ways
And I even took an oath, I think, to help the sick and save life
But then there was too much strife
I couldn't resist in medical school
They called me a fool

Don't even raise the issue; it's only tissue
And even if it's not, it's the law you know
It's a woman's right
But doc, she's alive I say, and look there's real red blood
No, it's just mud, just think of it as mud
It's a procedure called suction
Just suck it out—suck it all out and don't pout

It's a woman's right—you know
Just count them one by one
Nine, ten—got all the fingers
Eight, nine—oops, we've missed one of the toes
But maybe there were only nine—who knows?

A woman's right they say, once you pay, and pay, and pay

But the ultrasound showed ten
Then suck it out all again
We've got to do our job you know; obey the law
That way, they'll keep coming back, day after bloody day
And they'll continue to pay, and pay, and pay

A woman's right, they say, six, or seven or maybe ten thousand now a day
But wait, I'm a woman . . . well, I would have been.

Thomas sat staring out his window for some time in silence. He loved this view; he never got tired of it. The trees moving gently in the soft breeze danced gracefully before the backdrop of the mountains crowned with monasteries and adorned with various shades of green that contrasted perfectly with the whiteness of white clouds and the sky of light and dark blue. He went into a kind of trance, intoxicated by the otherness of the scenery beckoning to him. When he returned to a normal state, he instinctively reached for his writing pad and pencil and began to write without the slightest effort.

Although writing flowed easily, after he'd made his final decision to bring Jhansi to live next to him, two serious obstacles remained: the ending and the introduction.

"Time is running out," he constantly reminded himself. "I must submit for publication soon."

One afternoon, he confided in a friend who had read a good deal of the manuscript and who was encouraging him to publish it. "You see, Antoine, I want to publish it in India, but the one who promised to help is leaving in less than six weeks."

"That's plenty of time to do something; just get him the manuscript."

"It's a her."

"Then send her the manuscript. You said it's ready, didn't you?"

"It's almost ready. But there's no one to write the introduction, and I don't yet have an ending."

"Introduction?" his friend replied in amazement. "What the hell do you need an introduction to a novel for?"

"You know you shouldn't end your sentences with a preposition."

"Excuse me, Dr. Sleiman," he snarled back. "How's this? What the hell do you need an introduction to a novel for, smart ass?"

Thomas roared with laughter, and then got serious again.

"Well, if someone famous doesn't write the introduction, then no one will read it."

"You idiot. Novels are not to be introduced. People like to begin a novel with the author's own words, and they certainly don't want to be told what is going to happen."

"Oh yes," said Thomas, giving him a little of his own medicine by virtually ignoring his friend's remarks, "that reminds me—there's also the problem of the opening sentence. I just can't seem to get it right."

"The opening sentence?"

"Well, yes, of course! It's perhaps the most important sentence in a novel, don't you think? Didn't you just say how important it was? I know that I want it to be something about the power of the moon, so as to suggest the centrality of transformation, but in the context of dreams and love."

"Sounds like *A Midsummer Night's Dream* to me," his friend said pontifically; he prided himself on knowing Shakespeare so well.

"Well, transformation is one of my main themes, and you know my theory about the naming of that play, don't you?"

"No, I can't remember all your theories. That's your problem, Thomas; you're too much into theories."

Antoine only occasionally listened to Thomas anymore, as he had it in his mind that he had already figured him out. Thomas took it all in stride. Thomas was expected just to listen and learn, but never to teach, and for the most part that's what he had finally resigned himself to do since his friend was much older than he and extremely tired of books and theories and academic life in general. Thomas tried to tell him quite a few times that Shakespeare was a Catholic mystic, and that the feast of the "Transfiguration of Christ" came exactly in midsummer, on the night of August 5, but his friend just dismissed it as the result of Thomas's over-religiosity, and thus had forgotten all about it.

Thomas told him again, but his friend interrupted him with, "Now what were you saying about opening sentences?" Antoine wanted to get Thomas back to what they'd first been talking about and off the subject of Shakespeare. He especially resisted learning anything about Shakespeare from Thomas.

Thomas complied and said, "Well, when you think of any great novel you've read, the opening sentence comes rushing back."

"Yeah, you're right, and it somehow embodies the whole novel, doesn't it? Let me see," said his friend speculatively. "Oh, yeah, I remember this one from Murdoch's *The Sea, the Sea.*"

"Who?"

"Murdoch. Iris Murdoch. Don't tell me you've never heard of her?"

"Well, the name is familiar, but I can't really say that I know anything about her or her work."

"Impossible. I'm sometimes amazed at how ill-read you are. You must read something by her. I suggest you begin with *Nuns and Soldiers*; that'll be perfect for you. You'll fit right in."

Thomas made a mental note of it and did eventually go on, many years later, to read all of Murdoch's twenty-six philosophical novels, as they were called, only to discover later that his friend had only read one or two.

"Well, I'm waiting."

"For what?"

"For the opening line."

"Oh, yeah. Some say it's really a novel about philosophical aesthetics. It starts like this: The sea, which lies before me as I write, glows rather than sparkles in the bland May sunshine."

Thomas waited for his friend's assessment.

"Do you know when the sea glows and when it sparkles, Thomas?"

"Well, I suppose it has something to do with the month of May, and I guess when the sun shines on it."

"Right, and do you know the difference between sparkling and glowing?"

Thomas paused to contemplate.

"Don't tax your poor mind; I'll explain it to you. You see, Thomas, at high noon on a clear May day when the sun is most proud, its brilliance drowns out every other brilliance. The sea here only sparkles, but in the evening, when the troubles of the day have taught it humility and compassion, the sun makes room for other brilliances. It gives itself up in loving sacrifice so that the sea may glow rather than sparkle. This is why she says 'the bland May sunshine.' Do you get it?"

Thomas nodded and pointed out how close it was to something one of his favorite theologians had written about beauty while describing Schiller's reflections on Kant's work on aesthetics.

"You see, Thomas, my dear, how much you underrate me? I am in league with people like Kant and Schiller, only nobody knows it. Now go on, I know you want to read me something. I can see it in your eyes."

"That's right; how did you know?"

"I told you, I can see it in your eyes. Well, hurry up before I change my mind. I don't have all day to listen to you pontificate."

Thomas disappeared for a moment and then reappeared with a book in his hand, from which he read the following:

When beauty becomes a form which is no longer understood as being identical with Being, spirit, and freedom, we have again entered an age of aestheticism, and realists will then be right in objecting to this kind of beauty. They go about demolishing what has rotted from within, but they cannot replace the power of Being, which resides in the conferring of form. But so long as the form remains true—which is to say living, efficacious form—it is a body animated by the spirit, a body whose meaning and whose principle of unity are dictated and imposed by the spirit. The level at which form makes its appearance transcends itself interiorly, or better, it does not so much or so obviously transcend itself, as the spirit which is immanent in it manifests itself radiantly through it. Borrowing from Kant, Schiller has described the double dialectic of this sunrise of the spirit's splendor in the beauty of form. At dawn, heaven and earth are still as one. Earthly things are transfigured and become celestial, while the light of heaven has not yet appeared in all its particularity. Such is the charm of youth, in which the spirit plays in the body unselfconsciously. When the sun climbs to the very zenith of midday, heaven and earth are fully separated, but that which is earthly enters heaven's bright light to the extent that the spirit's sovereign freedom scorches and shatters the instrument and the medium of its appearing, and by this destruction proclaims its lordship. This is the age of dignity. The second dialectic is directed by the same impetus. Out of an existence fully governed by the aesthetic principle there breaks forth the ethical on account of the spirit's stronger radiance. But the ethical does not then question the legitimacy of beauty, rather does it reveal itself as beauty's inner coordinate axis, which enables beauty to enfold to its full dimensionality as a transcendental attribute of Being.

Somewhat dumbfounded by the sheer force of how the words were strung together, let alone by the muscle of their meaning, Antoine stared blankly at Thomas then said sardonically, just to torture him a bit, "So what the hell does that have to do with glowing and sparkling?"

"You're hopeless," Thomas shot back.

"I know that—thank you. Anyway, you'd better get back to your so-called novel if you're ever going to finish the damn thing. By the way, from what you've given me to read, it seems that what you're up to in that book of yours is very much like what Murdoch did in *The Sea, the Sea*, you know."

"No. I don't know. I haven't read it; remember how ill-read I am?"

A few days later, Thomas was meditating in his usual spot, an oasis of sorts in the middle of the city, where a little lake, a chapel, and scores of beautiful trees and flowers provided an ideal morning refuge from the angry cars of the modern city.

Why are they so angry? he wondered, and he recalled Rabindranath Tagore's description of the modern motor engine as "shouting its discourtesy to the silent music of the spheres." After he'd said his morning prayers and read the little portion of divine music included in Narayan's autobiography *My Days*, the idea of asking someone from Narayan's family to write the introduction flashed through his mind.

"But whom," he murmured. "Perhaps his grandson would be interested," he answered himself, recalling the amusing story Narayan had told about him in the autobiography. After receiving what he interpreted to be nods of approbation from the white and pink pedals of the little flowers adorning the tops of the trees in front of the stone bench supporting him, he took out a pen and pad and scribbled down the following letter:

Dear Sir,

Please allow me to introduce myself and to explain my purpose in writing to you. I am Dr. Thomas Sleiman. Well, my name is Thomas Sleiman, but as for who I am, that remains quite a mystery, even to me. In fact, this quandary is related to the purpose of this letter: to kindly ask you to read my book, which deals primarily with the question of personal identity as related to love, or something like that, but it's not prescriptive, at least I didn't mean it to be. Although sometimes I think I did mean it to be. I'm sending it with a very close friend of mine, who also carries with her some of my credentials, which I must warn you in advance are next to none. If you deem it at all praiseworthy, would you be so kind as to write an introduction explaining precisely why you found it so? This would mean a great deal to me aside from whether or not the book ever gets published, and regardless of whether or not many people ever read it.

I know not whether you are in the writing business, but I do know that you have written at least one important work—one paragraph, in fact,

which appeared in the final chapter of your late grandfather's autobiography
My Days, which, as you know, of course, he deemed important enough to
write a short literary criticism of—I believe one long sentence.

If you please, sir, kindly give my request some thought. I anxiously await
your answer.
Very cordially,
Thomas Sleiman

When he'd finished, the little friendly flowers were still swaying smoothly in
the wind, still nodding their heads in approval. Having handled the matter of
the introduction, Thomas wrote with even more ease now. He finished the book
two weeks later and sent it off to Jhansi with the letter, instructing her to find
Narayan's grandson and hand deliver both the letter and the book, in that order.
He called and told her to watch for an important package.

"But do you know whether he even lives in India?" she protested.

"Of course I don't, dear; do you think I've had the time to find out? I've
written virtually nonstop for two weeks. That's your job."

"Consider it done, oh great king," she said, giggling over the phone.

After such a long stint of writing, Thomas was exhausted. He decided to
spend a few days in prayer and silence at a well-known monastery in Syria where
the local people still spoke the language of Christ. Mr. Morrison had highly
recommended it as a place where one could allow the dry desert wind to "clean
the soul from all the debris it inevitably accumulates living in the pornographic
modern world." And Mr. Morrison was right. The modern Trojan Horse, as
Thomas called the television, was nowhere to be found.

The first day, Thomas immersed himself in blissful relaxation. He celebrated
the Catholic Sacrament of Confession, received Holy Communion, meditated
on his Rosary, drank nearly a bottle of good monastery wine with his simple
vegetarian Middle Eastern supper, finished reading Naipaul's *A Bend in the River*,
and went softly to sleep.

That night his dreams took him to India, but as he stepped off the plane,
he saw and smelled an India that somehow he'd failed to see and smell before.

He knew in the dream that he had brought Jhansi back to Lebanon from India after a great internal struggle, and also that he had already sent her back to India; for some reason it had not worked out. He could see her saying goodbye to the sisters at the convent where she had spent the last few months of her time in Lebanon; in the dream, he was sure it was Jhansi, but the nuns kept calling her Rupali. He was acutely aware of his own apprehension. The Jhansi that met him at the airport was not dressed in one of her beautiful saris, with her long black hair hanging down to her tiny waist. There was no jasmine in her hair. In fact, she had no hair at all. The chemo treatment had changed all that. Her once tiny waist was bloated and marred by the ugly scar of an emergency stomach surgery that hurriedly sought to remove a stubborn cancerous tumor. Her eyes had sunk deep into their sockets and lacked the playfulness that had once animated them. He noticed that her neck, now laid bare, was short and somehow deformed. The smell of human shit and urine permeated the airport, the car, and the house where they put him. The room was like a furnace. The bed he slept on was crawling with lice; the mosquitoes were virtually swimming in his sweat.

A copy of Naipaul's *India: A Wounded Civilization* adorned the only other furniture in the room, a small broken bookstand that was propped up by a box of old British magazines. He tried to escape from the little prison, but for some strange reason, Indian immigration police were guarding the house, waiting to arrest him. He climbed out a back window into an alley only to step on a miserable old man dying in his vomit. Thomas's weight was too much for the pathetic creature, and he let out a final cry of agony, his eyeballs pornographically protruding in an abhorrent way, his tongue quivering obscenely as it slid softly out of his mouth, the bloody saliva providing an ideal slippery slide. Thomas ran out into the night where he spotted his home. Hope returned. He dashed across the slimy scum of the ill-lit street toward the house, his heart beating with a desire to hold Rita and the children. He pounded on the front door, as he heard the sirens of the immigration police getting nearer. It was hot and horribly humid. Rita opened the door, her face taut with rage. He tried to enter, but she barred the way. His legs felt leaden; he'd lost all of his strength.

"You lying bastard," she screamed effusively. "Some priest you would have been. I wonder what your children will say when they've found out you've been screwing our maid. Do you think you could have stooped any lower?"

"Oh, my God in heaven! Don't speak like that, for God's sake, Rita; please, the children will hear. Please, for God's sake, help me! I'm in trouble."

"Don't bring God into it. That's your favorite trick, isn't it? Deceive them with God talk and you win them over. Your whole life is a lie laced with talk of God and prayer."

"Please, Rita, I'm begging you."

"Do you pray with your lovers after you screw them? Everyone thinks you're so pious. You're a hypocrite, that's what you are."

"Stop it, Rita; stop it, please. Let me in. They're coming to arrest me."

"Good. That's exactly what you deserve. You're an adulterer; you're no better than a murderer. Go to jail, and then go to hell. I hate you. I no longer respect you. I don't ever want to see you again. Let your bald, stupid, dying maid with the deformed neck help you."

"Please, I've got to get out of India," Thomas pleaded, but she slammed the door in his face.

"Rita!" he screamed. "Please, this is my house too," he begged, confused as to why it was in India. "Please, I need to see my children, and then I'll be okay again. Please!"

But it was too late. The police had set their dogs loose, and he saw a severed hand appear in the sky that wrote in big bold letters: THE RAKSHAS HAVE COME TO CLAIM ONE OF THEIR OWN. Thomas tried to run, but his legs were just too heavy; one of the ferocious beasts bit him hard in the calf to bring him down.

A cramp in Thomas's calf awakened him. It took him a few minutes to remember that he was at the monastery. He stayed in bed staring at the ceiling for a long time. A few days after he'd returned home, he had the same awful dream. And again he was aware in his dream that he had managed to bring Jhansi to Lebanon, but he had sent her back to India once and for all because their plan to have a platonic relationship, with Jhansi living in the monastery, had not worked out. As the dogs brought him down, the same cramp awakened him. But this time Rita was sleeping gently beside him. He put his hand on her arm tenderly so as not to wake her, and thanked God it had all been a dream. He prayed it would not return a third time. He noticed how beautiful Rita was, sleeping so peacefully. He thought back to the days when he first fell in love with her and her Lebanon. Lebanon had become his home now too. He thanked heaven for giving him such a faithful companion; he felt a sincere appreciation for her as his wife and the mother of his children.

At the same moment he awoke, Jhansi too, some thousands of miles southeast, awoke, but to the sound of her mother's animated and comforting voice.

"The postman has just brought a package, Jhansi. Hurry, you need to sign for it. It's a registered parcel. Must have been expensive to send it like this."

Jhansi took the plain brown package reverentially into her hands and gazed upon it as if it contained prized green emeralds or precious red rubies.

"Who's it from?" her mom asked impatiently.

Jhansi knew it was from him. She opened it carefully without answering her.

"Is it important, dear?"

"Yes, very. It contains my ticket, my visa, a money order, a letter, and a book to be delivered," and she added silently, *to someone I don't even know*. She enjoyed the mystery of her impending errand like a delicious secret.

"What else?"

"Instructions from Dr. Sleiman."

"When are you leaving?" her mother cried in a panic.

"About a month from now," Jhansi said without looking up.

Tears welled up in her mother's eyes. Though she'd been praying for this moment to come, the reality of her daughter leaving was overwhelming. Jhansi failed to notice because she was diligently reading his instructions. When she finally threw a glance at her mother, they simultaneously burst into tears and embraced. Jhansi cried for joy, but her mother's tears were a mixture of joy and sorrow. The commotion caused a stir in the whole household, which eventually spread to the entire building and then to the relatives.

The next few days brought well-wishers from many quarters, most of them voicing opinions on the advantages and disadvantages of sending a daughter off to get married to a foreigner. Even the priest came over to advise and admonish; hardly anyone congratulated, except Sita, the only other living soul in all of India's one billion people who knew the real story. But even Sita had mixed feelings.

"I'm shocked that you're really going through with it, my dear friend. It's so unusual. Your future now is so uncertain."

"Unusual, yes, but why do you say uncertain? Is anyone's future certain?"

"I hate to say this to you now, my love, but it'll never work. He's married, with six children. Please reconsider."

"What do you mean by work? Do you think I'm going there to break up his family?" she said sharply, revealing her pain at her friend's misjudgment of her.

"No. No. I didn't mean it that way. I'm just worried about you. Stay here with us."

"And do what? Allow my parents to force me to marry someone I don't love?"

"Perhaps with time, Jhansi, you'll learn to love."

"Stop it, Sita. Stop it, please. You of all people! You've seen our letters; you know my heart."

"I'm sorry, honey," she said apologetically.

"I'm sorry I raised my voice," said Jhansi. "Forgive me, sweetheart," she added, and took her into her arms.

"I'm just worried, that's all. And I'm going to miss you terribly, as everyone here will."

"I know, my dear. Thank you. I love you. I'll miss you too; you know that. You've kept me sane these last two years. What would I have done without my Sita to share my heart with? But I've been living for this moment; can I ignore it?"

"Of course not. Go. God guide you. May he be with you both. I'll never forget you. You're my best friend forever. You'll write, won't you?"

"How can you even ask?"

The reality of leaving family, friends, and India began to sink in. She started saying goodbye to all the people she loved.

"Sita was right," she speculated. "The future is so uncertain, but at least now I have one. Before, I had nothing."

Her mother's brother was notably disheartened, as he'd never given up hope. He'd always banked on her changing her mind. Her mother showed signs of slight depression, and her father, his natural disposition being inclined to silence except when he drank, withdrew into periods of solitude. But deep inside, her parents were relieved. They trusted Thomas and felt that, even if the marriage with Thomas's brother didn't work out, Thomas himself would be sure to care for her as one of his own. She made one last bus trip to Bangalore to say so long to her grandmother and aunts and uncles, the eldest of whom insisted she stay for a while in order to celebrate her birthday there.

"This may be the last time we get to celebrate your birthday with you," he argued.

"God knows when you'll return to India. You've never spent any extended time in Bangalore. Give us the pleasure of seeing our favorite niece."

Her time passed quickly there. She cried when they did, but her tears were always mixed with joy. The return bus trip to Madras was full of memories of *him*. She tenderly remembered how she'd laid her head on his chest and how their feet had been entwined on the same return trip months before.

Was he really here in India? she thought. *Did he really come all this way just to see me?*

She couldn't believe that her dream was coming true.

"It's too good to be true," she kept repeating to herself. "When am I going to wake up?"

She finally fell asleep and had delicious dreams of him kissing her with his well-shaped lips that she loved so much. When she awoke, the bus was just pulling into the Madras station; she was able to pick out her father in the crowd immediately. She cherished the ride back home, saying farewell to all of the familiar streets and shops as she passed them. The little odds and ends in her house began to take on new meaning now. The Hindu shrine in the kitchen and the Christian altar in the main room grew in significance. She cherished watching her father perform his prayers and rituals in the morning. She tended to her mother's daily needs in an exceptional way now.

She was especially tender with Meena, who asked her each day, "How will I continue without you, sister? Who will I pour out my heart to? With whom can I share all my thoughts?"

"We'll stay in touch, Meena. I'm not being cremated. I'm just leaving the country. They have phones where I'm going. I'm sure their postal service is as good or better than ours. You must continue your studies, Meena. I'll be able to help you with the payments for university; don't worry about the money. Help our mother. Set a good example for the younger ones."

"I shall. I promise."

Shivani, for her part, was quite curious upon hearing the news, but Jhansi would not reveal much.

"Will you stay in the Middle East for long, or go on directly to America?" she asked several times.

Jhansi avoided giving a straight answer until Shivani finally got the hint and quit asking. Anyway, she had her hands full with the baby, with trying to please her husband, and in performing her duties as a daughter-in-law. She was content enough and had resigned herself to making the best of her situation. When tempted to complain, she reminded herself of the awful situation she'd been in before, and quickly counted her blessings. Her little boy, Thomas, was the great joy in her life. He sustained her through any and every trial.

Jhansi began immediately to inquire into the whereabouts of the potential introduction writer. A journalist friend of hers gave her a few leads, which she pursued religiously until she found him. A few days later she called Thomas to tell him that she'd found him, that she'd explained everything briefly, and that he agreed to give her an appointment on the fifteenth of November.

"Will this give him enough time to read it?" he asked doubtfully.

"I don't know. Depends on how fast a reader he is and whether he finds it interesting."

Pausing, he asked, "And did you find it interesting, sweetheart?"

She remained silent.

"Hello? Are you there?"

"Yes, I'm here."

"What is it, sweetheart?"

"It seems you've used that term often, and not only with me."

"Ah, I see now. So you've read it then. Would you rather that I'd not written about Juliet?"

"No, it's not that. I think it's admirable that you did. You've had a lot of courage in writing so truthfully, but it still hurts to read it."

"Look, Jhansi, I told you a long time ago to forget about me, didn't I?"

"Is it so easy for you to do the same?"

"To be honest, dear, I've tried, but I can't. You know that. Do you still want to come?"

"What a silly question. Even if my great king drives me out into the cold night and brings others in my place, I shall always love him. I am him or else I am not."

"Are you real, Jhansi? Do you know what you're saying?"

"Yes, I do know, but I hope and pray that I'll never have to show you that I'm serious."

"Oh, Jhansi, my angel, I've never known or loved anyone like you before. Only a few more weeks now, and we shall finally be together."

"Yes, my king, just a few more weeks."

The fifteenth of November arrived. She cautiously made her way up to the medium-sized Madras apartment and found the man waiting for her. She briefly told him in Tamil a bit more about Thomas, and handed him the letter. He read it twice, folded it, gave it back to her, and asked politely in English, "Where's the manuscript?"

Jhansi produced it directly.

"Do you have a phone at home?" he asked.

"Yes, here's the number."

"Fine. I'll call you in about a week with my answer."

"Thank you kindly, sir. Thank you kindly."

"More than welcome. Good day."

He called less than a week later and asked her whether Dr. Sleiman had written anything besides the novel she'd given him. When she told him that he'd written some poetry and a few short stories, he asked whether he could see them. After getting Thomas's permission, she delivered what Thomas had sent her. His vanity convinced him that the grandson had enjoyed the novel so much that he desired to see the ending. Thomas was sure of the fact that not only would he write the introduction, but he would agree to help publish all of his writing in a handsome volume titled *The Complete Literary Works of Thomas Sleiman*.

In fact, he did enjoy the poetry. The first poem he read was titled "The Horse." It pleased him when he read:

The princely horse so proud and tall
So steady in his stance
So rarely does he trip and fall
His nature is to prance
His steps are sure and full of strength
His coat so smooth and white
His beauty's of unmeasured length
His eyes as black as night
The prairies bow before his grace
The fields and farms acclaim
That here's one who's born to race
His heart shall not be tame

The poem he enjoyed the most, however, and considered to be somewhat of a masterpiece, was "The Rain." He then turned to some of the short stories. He read only the first few lines of each story before deciding whether to continue. He opened to the one titled "Just a Small Miracle" and read:

"No! Absolutely not; it's out of the question, daughter. If you mention it again, I shall bring it to the attention of your father."

"But mother, I . . ."

"Silence, girl, you know how I feel about it, let alone the problems it could bring to our community. You are a high-caste Brahmin girl; your father has great respect in this village, his father is a living legend, not to mention the status of my own family."

"Mother, I just want you to meet him, and then. . ."

"It's impossible. It won't work. Why can't you see? Forget him once and for all. If we'd known it would come to this, we never would have sent you to Delhi for your university studies."

Sita retreated reluctantly through the poorly lit passage of her ancient home to the pyol where she sat on her mat and gazed despondently at the dusty dirt road. The voices of young girls playing in a nearby schoolyard took her back to more innocent and carefree days, when love-problems were unimaginable. Part of her yearned to be young again, and another part. . ."

After this, he read the story titled "January 12th" and simply could not put it down. He then turned to "On Precious Stones":

"How the hell do ya tell the difference between a fake one and a real one?"

"The only way I can tell is by the size of the damned dent it puts in my wallet," his friend answered obnoxiously, "and occasionally," he murmured, nudging his friend's side, "by the way my wife responds in bed on the night of the gift."

The store's owner secretly despised their distasteful public conversation, but managed to forge a friendly smile. He'd forgotten just how hard it was to endure front-line sales, and took comfort in the fact that, as one of the most important jewelers in Bangkok, he no longer had to slave away behind a counter all day long listening to the shallow and offensive jabber of the nouveaux riche. Though he too was among those who'd recently come into big money, he strove to separate himself from them by improving his intellect through the reading of philosophy, poetry, and literature. He'd just finished reading Thomas Hardy's *Jude the Obscure* and was presently engrossed in the reading of Cervantes' *Don Quixote*, a book he'd heard about as an undergraduate, but had never got round to reading.

The two men continued their meaningless discourse as their wives asked silly questions. Longing to get back to Cervantes, Mr. Withisin focused his energy on getting them out by encouraging one woman to purchase, without delay, a pear-shaped emerald ring with diamonds set in eighteen-carat gold, and by convincing the other to settle upon an oval ruby and diamond necklace in fourteen-carat gold.

"Did you not say, madam, that you were soon to celebrate your fifteenth wedding anniversary?"

"Why, yes, I did mention that, how perceptive of you."

"Well, then, it only makes sense to purchase the ruby, as it's the recommended gem for both the fifteenth and the fortieth wedding anniversaries. Besides, it's July, and the ruby is the birthstone for July."

"Oh, isn't he slick," said the other woman disrespectfully. "But what our little salesman here doesn't know is that the real reason you'd better buy it now is that you'll never make it to your fortieth."

"That's for damn sure," said her friend, "but after four husbands, it's rather nifty to finally make fifteen with the fifth," she blurted out laughingly.

He refrained from telling them that he was not a little salesman, but the owner of the store, and that he would now like them to leave. Instead, he forced a laugh, privately loathing their presence. Before they were out the door, he phoned the back room and ordered an employee to watch the floor. He seized his book, as if more precious than all his beautiful stones shining so brilliantly in their displays, and retired to his lush apartment directly above to avoid any more interruptions. He poured himself some eighteen-year-old gold-label scotch, lit up a Cohiba, and reclined deep into his black leather reading chair. Before long, he was back in Medieval Spain, in a world of chivalry, saints, sinners, demons, mystical poetry, proverbs, philosophy, old-fashioned tragic love affairs, inns, and horses, comfortably safe from the modern world. But then the phone rang.

"Didn't I tell you not to disturb me?" he howled without saying hello, as he knew the call had come from below.

"But sir, it's the—"

"I don't care if it's the Sultan of Brunei, I'm reading, and if I've told you once, I've told you a thousand times, don't disturb me while—"

"Sir, excuse me for interrupting, but it's him, sir; it's him, and he's asking about you."

"Oh, I see; well, why didn't you say so, for heaven's sake?"

"I tried to, sir, but—"

"Enough excuses, my friend, just send him up immediately; what are you waiting for?"

"Yes, sir. Of course, sir."

Mr. Withisin placed his book carefully on the custom-made wooden bookstand, cleverly carved out of genuine oak, and prepared himself to meet his hero: a retired professor emeritus who'd spent the better part of his life at a Jesuit university in the Philippines after receiving an excellent education in India, Britain, and America. Within moments, he heard the gentle knock and rushed to give the professor a gracious welcome.

"Why, Professor Lorenzo," he said warmly, "where have you been? I waited for your weekly visit last Wednesday and tried to call several times when you didn't show up, but—"

"Please excuse me, my good man; you won't believe what happened."

"Was it another one of your unexpected sallies to the mountains in the North, where there's no telephone reception?"

"Half right. It was an unexpected excursion all right, but not too far out of Bangkok this time, though quite far enough. You see, I met up with an old friend of mine, a professor of history now teaching at Columbia, with whom I'd spent the better part of my life as a graduate student at the Jesuit University of Calcutta. Believe it or not, we met on the public bus last week, after all these years; can you imagine? He was on vacation here. We got so carried away catching up on old times that we failed to notice we'd missed our stops. It's been nearly three decades, you know? When we finally did get off, it was quite late, and we found ourselves in the middle of nowhere, with only a beggar and a couple of prostitutes to keep us company—a company, mind you, from which we promptly distanced ourselves. Absent-minded professors they call us, and for good reason," he said musingly. "Do you think it's meaningful to speak of a philosophy of history, Mr. Withisin?" he suddenly whispered, recalling the stimulating conversation he'd had with his friend that night. Not waiting for an answer, as if certain Mr. Withisin didn't comprehend the question, he emphatically declared, and not without a tad of lunacy in his voice, "I think it is, but that poor fellow over there, in the midst of all those specialists, doesn't think so. Oh, don't get me wrong, he's a damn good historian per se, but he's lost, lost I tell you! Should have stayed in India; would have been better off. Of course I wouldn't mind having constant recourse to those New York libraries."

"Well, you could have called me, sir. I was quite worried."

"That's kind of you to worry about me, my friend," he said softly, his voice returning to normal, "but after he'd decided to make his way back to town, and I'd found a cheap hotel, it was an ungodly hour, and my thoughts kept returning to those prostitutes we'd seen. One was extraordinarily beautiful with some sort of strange charisma. I couldn't have very well called you at that hour, but I did consider it."

"Well, if your conversation had been so interesting, and you were so much enjoying his company, why didn't you just return with him?"

"I was exhausted and just had to close my eyes. You knew I was the keynote speaker at that international conference on metaphysics and mysticism last week, didn't you?"

"Yes. I'd love to see your paper."

"Fine, fine, here it is. I thought you might want to take a look at it," he muttered as he threw a copy onto the couch. "But my point was that the conference literally exhausted me. I'm still recovering, and after getting lost, I just couldn't face another long bus ride back to town. Besides, I kept entertaining the thought of employing one of those ladies for the night, you know, the beautiful one, but I was able to resist the temptation long enough for it to go away."

Mr. Withisin wondered secretly why such beautiful prostitutes had been out in the middle of nowhere and how, if he had been so tired, he would have gotten the energy. And he was dreadfully disappointed at the professor's confession, because he'd practically worshipped the professor as the embodiment of learning and virtue ever since he'd met him about a year before. He respected or feared the man too much to say anything, though.

Noticing his discontent, the professor became more serious and said, "Mr. Withisin, have you never been tempted in this way?"

"Why, yes, I have been, and not only tempted. I have succumbed to temptation, and used to quite regularly, until of course I met Patcharee. She cured me of all that."

"Then why are you so surprised? I've not yet met my Patcharee."

"But you have the love of your life in your learning, sir. Wisdom is your lover, as everyone who has ever met you proclaims." He felt confident making such a bold statement.

"Well, if it's any consolation to you then, I must say that through some unearthly grace, I have managed to live a life of virginal chastity for these last fifty years, but it hasn't always been easy. If I'd concealed this little episode from you, it would have grown into something much larger, and one day would have become unmanageable. As it is, I acknowledged her beauty and my desire for it, and for her, or at least I felt I did, and now it's gone, that's all. I know that sex without romance is deadening, but it doesn't mean that the culture of death isn't sometimes deceptively attractive."

"You can say that again," Mr. Withisin declared thoughtfully. "So what exactly do you mean by a philosophy of history?"

"I was wondering when you'd come back to that, Mr. Withisin, but perhaps it's still too early to explain. You must first complete the reading list I've given you; then we'll talk about it."

"I'm nearly done, sir. And please call me by my first name," he added, desperately hoping to cultivate an intimacy that was not yet present. "Now, as I was saying, I've almost completed your latest suggestion." He picked up the book just as reverently as he'd placed it down. "You see, I've nearly finished *Don Quixote*," he affirmed proudly.

"Impossible," the professor barked, taking Mr. Withisin completely by surprise.

"No, sir, it's true! Look where I am already," he said, gently removing his bookmarker and pointing to a page near the end of the novel. "I'm almost finished."

Professor Lorenzo glared at the jeweler then said with the utmost gravity, "Mr. Withisin, or if you insist, Mr. Kim, I beg you never to utter that same sacrilege again—neither in my presence nor in the presence of any respectable man or woman. This blasphemy confirms my judgment that it is still too early to enter into conversation with you about the philosophy of history."

Rather confused by the professor's abrupt behavior and not detecting the rage that was beginning to boil beneath the professor's skin, he casually stated, "All I've said, sir, is that I'm nearly finished. . ."

"One is never finished with *Don Quixote*, I tell you," he screamed at the top of his lungs. "Do you dare fancy yourself better than Melville and Faulkner, Dickens and Flaubert, or Fielding and Sterne, all of whom religiously reread it once a year? What is this nonsense? Have I trekked clear across town to be told that you've finished with *Don Quixote*?"

Mr. Withisin was too shocked to answer, never having seen this psychotic side of his newly found friend-hero. He felt like poor Sancho himself receiving an unjust rebuke from the mad Quixote.

Professor Lorenzo realized that he'd gotten out of hand, and composing himself, said in a soft and more sane voice, "Please excuse me, Kim, I'm awfully cranky today. You'll have to put up with these outbursts of mine from time to time—that is, if you're up to it." He smiled, but it seemed rather unsettling to Mr. Withisin, who was hurt, and even began to feel some anger, but he said politely, "I understand, sir. Perhaps we can meet next week, as you do seem a bit under the weather today. Which commentary do you recommend I read once I finish with . . . I mean, once I have completed . . . I mean, before I start the second reading of *Don Quixote*?"

"I'm glad you've remembered to ask. Look, this is a must for you," the professor said, pulling out a small red book from his briefcase, inwardly pleased and relieved that Mr. Withisin had not uttered the blasphemy again. The book was an obscure masterpiece titled *Theory of Don Quixote: Its Hispanic Mysticism*, by a little known Spanish mystic whom the professor had met in Queens, New York, where the mystic happened to be residing.

Mr. Withisin thanked the professor kindly as the latter walked toward the door to leave. Before he opened the door, he turned and said, with all the sincerity and innocence of a child, "Mr. Withisin, I really do apologize," and with that, he left before his friend could answer. After the professor was gone, Mr. Withisin picked up the paper titled "The Heavens Declare the Glory of God." He quickly read the opening paragraphs:

> We find ourselves in a fix. The impetus that draws us together is a crisis. To be precise, it is the calamity of the devaluing of human life. And perhaps there is no one present here today who doubts the seriousness of the situation. We're all aware of its catastrophic dimensions, but many sound-minded and good-willed people don't share our assumptions. Their assumption, rather, is that things weren't much better, and probably were even worse, in medieval and ancient times with respect to the value of human life. Some would argue that we exaggerate the ills of Western modernity's materialism and consumerism and claim rather that modernity itself has given us a heightened sense of human dignity, and has made us more sensitive to the value of human life. I don't think there are any winners in such arguments. Each side can mount convincing arguments aided by their historian gurus.
>
> Thus, I won't spend much time proving my assumption that the nature of the present crisis is substantially different and more serious than that which the world has hitherto seen. Neither will I address the philosophical roots of Western modernity's formalistic sense of freedom, exaggerated individualism, and impersonal materialism and consumerism, since they are

already well known. I would like rather to dwell mainly on solutions and to consider the possibility of providing a solid philosophical foundation for an experience of the holy—a category that is usually considered to belong only to the realm of emotions or opinion.

As I see it, to be a human being means to be, first and foremost, open and oriented to the mystery of transcendence. But modern Western thought has tended to treat mysticism as a sentiment at best and as a delusion at worst. Again, we are all familiar with the rationalistic roots of this Cartesian tendency. Until the middle of the last century, it seemed as if this bent had gained so much momentum that there was no way of curbing it. Philosophical reactions to Mechanism had not been wanting even as early as the late seventeenth century, but most philosophers and theologians simply chose retreat over resistance, resulting eventually in various sundry forms of nineteenth-century spiritualism and idealism.

One notable exception was the philosophy of Bergson, who chose not to retreat, but to attack. But in its desire to sweep away the intellectualism of the mechanical philosophy, Bergsonian philosophy mistakenly assailed the very rock-bottom principles of all thought, throwing out, as it were, the baby with the bath water. If the laws of non-contradiction, of identity, or of the excluded middle are challenged, then thought and language are impossible. For all of the havoc it caused, at least the mechanical philosophy, to its credit, knew better than to challenge these first principles.

Surprisingly enough, serious resistance finally appeared from the least likely quarter: from modern science itself. The revolution in physics was not merely a revolution in physics, but a revolution in science. When the Newtonian world of determinability and predictability came crashing down, many serious thinkers questioned the rationalism on which it was founded. Quantum Theory gave philosophers new courage. Traditional philosophical categories that had been all but outlawed in the deterministic system of mechanism, such as the concept of free will, were suddenly in vogue again. But if the new spirit of Quantum Theory offered dispensations in the territory of philosophy it also stipulated its conditions. That is to say, in exchange for withdrawing its resistance to free will, it demanded that philosophy should surrender its principle of causation. Ironically enough, the very same schools of philosophy that were intimidated by determinism are now cowed by Quantum Theory. The lesson: philosophers must recover and have confidence in what I think Gilson called many years ago the Unity of Philosophical Experience.

If philosophy hopes to have any success in advancing the claim that the experience of the sacred or the transcendent is not to be reduced to a mere sentiment, opinion, or delusion, it must first avoid the mistake of looking to contemporary scientific theory as its guide. The philosopher must know Quantum Theory, Set Theory, Chaos Theory, and Uncertainty Theory. He must be cognizant of the revolution in physics that took place in the first part of the twentieth century, and be equally aware of the significant ramifications of the genetic revolution in the latter part of the century, but he mustn't be carried away by their possible philosophical implications.

Philosophy must continually drink from its own rich and deep well, a timeless resource that promises never to run dry. This in fact is precisely what some of the most important contemporary philosophers have done in their attempts to ground mystical experience. In particular, I refer to the philosophy of the contemporary Spanish philosopher Fernando Rielo, whose new and vital metaphysical model promises to guide us to an exceedingly rich land flowing with milk and honey.

Mr. Withisin paused here to consider what he had read. He wanted to call his friend immediately, as he had many questions, but thought twice about it after remembering the outbreak of lunacy. Attributing, finally, the unusual behavior to fatigue and recalling the gentle apology, he picked up the telephone and dialed the professor's number.

"It's splendid, sir; it's absolutely splendid. I have many questions."

"I'd be glad to answer them, my friend, once I finish this piece on the role of the angels in the theology of history. You see, I am struggling with the whole question of how . . . well, never mind, it's an ontological problem of the first order related to Pannenberg's new theology of history, which, for all its newness, nonetheless gets bogged down in Hegelian rationalism."

Mr. Withisin had no idea what the professor was talking about.

"And I need to revise the talk I gave in China last month on Tagore. Listen, if you have a moment, I'd like you to hear the introduction of that piece; I have just put the finishing touches on it."

"I'd be honored, sir."

"Okay, it begins like this," said the professor, catching Mr. Withisin off guard, as he didn't expect him to read it over the phone.

"Are you listening?"

"Yes, sir, I am."

The professor read the introduction to him:

In 1924, the Beijing Lecture Association invited Rabindranath Tagore to China, where he gave talks in the months of April and May to students and teachers on a variety of subjects ranging from progress and civilization to the meaning of beauty. In one particularly powerful and, I would say, prophetic moment, while expressing his deep gratitude to his hosts he said, "Among you, my mind feels not the least apprehension of any undue sense of race feeling or difference of tradition. I am rather reminded of the day when India claimed [the Chinese] as brothers and sent you her love. That relationship is, I hope, still there, hidden in the heart of all of us—the people of the East. The path to it may be overgrown with the grass of centuries, but we shall find traces of it still.

When you have succeeded in recalling all the things achieved in spite of insuperable difficulties, I hope that some great dreamer will spring from among you and preach a message of love and, therewith overcoming all differences, bridge the chasm of passions that has been widening for ages. Age after age in Asia, great dreamers have made the world sweet with showers of their love. Asia is again waiting for such dreamers to come and carry on the work, not of fighting, not of profit making, but of establishing bonds of spiritual relationship."

The time is at hand when we shall once again be proud to belong to a continent which produces the light that radiates through the storm-clouds of trouble and illuminates the path of life. For some, phrases like "making the world sweet with showers of love" will sound far too idealistic and perhaps even superficial, but Tagore was aware of this, and that's why he referred to those who believed in such projects as "dreamers." However, he then describes such "showering of love" as the work of "establishing bonds of spiritual relationship." Thus, Tagore, although a dreamer himself, operates under no illusion: he knows that the most important work requires the greatest amount of effort, self-sacrifice, and even suffering.

I want to suggest that Tagore's understanding of sacrifice is somewhat commensurate with that of St. Augustine's, and with many of the early Christian Fathers, who understood sacrifice as transfiguration. Sacrifice here means making room for the divine spirit who enters into the deepest recesses of the creature in order to transform and perfect the creaturely nature. Such making room necessarily involves suffering and self-denial. Though the divine is understood here as purely spiritual and thus higher than any creaturely spirit or matter, its role is understood not as destroying the creaturely nature, but in perfecting it. Thanks to the efforts of the great German theologian, Matthias Joseph Scheeben, Catholic theology was to recover this more dynamic sense of sacrifice, as the greatest Catholic theologian of the twentieth century, Hans Urs Von Balthasar, has taught us. Von Balthasar's own monumental effort, in fact, to restore beauty to its proper place in Christian Theology, is also somewhat commensurate with Tagore's vocation in trying to restore beauty to its proper place in Hindu discourse on the divine realities.

Although Mr. Withisin didn't really understand much of what he heard, he responded enthusiastically with, "That is brilliant, sir, just brilliant. I'd love to get a copy of that when it's published."
"All in good time . . . all in good time."
As the time for their next meeting drew near, Mr. Withisin became more and more pensive. He wondered whether his newly discovered desire to improve his mind through reading and conversation with the professor was all really worth it. He couldn't deny that an entirely new and exciting world had opened up to him, but at times, he was discouraged. There was so much to read, an entirely new linguistic apparatus to master, and a plethora of academic commentary that seemed simply too vast and complicated to sort out. It wasn't at all like buying and selling precious stones, although at times he was able to perceive certain mystical parallels between the two activities, at the very purest level—something that absolutely none of his other friends understood—but the professor seemed to understand perfectly. And although he admired greatly his professor friend, and at times felt great joy and even hope in his presence, he couldn't deny that the professor seemed to be on the verge of insanity. Lately, things had gotten worse. The latest outbreak of near lunacy was still in his mind as he prepared himself for the coming meeting. "Will he explode again," he wondered, as the meeting drew near. "I must be careful when talking

about Cervantes. Perhaps it is better not to even mention the name Cervantes at all; he gets irritated when I utter this name. Maybe I should always say the great Cervantes, or simply Cervantes the Great. Yeah. That's it. That sounds better too."

And so it was.

"Hello, my good friend, how's business these days?" the professor warmly greeted him when they next met.

"Excellent. I'm not sure what to do with all the money I'm making lately. There seems to be a passion for emeralds these days."

"Well, you could always invest in the acquisition of books for my, I mean, our library."

"Invest?"

"Sure. Invest. What could be better for posterity?"

"I'm not sure what kind of investment that would be; many are saying that the days of the book are over. Today only the e-book matters, it seems, and besides, there's so much out there. In fact, I've been a bit overwhelmed lately. How do you choose which books to read? How do you know which books to buy and put in your library?"

The professor didn't bother to answer since he didn't hear the questions. He entered instead right into the proposed reading for discussion and asked, "So, what did you think of the events surrounding the death of Don Quixote?"

"Oh, I was deeply moved, but a bit confused."

"Why?"

"I mean, did he really regain his sanity?"

"Very good question! Very good! I like the way you've put it."

Encouraged by this compliment, Mr. Withisin continued. "Which Don Quixote did the great Cervantes, or should I say Cervantes the Great, want us to sympathize with?"

"Oh, another great question, wonderful. I like your mind, my boy. I like your mind. You have great potential. Go on, continue."

"Is it Alonso Quijano the Good, or Don Quixote the madman that Cervantes, I mean, Cervantes the Great, wants us to remember?"

The professor was beaming with joy. He seemed ecstatic. *I wonder if it's my question, or the way I'm referring to Cervantes, that's making him so happy*, he thought.

"Mr. Withisin," the professor said after some time, "your mind is really beginning to mature. Your spirit will soon be soaring in the heights. You are approaching enlightenment, my friend, with such questions. But you must wait for the answers. Do you hear me? Wait! Repeat that word a thousand times a day. For the Lord delights in those who wait for his love. You must not presume anything. Just wait. Be silent now. Just wait a few weeks, months, or even years, and you will find the answers you are seeking. Yes. Seek and you shall find; knock and it will surely be opened to you."

Mr. Withisin felt the lunacy building and changed the subject, but the professor overpowered him. "While you are waiting, I want you to read this," he said softly, and he reached into his old and tattered brown leather briefcase. "I had a premonition that you just might be ready for this. No one has seen this yet. I repeat. No one, except me, of course, and my guardian angel, who helped me write it."

Mr. Withisin looked straight at him to see if he was joking or not, but couldn't really tell, and so decided to let it pass, since he perceived a return to sanity in the tone of the professor's voice. He took the manuscript with gentle hands when the professor offered it to him. Kim glanced at the title.

"Not so fast. It's important that you sit down and read the title out loud slowly and carefully. Go ahead." Doing exactly as he was told, he sat down and read out loud, "The Life and Times of Sancho Panza, After the Death of Alonso Quijano of La Mancha, also known as Don Quixote."

"Yes. That's right. This is a revelation, my friend. I have had a vision of what life was like for the great and stupid Sancho after his master died. And you will not believe what you will read in this book. It will overwhelm you, and I suppose even take you entirely out of this world. You will be transported to another world when you enter it—a better world, I assure you. What did Sancho do the very morning after his master died? How did he spend that sad day and the many days that followed? And how many days did follow? What were his dreams that night? When did the great and stupid Sancho die? Did death take him like a thief in the night, or did he die slowly and painfully? Did his dear Teresa expire before he did, or did he leave her and his dear daughter, Maria, to mourn his death? What was the cause of his death? Was it the relentless nagging of his dear and intolerable Teresa, or did he die because she suddenly stopped nagging? Did he go on another adventure? Did he ever penetrate the mystery of the cave of Montesinos? Was he overweight when he died, or withered and emaciated from all his mourning and fasting after the death of the great and good Don Alonso Quixote Quijano?

"Did he regret losing his island? Did he ever really have an island to lose? Did he rise in the middle of the night and shed tears of repentance—tears laced with the memories of the good and mad master? Did he ever open the subject of chastity with his daughter, Maria—pointing out to her the fine distinctions between marital and virginal chastity. Did his daughter respond by giving herself body and soul to the divine Bridegroom? Was his Maria among the mystics of Spain who disappeared into the convent to reap the joys of spiritual ecstasy with Christ, or was she lured into a life of intense sexual pleasure that finally consumed her in an empty orgy of disgusting desire? These are but a few of the mysteries you will read about here, my friend, but I warn you: read it slowly, and not too much at one sitting, but if you feel strong, you may read on. You must not discuss it with another soul or you will be led southwest against your will, deposited into the ocean and swallowed by a whale, where you will dwell in its belly for three days. Yes—in its belly."

Mr. Withisin was waiting for the professor to laugh, but no such laughter came. He stared at him, rather, with a chilling seriousness, and repeated, "Absolutely no one; at least not now. Read chapter one tomorrow night, which will be the first night after the full moon. Never read this, my dear Sancho, I mean, my dear Mr. Withisin, on the night of a full moon—never. Do you understand? The first chapter is only seven pages. You may read this at one sitting; it's all about Sancho's family name Panza, which means literally . . . do you know? Of course you don't. It literally means belly in Spanish. Goodnight, my dear friend. I must leave you now to face my own battles, and yes, all alone . . . so alone. See you next week."

When Mr. Withisin had time to reflect the next day on the events of the previous evening, he decided that his professor friend was indeed a madman. The talk of guardian angels and full moons and the bellies of whales was enough to assure him that he was dealing with a lunatic, but he could not deny that this madman was the most interesting person he had ever met and, at times, was very compassionate; a person whose presence exuded a kind of peace, an otherworldly hope; he was insane, but he was an extraordinary lunatic.

He thought back on why he had gotten mixed up with the professor in the first place. He remembered that he'd been drawn at first to his face, a very handsome and softly masculine, intelligent face, a face filled with light and understanding. The professor's nephew had appeared with him in the shop one morning searching for a wedding ring. He was instantly drawn to the professor's face, so different it was from the plethora of faces he'd seen in the nouveaux riche who were constantly in his shop. Just the thought of these superficial types convinced him that the madness of his professor friend was preferable to their lustful emptiness. They bored him and left him with an indescribable loneliness that was all the more painful because he knew that it was partly his. No. Better to dwell in the midst of the madness than to die in the presence of the living death of the nouveaux riche.

It was this latter thought that motivated him one day before their scheduled meeting to call on the professor at his own home.

"Why, Mr. Withisin, what a surprise. I didn't expect to see you until tomorrow."

"I'm sorry for barging in on you, sir, but I simply must know whether Sancho ever discovered the secret of the cave of Montesinos."

"I see you have read well beyond what I've suggested."

"I couldn't help myself, sir. I couldn't control my own desires. I am mad with anticipation. I am sick with the pleasures of this world; they mean nothing to me now. I want the infinite. I want the raptures of joy that Don Quixote experienced on that very first morning when he left his home. Do you remember, sir, that he himself was amazed at how easy it was to fulfill his dreams? Do you remember this, sir? Can it be so easy?"

With much delight, the professor invited him in and encouraged him to continue. "Go on, son, go on. Let it out. We have all been through this initial fascination. Enjoy it while it lasts, because it will certainly fade."

"Excuse me?"

"Oh yes, there will come a time when the very sound of the name Don Quixote will disgust you. But no need to worry, that will pass too. It is all part of the necessary purification before the deeper illumination takes place. And then, my boy, you will not only be filled with anticipation and excitement as you are now, but you will enter into the cave of Montesinos and penetrate its secrets hidden from the ages. Yes, you will experience it from the inside, so to speak. But that will come later. Come now, enjoy the present infatuation; this is good too."

Not knowing what to say, as he was still considering what the professor had just told him, he simply stared at the clutter in the apartment and remained silent.

After reading these short stories, the grandson took a long break. Jhansi was getting nervous and wondered whether she should contact him. She decided to wait a few more days. He next picked up "The Turtle of the Sea or the Net" and was pleasantly surprised as he read:

The sun and their net rose simultaneously. They had caught next to nothing all night long. Suddenly, as the net neared the boat, the groggy-eyed fisherman was jerked so violently that he nearly went overboard.

"What the hell was that?" cried his partner.

"How the hell would I know; it felt like a damned whale."

Before he could balance himself, he was jolted again, and this time did go overboard. His partner quickly threw him a life jacket and eventually pulled both fisherman and net aboard.

"We've caught something down there that ain't been in these waters for a long time."

"Like what?" the other asked.

"Only God knows, but whatever it is, it . . ."

He wasn't able to finish his sentence for the mystery then revealed itself: the smooth shiny surface of what would later be identified as a two-hundred-year-old turtle of a species thought to be extinct slowly emerged from the dark blue waters. The radiant reflection of its dark green shell shone brilliantly in the new morning sun as the two old men stared in silence. The circle enlarged until its entire five-and-a-half-foot shell was fully exposed and they could see its head and feet fighting furiously against the faded white cord that they had twisted with their own hands many years before as a symbol of their newly established partnership. But in all its years of hard work in the depths of the sea, the net had never witnessed anything like this.

"Well, what are you staring at? Let's disentangle it and set it free before it shreds our net into pieces or something worse; with its size, I reckon it could even damage the boat."

"Set it free?" the slightly younger man exclaimed in surprise. "What the hell for? Maybe it's worth some money."

"What money? Who would pay us?"

"Let's get it to shore and find out."

They argued for a few moments more and finally decided to bring it ashore. Still in the water, as it was much too heavy to bring aboard, they managed to drag it ashore after a vicious struggle, which saw their hands and net nearly torn to shreds. The older of the two had not stopped cursing—resenting that he had been coerced into what was becoming a rather bloody and painful ordeal for all involved, not excluding the turtle of the sea. Not a few of their comrades had noticed the commotion, and within minutes a crowd of fourteen or fifteen fishermen surrounded them—all shouting directions and giving orders to one another in vain.

Visibly distressed and embarrassed, the miserable creature mustered up all its remaining energy and made one last valiant effort to escape. The haste with which the ancient sea monster moved back to the water shocked them. No less than seven strong seamen were needed to subdue it, drag it onto the dirty beach, and tie it next to their shabby living quarters, wherein a long and complicated debate took place regarding what to do next. Vast quantities of beer were consumed as the fishermen debated the creature's future.

Mercilessly exposed to the blank and pitiless gaze of the sun, its head and feet sizzled, and the ancient turtle of the sea began to die. Its long and rich life passed before its eyes. Images of happy, youthful days in the company of friendly and familiar shells came as a welcomed distraction, but other images rekindled old and forgotten fears, like the one of a companion turtle bleeding to death after biting into a fish bait that concealed numerous nasty hooks and poison. The combination of beer, cheap gin, and muddled legends of an ancient sea monster that'd once consumed stolen treasures of precious gems from a sunken ship off the coast of the Mediterranean caused their imaginations to run wild, and eventually had their evil effect. Without warning, and in spite of the best effort of the elder partner, they attacked the now wretched creature and mercilessly cut open its belly looking greedily for the lost treasures. Later that night, the old fisherman packed his few belongings and walked quietly away from the only profession and partner he had ever known, leaving behind a pathetic trail of nylon net, which he angrily shredded as he walked along the coast.

The grandson steadily became more and more interested in Thomas's work because of how versatile his writing was. The next title, "The Darkness Drops Again," really grabbed his attention because he recognized it as a line from one of Yeats's great poems, but he put it aside for the time being. He turned instead to a critical piece of scholarship titled "The Brilliance of Marie Corelli: A Critical Study of the Romances of Marie Corelli," and read the introduction to that work:

> Since no one has attempted a thorough and serious study of her works, I am hopeful that this study may fill a real vacuum in the literary scholarship of the era. Not only was Marie Corelli (1855 – 1924) one of the most widely read authors of fiction in her days, but there is solid evidence of her influence on twentieth-century greats, Narayan and Naipaul not excluded. My work is novel in that I not only supply a critical analysis of everything Corelli ever wrote, but I suggest that the hermeneutical key to unlocking the real genius and message of Corelli can be found in two of her lesser-known works, *The Soul of Lilith* and, perhaps more importantly, *Love and the Philosopher*.

When he finished reading the entire thirty-page work, the day had drawn to its end. He rested a bit, took some light refreshments, and retired to his bedroom, bringing with him "The Darkness Drops Again," filled with anticipation at what it could possibly be about. He was pleasantly surprised and duly impressed to learn that it was a kind of running commentary on the three great works of the famous Nigerian author Chinua Achebe. He learned that Achebe's works, one of which he had read, formed a trilogy. *The Arrow of God*, which was published after *Things Fall Apart*, should be read before the latter, as it was set in the early stages of imperialism in Africa, wherein the setting of *Things Fall Apart* presupposed that this imperialism had already won the day. The final work of the trilogy, *No Longer at Ease*, represented the point of no return for Africa, according to Sleiman. What really fascinated the grandson, however, was the depth with which the assistant professor read Achebe's work, and in doing so, shed light on revelations that transcended the intentions of Achebe himself. In one place, commenting on the critical moment in *Things Fall Apart*, Sleiman wrote:

> When one is dealing with themes as profound as the modern dissemination of Christianity into Africa, and the necessary drama that ensues due to the complex interplay of both the resistance to and the acceptance of the new religion on the part of the recipients, one is bound to enter territory that is much bigger than oneself. One may even unwittingly fall prey to being used by the competing spirits as so many arrows in the hands of contending gods. I am convinced that not even Achebe himself realized the depth and power of the central event in the novel when he described how the main character's "son" ran to his father for help, screaming, "Father, they are killing us," only to be chopped down by his own father for the good of the tribe. One shudders at the profundity of such writing.

Early the next morning, even before he'd had anything to eat or drink, he immediately delved into "That Man in His Car":

> "Baba," she said, "why does that man live in his car?" Her voice was tinged with sadness yet filled with great animation.
>
> "Good question, angel," said her father, as he hurriedly rounded up his six children and walked them down the rugged road to their school.
>
> "Why, Daddy?" she insisted.
>
> "That's his home, sweetheart."
>
> "What?" exclaimed his eldest son. "He can afford a car, but he can't afford a house?"
>
> "Well, how do you know it's his car, brainless?" another son asked challengingly.
>
> "Hey, watch the way you talk to each other. How many times must I say it?"
>
> The little girl would not be denied.
>
> "Why, Daddy? Tell me. Tell me now, Daddy."

"How do I know, princess? That's where he lives; that's all I know."

"Poor man," she cried with compassion.

"How does he eat and wash? Where does he cook?" inquired the other children, "and what about his clothes, Daddy?"

"You see how blessed you kids are? The next time you want to complain about Mommy's food, or about not having the best name-brand shoes, just remember the man in the car, and thank the good Lord for all he's given you."

"Yes, Daddy," they sang in chorus.

"But why didn't the good Lord give him good things too, Daddy? Why, Daddy?"

Mr. Mousa pretended not to hear the question. On his way back to his own car, after getting the children situated for their long school day, he found himself wondering about the man in the car.

Perhaps he was a war refugee, one of those unlucky souls who lost family, house, and all his possessions, except his car, in one horrible instant when an enemy shell slammed into his home one bright sunny morning. *An enemy shell*, he reflected. *And who was the enemy here in Lebanon during that senseless twenty-year war? It could have been a Syrian shell, a Palestinian shell, an Israeli shell, or even a Lebanese shell. Who knows, and who cares now?*

So occupied was he by these thoughts, he failed to notice that the man got out of the car to follow him and was now but inches away. Turning around abruptly, he declared himself:

"May I help you, sir?"

"No one can help me," the man barked in a rough voice.

"Then may I ask why you are following me?"

"I'm not following anyone," he said, practically yelling this time, "at least not anymore," he added in a more subdued voice.

For some reason the man evoked a sense of sympathy in Mr. Mousa. He felt a strange compulsion to reach out to the miserable creature. He wanted to ask him what he meant by not anymore, but for some reason he resisted, turned away quickly, and headed toward his car. As he sped away, he glanced back through his rear-view mirror, and to his surprise, saw the man waving goodbye with what seemed to be genuine affection. Mr. Mousa was visibly irritated the rest of that day as the image of the man returned time and time again. That night he dreamt of the man. The dream was bizarre; it began with images of . . .

At this point, losing interest, he left off for a cup of coffee and a little morning walk. He wondered about this Dr. Sleiman as he walked along, and he tried to picture him.

"I wonder why he wants my opinion of his work," he mused to himself. "I suppose he has idealized my grandfather to the point of an almost unhealthy obsession, and just wants any connection to the family that he can get, or maybe he just wants an endorsement for marketing purposes. Or maybe he really is both healthy and sincere and meant what he said in the letter."

By the time he arrived back home, he'd settled on the latter position and all but decided to go ahead and endorse the work. He then looked at one of Thomas's critical essays titled "Ibsen's *The Wild Duck*: A Critique of Idealism." The essay was rough going for him, as it was geared more for professional philosophers and literary critics; it sought to undercut the philosophical foundations of idealism found in a good deal of nineteenth-century thought. He did manage, however, to glean the main point of the critical essay, namely, that having heroes and attempting to live one's life according to high ideals are two-edged swords.

He then read "Slightly South of the Equator," attracted especially by the title:

I had heard about the beauty of Brazilian beaches and about the wild lush of her ferocious rainforest, but until that auspicious night in late June, I had never known they literally touched one another. It was more than a touch, actually, it was a kiss—a kiss that led to an eternal night of fervent lovemaking, bearing abundant fruit in a bright morning of infinite fecundity. As soon as I opened my eyes the next morning, I wondered if it had all been a dream. We arrived from São Paulo at night, and she insisted we take a walk along the ocean shore immediately after unpacking, so anxious was she to share with me the place she had spent her summers as a girl. Somewhat worn out by the four-hour drive, and looking forward to being totally alone with her for the first time in the year I had known her, I suggested we rest a while before venturing out. And so I opened a bottle of young Argentinean red as she cut up a few tomatoes, which she served with olive oil, French bread, and some white Brazilian cheese. Halfway through the bottle we fell silent, and the ocean waves seemed to get louder and closer by the minute.

"Let's go," she cried. "I can't stand it anymore."

"Alright," I said, in spite of my reluctance to leave the little bungalow we had rented for the week, which was already beginning to feel like home. We walked quietly in the dark toward what had now become a roar of ocean waves. Stepping off the pavement onto a field of dark and deep spongy grass, the water's white waves could now faintly be seen in the distance. The grass gave gradually away to the soft clean sand, and silhouettes of Rainforest Mountains rising from the ocean now appeared. She squeezed my hand and tucked her face into my chest, filling my senses with the fresh scent of her smooth silky hair. We stopped and embraced as the wind graciously fed locks of her thick golden hair into my mouth, now forced slightly open in awe of a scene of natural beauty I had thought existed only in dreams. That hair, in fact, had been legendary in the small community inhabiting the area, not only because of its unique rich thickness, which fell just below her belly button like a flowing river of gold, but because the source of this river, her perfectly proportioned head, supported a slightly dark Asian face, which usually complemented coal-black hair. Still clutching my hand, she led me toward the water as we removed our sandals to walk barefoot under the moonlight, allowing the splash of the waves to caress our feet. We walked south for about twenty minutes until the forest prevented us from going any further.

"I had no idea the rainforest actually touches the ocean here."

"Not only does he touch her," she said, "but he kisses her."

Delighted by this personification, I played with it and asked, "Where?"

"Where what?" she said.

"Where does he kiss her?"

"Well, he begins with her feet," pointing to the rocks on the shore covered with the growth of the forest, which really did resemble human feet, "and works his way slowly out and up until he penetrates her very depths."

Intensely animated by her answer, I fell to my knees kissing her feet gently and honestly, and worked my way up her slim ankles toward her inner thighs. When my tongue touched the inner thigh of her left leg, she let out a soft moan and whispered, "Not here, my love," and raised me softly to my feet, kissing me tenderly on my left cheek.

"Look," she said, pointing to the ocean, "he penetrates her so deeply and so honestly that he becomes one with her. Can you see how the forest emerges from inside her?"

Noticing I was not quite following, she pointed and said, "Look here and over there; that's the fruit of their love. They say there are nearly four hundred of them. Geologists call them islands, but I just call them children conceived of rainforest and ocean water. A great combination, yeah?"

"Marvelous," I said. "Marvelous. Thanks for bringing me here; what a magical place. I can't wait to see it all tomorrow in the light of day. Should we go back now?"

As we walked back to the bungalow, my desire for her grew with every step, still not believing that we were going to be totally alone for the first time. As soon as we closed the door behind us, I could resist her no longer, and firmly but gently pushed her up against the door, kissing her with the kisses of my mouth. Her tongue met mine for just a split second before she tucked her face into my chest once again, saying, "Not now, my angel."

"When?" I asked in a slightly frustrated tone. "You know how much planning went into this so that we could be alone here for the week."

"I know, my love, but not now, sweetheart, please."

"But when?"

"When we are married," she declared.

"You are so un-Brazilian," I said sarcastically.

"Since when did you become an expert on what it is to be Brazilian, especially on what it means to be a Brazilian woman? You've only been here for a year now, and I know you miss most of the subtleties in Portuguese."

"It took much less than a year to learn this about Brazilian women," I said chuckling, "regardless of the level of my Portuguese."

"Well, don't forget: the women you know and deal with at your company are all higher upper class and could not care less about traditional religious values, but many of the middle to lower classes, which make up most of the women in this country, still take the teaching of the Church very seriously when it comes to marriage and sex."

"Of course, the poor are always religious. They use religion as a drug to help them get through their miserable lives."

"Is that so? And what about the middle class?"

I didn't answer.

"And which drugs do the rich use to get them through their miserable lives?" she asked challengingly.

"Look, my angel, let's not waste time talking about this," I said, and I gently moved her up against the door again.

"Please, sweetheart, let's wait."

"Why do you want to wait? Just because your Church teaches you to?"

"My Church is your Church too, isn't it? You told me your parents were both Catholics and they raised you Catholic."

"That's true, but my beliefs have changed a lot over the years."

"Your beliefs? What do you believe in, honey?"

"I believe in your love and beauty and in our desire for one another."

She led me to the couch where she sat me down softly then put her head on my lap, asking me to play with her hair.

"Have you thought about a date yet?" she asked. "You proposed over six months ago now."

"Yes, I know. I'm almost ready." At thirty, I thought I was really too young to get married. None of my friends back in England were even considering marriage yet. Why had I proposed in the first place? A moment of weakness, perhaps?

"Are you having second thoughts?" she inquired, as if reading my mind.

"No. I'm ready whenever you are. As of next month, the remodeling of my apartment will be finished. We can live there, if you wish."

"At first, sure, but what about when the children come?"

"Children? We don't have to think about that for a long time, do we?"

"What do you mean by a long time? Anyway, we must be prepared. God knows when they will come."

"Well, yes, but . . . well . . . we must control that ourselves; it's in our hands."

"Are you strong enough? I've told you before that I will not use any form of artificial birth control, nor will I let you. And that means you must patiently learn and then submit to my natural cycles, if, that is, you don't want children right away. But why should we wait, anyway?"

I could see we were heading toward a serious many-layered disagreement and didn't want to argue with her. All I wanted was to make love to her. I was deeply in love with her; she was so different from all the other women I had had before. At first, I thought my love had something to do with her still being a virgin at twenty-six—a small miracle in Brazil, and a big one in the UK. I thought my intense desire for her grew mostly out of the way she resisted me. But as time went on, and I got to know her better, I knew it was much more than this. I couldn't live without her; she was just so different and her beauty so unique. I loved everything about her. I even loved the things I didn't like, which was a constant puzzle to me. She was always more real, deeper, more beautiful and more precious than even the things that bothered me. Our minds appreciated the same truths and rejoiced in the same beauty, though we disagreed on some important things. In the course of the year we had been seeing each other, we had only really argued once, and it was about these very things: marriage, sex, birth control, and children. I wanted children, but not right away. And I just couldn't see the difference between artificial and natural birth control, which she made such a big deal out of.

I got up to retrieve the wine in an effort to change the subject, but she insisted that we talk. I sat down on the couch, and she again put her head on my lap and asked me to play with her hair. I listened patiently as she explained to me how using artificial birth control was a betrayal of true love, since it prevented the bodies of the lovers from fully touching.

"When I give myself to you, body and soul, I want to receive you completely too, body and soul. We should hold nothing back. Just like that rainforest out there, who plunges deep into the ocean without holding anything back, nothing artificial preventing their union—no holding back. I want every fiber of your being, body and soul, to be united to my being, body and soul, so that our lovemaking might be total and pure and divine—open to life each time—the very same life we are exchanging with one another. If not, it is so mechanical and artificial and dishonest and impure and so . . . I don't know . . . tending toward pain and fear and death."

I became more and more convinced and physically excited as she continued; she sat up to drink some wine then put her head on my lap again. The more wine she drank the more articulate and passionate she became.

"Isn't it strange, my love, that in this day and age, when all the rage is for things natural—natural food, natural drink, natural landscapes, natural everything—but when it comes to what is most natural, procreation, we prefer the artificial? We want artificial birth control and in vitro fertilization, and even claim that these are personal rights."

"But what if a couple can't have a baby naturally?" I objected. "Don't they have a right to have a baby another way?"

"There you go now. A right? No. Babies are not rights; they are gifts. It is so highly clinical, and unnatural, and even horrendous to be conceived in glass, as a right, and outside the warmth of a loving mother's womb, accompanied, we hope, by the passionate and honest mutual self-giving of a man to a woman and a woman to a man. And besides, don't you know how pro-death it is?"

"What do you mean?"

"Oh, you surprise me sometimes, my love. You're so uneducated in some ways. Don't you know how in vitro works? Do you know how many zygotes are destroyed before getting the one that has the best chance of surviving when transferred to the uterus? Those zygotes are eggs that have been fertilized and are alive, you know, and many are killed before finding the lucky one to be moved into the mother."

"But those zygotes aren't really human persons, are they? You can't literally say that you are killing human life."

"Then tell me, my dear, what kind of life it is. It is alive, we know that."

"Yes, it's alive, obviously."

"Then what kind of life is it? Cat life? Fish life? Apple life? Carrot life? It is human life, the result of a human sperm fertilizing a human egg."

"But the guy who developed IVF won the Nobel Prize in medicine for this."

"Oh, is that your argument? You are really so superficial sometimes, sweetheart."

At this, I became a little angry and stopped playing with her hair. I got quiet as some of the excitement of being alone with her wore off. Before I could start brooding, however, she raised her head and brought her face close to mine, and looked at me deeply with her light green eyes that contrasted so magically with her dark Asian face and complemented so outstandingly her golden hair. She brought her lips close to mine and opened them slightly, kissing my bottom lip and placing her right hand on my chest.

"Don't fret, my angel," she whispered, as her other hand began playing with my hair. "I love you even in your superficiality, because I have seen your depth and honesty. I have seen the beauty of your soul, and I am crazy about your body and these dark black eyes of yours, which hide many profound secrets."

My anger dissipated immediately, and I began kissing her all over her beautiful face until my mouth met hers and we kissed deeply; this time her tongue was more liberal as she explored my mouth. I led her to the bedroom where we collapsed onto the bed, and I spent what seemed an eternity examining every inch of her face. She had high cheekbones, but not too high. Her lips were full and perfectly formed. Her nose was delicate, small, but not completely Asian, as it did protrude from her face well enough. Her eyes too were Asian, but were larger and more almond shaped than most. The dark color of her skin remained a mystery; it could not have come from her father's side, like her hair, but her mother's side was fair-skinned as well. Someone did say once that her maternal great grandmother was from the south of India, but I never did get the details. My deep gazing into her face was punctuated by kisses. I just couldn't get enough of her, and as the night grew, so did the silence. From the bedroom, we could hear even more clearly the sound of the waves, to which we eventually fell asleep.

When I woke up, I wondered if it had all been a dream—the soft splash of ocean water caressing our feet, the rainforest kissing the ocean, the islands rising out of the water in the moonlight, her passionate tender kisses.

She was sound asleep, so I slipped out and headed to the ocean for a swim; it was still a bit dark, about an hour before sunrise. I followed the same path we had taken the night before, excited to gaze at the natural beauty in the light of dawn and then day. It had not been a dream; it was just as we had left it, but now I could see better the thick foliage on the many islands that emerged from the water. It was almost silent; only the soft sweep of an easy wind and downy waves could be heard. I was breathless as I slowly walked into the ocean up to my hips. I left my feet and swam toward one of the islands for what seemed half an hour. The sun announced its coming, and the clouds began to blush, bright red at first, and then a soft orange, and then finally a brilliant clear white. I floated on my back with my head raised out of the water so that I could see the sun rise over the Rainforest Mountains. They seemed endless, stretching out in all directions as far as the eye could see. "Amazing," I said aloud, and tried to picture where I was on a map. I knew I was slightly south of the equator, not far from the place where the slaves from Africa had been brought by the Portuguese to be sold to the highest bidder.

How could such a magical and beautiful place also be the site of such horror, I thought as I pictured the coast of West Africa where that infamous journey across the ocean began for millions of African slaves, many of whom died before reaching this shore. I had spent two years in Accra, in Ghana, and occasionally made the trip down to Cape Coast where the slaves were kept before boarding the ships. I tried to get these negative images out of mind; they seemed so obscene in such a place of beauty, but the thoughts kept forcing themselves upon me.

Now I've seen the place of origin and the final destination, I pondered as the sun finally showed its bright face. I could stare at the sun this morning without turning away. I wondered why it wasn't blinding my eyes.

At the thought of Ghana, I remembered my dad, who had arranged for me to spend two years there after finishing my master's degree in architecture in England. He was British, my mother Brazilian. They had met in São Paulo, where my father had gone as a young architect to assist in the construction of some cutting-edge sky-rises. In those days, most of the foreign architects were from the United States; only a few from Europe managed to excel, and my dad was one of them. After falling in love with and marrying my mom, they lived in Brazil for a few years but eventually settled in London, where my father established himself as one of London's finest architects. My mom visited her family and friends each summer, wintertime in Brazil, and I always insisted on traveling with her. I looked forward to those trips—greatly preferring the winter in Brazil to the summer in England.

That is how I first met Patcharee. She lived in the same neighborhood as my mother's family. Her mother was Japanese and was friendly with the friends of my mother's family. We had met each other on a few occasions and had kept in touch through letters for about a year before I took my present job. Her mother was part of an older wave of Japanese immigration to Brazil, and a dedicated Buddhist. Her father was a Bavarian who had been raised in a devout German Catholic family. He moved to Brazil for an excellent opportunity in civil engineering and soon after met the love of his life. When he married her, his family in Bavaria mourned and fretted for a long time since he was the first in their long tradition of Catholic Bavarian families to marry a non-Catholic. His family considered it a disaster, but they were a perfectly happy couple and lived in great harmony.

There was a slight tension when their daughter was born, however, since her father wanted to give her a traditional Christian German name, and to raise her exclusively in the Catholic tradition, while her mother saw no reason why she couldn't be given an Asian name and be exposed to both religious traditions. Eventually they worked it out in a typically Brazilian kind of way. She was called Patcharee and raised in the Catholic tradition, but accompanied her mother to the Buddhist temple on all the important holy days. For her part, she considered herself neither Japanese nor German, but simply Brazilian, and in this regard she was like most other Brazilians, fully integrated into the local culture, which was a highly complex combination of indigenous native culture, semi-colonizing Portuguese culture, and African slave culture.

My time in Ghana was liberating in many ways; it was the first time on my own making good money, and I had numerous love affairs with many African women. My father had set me up with a well-known architectural firm; I had excellent living conditions, not only as compared to many of the locals, but even as compared to other foreigners. I had a live-in maid, a driver, a live-in cook, and a butler. I made more in one hour than they made in an entire month. Everyone called me sir and went out of their way to please me. For the first time in my life, I felt invincible.

Ten minutes after the sun rose, I started swimming back to the shore. Just before I got there, I thought I saw a figure off to my left where the rocky part of the forest touched the ocean. I looked more closely and saw a young woman, who quickly disappeared into the rainforest. Without warning, a great mist appeared out of the forest and saturated the area so thoroughly that the sun could no longer be seen. It suddenly got chilly, so I quickly dried off and hurriedly made my way back to the bungalow.

On the way back, I thought of bits and pieces of conversations we'd had the previous day. I felt a bit of anger again remembering how she called me uneducated and superficial, but it quickly went away when I recalled how she spoke about my depth, and especially when I recollected how she expressed this with her kisses. I thought about our talk during the long ride from São Paulo, and about her tears upon seeing that parts of the rainforest were disappearing due to the huge multinational companies that cut down large sections in order to feed and breed cattle to produce large quantities of beef for fast food conglomerates. She told me that some of the owners of these companies had purchased parts of the rainforest next to the ocean and then privatized the area, forbidding even those who had been raised there from entering. She told me how one of their sons had pursued her one summer, and proposed to her. The money was a temptation, she told me, but she couldn't get herself to love the boy, and besides this, she was appalled at how he and his family treated the locals. All these thoughts ran through my mind in the brief walk back; I wondered for a moment if the young woman I saw had been one of those locals prevented from entering the area.

The distinct aroma of breakfast welcomed me when I entered the bungalow. Patcharee was in the kitchen and hurriedly ran to me, thrusting her arms around my shoulders, kissing my neck. I wrapped my arms around her waist and lifted her high off her feet, swinging her around a few times before letting her down.

"What time did you leave?"

"Oh, about an hour before the sun rose."

"Did you know the way?"

"Of course."

"Did you swim?"

"Yes, for a long time, and then I watched the sun come up."

"But could you see the sun in all this mist?"

"Well, the mist only came up about ten minutes ago, and so suddenly. It was crystal clear before that, only a few clouds."

"Yes, that's how it is here, especially during these winter months. Do you like it here, honey?"

"I love it, baby. And I love you too." I took her in my arms and kissed her cheeks and forehead.

"I would love to live here, Michael. What about you?"

"Of course I would love to, but how could we ever afford it? And what about my work?"

"I know, honey. I'm just dreaming. It was affordable at one time, before the nouveaux riche came in and practically kicked everyone else out. When I was a girl, it was so different. People like my parents, who came here for the summers or just to get away from the city, respected the locals, got to know them, and learned from them. My parents were very fond of them and became quite close to many of them over the years."

"Tell me, sweetheart, where did the locals go when they were forced out?"

"Different places. Some remained around here, as they couldn't bear being torn away from the place they had lived for centuries."

"And how did they live before?"

"They farmed in the forest and fished in the ocean."

"And what did they do when they were forced out?"

"Some tried to farm; a few still farm around here. They harvest sugarcane and make flour, but it's nothing like it used to be. Their whole pattern of life was disrupted. Some continue fishing, as they have for generations, but all the new privacy laws make it very difficult. And worse than that, the huge fishing industries have upset the natural migration of the fish, which really confused and hurt the local fishermen."

"How so?"

"Well, their fishing was based on the natural migration of certain fish at certain times. I don't remember all the details, but if we meet some of the old-timers this week, they can tell you all about it. I remember them talking to my dad about catching certain fish during certain months. I think they used to catch sharks during certain months."

"Sharks? I was wondering about that while swimming this morning."

"No. Don't worry," she said laughingly. "I think the shark migration is in December, and they aren't very big sharks. And I think in January, the fishermen used to get tons of small shrimp. But the locals say that the varieties of fish have all but disappeared because of the fishing methods employed by the huge companies."

"Well, there's more demand now because of the population explosion; you can't really blame those corporations, can you?"

"You're joking, right?"

"Not entirely, no. You see why we need birth control? Okay, maybe you're right about preferring natural birth control to artificial methods, but you've got to admit how idealistic this is; it's unrealistic for most people, so we have to control birth using artificial methods, or else the planet and its resources will be ruined forever. There are only a limited number of resources, you know."

"You are serious, aren't you?"

I remained silent, as I'd already detected a flaw in what I'd said, but since I wasn't quite sure where I had gone wrong, I stood my ground and waited for her response. "Was there something wrong with what I said? A flaw in my logic?"

"There are so many things wrong with what you said that I don't quite know where to start."

"Well, let's start by sitting down to breakfast, and I will listen patiently to you; I'm dying for a cup of coffee."

She poured my coffee and served the breakfast. We ate quietly for a few minutes until she broke the silence.

"Michael, do you know how wasteful those conglomerates are? But even more than waste, their methods have disrupted the natural migration patterns so radically that the fish are practically disappearing; the locals say there are hardly any fish left."

"Okay, perhaps I overstated my point. I would agree there's a lot of unnecessary waste, and greed is a problem everywhere, but my point is that these huge corporations exist precisely because there are seven billion people occupying the earth; mass production is a necessity. For better or worse, we need such companies unless we drastically reduce the earth's population."

"No. That's where you're wrong, sweetheart. We don't need them. First of all, if it were left to local communities, there would be many more fish and hardly any waste. The problem is not too many people; the problem is too many greedy people. The gap between the filthy rich and the poor is staggering and gets greater and greater all the time; and it's directly proportionate to the way the new science has tried to master nature rather than cooperate with it. Nature will provide for us if we respect her and not rape her."

"So what are you saying? The more the merrier? No population control?"

"Of course not! I want ten children; what do you say?"

"Ten?"

"Well, at least eight! You know the local woman I told you about who was so close to my parents, and from whom we learned so much about this area."

"Yeah, I think I remember you telling me something about her."

"Well, she is one of seventeen children."

"Seventeen? From the same mother?"

"Yep. But they have all been dispersed now. They had a wonderful life here between the ocean and the forest."

"Where did they all go?"

"Some took menial jobs in town since fishing and farming was all they knew; others work as maids or cooks for the very people who forced them out. Most of them lost their dignity and their balance, of course, since this land had been theirs. It's a very sad story."

"Do they still come to this area?"

"In this particular place, they can't; they are forbidden because this area is all privatized now. If they are caught, they are usually charged with attempted theft, or worse. Didn't you see all the security guards this morning?"

"Yes, I saw a few, but I also saw a young woman while I was swimming who quickly disappeared into the forest as soon as I spotted her, and I was wondering who she might be."

"It's possible that she's from the Caiçara community."

"Who are they?"

"They're the local people I've been telling you about; they inhabited this area for centuries. I believe they're the indigenous natives who eventually intermingled with the Africans and the Portuguese. Their culture was developed between the forest and the ocean."

"I see."

"Want some more eggs, honey?"

"No thank you. I'm stuffed. It was delicious, thanks."

"You're welcome, sweetheart. So, did I convince you?" She asked this mischievously as she got up to clear the table and brought her waist alongside my shoulder.

Memories of last night erupted in my imagination, and I wrapped my arms around her and pressed my chest against her stomach.

"Oh, not so hard; I've eaten a lot too." I released her and got up to help her clear the table.

"Well?" she said. "Convinced?"

"About what? Eight children?"

"About everything."

"I'll think about it. But I do know that your beauty makes all your arguments more convincing," I said, following her into the kitchen.

"Why don't we walk down to the beach and soak in the sun," she said, turning to me at the sink.

"Sure. I'm ready when you are."

"Let me clean up and get ready."

"I'll help you."

"You'll help me what? Clean up or get ready?"

"Both. I'm dying to see how that new blue bikini looks on you."

"I'm a big girl," she said smilingly. "I can get ready on my own."

"Are you sure?" I said teasingly as I reached out and held her face in my hands.

She was in pajamas and wearing a beautiful silk red robe. I began kissing her neck softly and let my hands slip down from her face to feel the heavenly curves of her body. She leaned up gently against the sink, allowing my hands to first explore her breasts and then her stomach and then her hips. She closed her eyes and wrapped her arms around my waist while giving me the full length of her long and stately neck to kiss over and over. The blood rushed to my head; a deep joy possessed my heart, and I playfully whispered in her ear, "I don't know about eight, but why don't we get started on one right now?"

She giggled a bit while slipping out from under me then went back to the dining area, slowly clearing the rest of the table. She went back and forth before finally settling down to wash the dishes. As if mesmerized, all I could do was watch her graceful movements and her methodical cleansing of the plates and utensils. She furtively glanced my way with a slight smile on her face as if reading my mind. When she finished, she made her way to the bathroom saying, "Give me about twenty minutes, and I'll be ready to go."

I remained standing in the kitchen, burning with an earnest desire to please her and be pleased by her. I was genuinely grateful that she was in my life and took great joy in the idea of her being my wife. I began to entertain her dream of living in this area and raising a family here; it was unrealistic, but appealing nonetheless. The image of the young woman I saw in the morning dashed through my mind. I thought too about living permanently in such a beautiful place, starting each day with a long swim in the ocean, surrounded by the rainforest; it sounded too good to be true. But what about my job? No; it could never work, but perhaps we could spend a lot of time here, and maybe even get a small place of our own someday. I wondered what kind of life we would have together, and whether we would always be so in love. I wondered too if I could love only one woman my entire life.

So occupied by these ruminations, I didn't hear or see her until she was right next to me. All these musings vanished at the sight of her in her turquoise blue bikini, which I could see under the thin white beaded beach shirt that she wore over it.

She grabbed my hand like a little girl, saying, "Ready?"

"Sure. Let's go."

I started down the path I had taken that morning, but she pulled me in another direction.

"Aren't we going to the beach?"

"Yes. But not to the one you know. I want to show you another one."

"There's more than one around here?"

"More than one? There are about twenty."

"Twenty different beaches? Amazing!"

"Oh, and each one is a bit different depending on how and where the rainforest has decided to touch it."

"You mean kiss it?"

"Yes, my love, I mean kiss it," she said, leaning her head against my shoulder.

In ten minutes, we were there. This beach was quite different; it was considerably smaller, with one border caused by what seemed to be only a slice of the rainforest, mostly rock, and the other border, mostly vegetation, formed by a vastly wide part of the forest from which a number of streams poured into the ocean through waterfalls of varying heights.

"Unbelievable," I said. "Too good to be true."

"Yeah, all the best things in life are like that, aren't they? Too good to be true. But guess what, my angel? They are true."

"Such a beautiful place, and we are all alone. I can't believe this. Where is everyone?"

"It's winter, remember?"

"Somehow that just doesn't sound right," I said, remembering what the word winter meant in England. Today it was about thirty degrees Celsius; the mist had dissipated, and the sun was shining brightly again.

"I should have come here sooner. What a shame that I've been in Brazil for a whole year and have never come here before."

"We can come often after we're married, even if we can't manage to live here."

"What a splendid idea, my love," I said, kissing her shoulder.

We walked out together into the water. She stopped when it got waist deep, but I continued until I was in up to my chest, at which point I left my feet and swam toward one of the small islands only about a hundred yards away. It was more challenging than I anticipated, and I was completely worn out when I finally reached the shore. I rested on the sand facedown for a few minutes thinking that I should have told her I was going to swim all the way out here rather than just leave her suddenly and without warning. I got up and looked back to see her, but she was nowhere to be seen. The mist was thicker now, and made it more difficult to see clearly.

He was dying to continue reading, becoming more and more convinced that he was dealing with an exceptionally gifted writer who could write in truly diverse ways, but he had business to attend to at the Madras airport. When he returned late in the evening, he was planning to continue reading "Slightly South of the Equator," but in searching for it, fell upon another short story titled "Lake Victoria." This was a prelude to what Thomas often mused about turning into his second and final novel: his African novel. The background was set in Uganda, shortly after the era of Idi Amin, in the early eighties. Most of the story unfolded on the shores of beautiful Lake Victoria not too far from the town of Entebbe. The plot was narrated by the son of a famous writer, who'd discovered his father's diary after the latter's untimely death in Northern Uganda at the hands of rebel gangs from the Sudan. The son finds himself the center of worldwide media attention after his father's death, when someone tips off the press about the exciting discovery. The plot unfolds as the son learns about his father's hidden life and begins to understand who he is as his father's son. The main themes were man's basic need to define himself in relation to the other, the I-Thou relationship with the Divine as manifest in love between man and woman, or in the case of the main character, between one man and many women. The plot's climax revolved around his chaste love affair with a beautiful black maiden who finally satisfies his yearning to love and be loved to the point where he risks his life for her and her people. The grandson was impressed with the way Thomas began the story: "The world is what it is; men who are nothing, who allow themselves to become nothing, have no place in it." To the learned, this was a short but profound commentary on the opening lines of Naipaul's great novel of Africa, *A Bend in the River*.

He was also impressed with the way Thomas was able to integrate themes and insights of great novels set in Africa into the main movements of his story. Though the grandson only read the first seven pages of what was a thirty-page short story, he could already see how Thomas had forced authors as diverse as Graham Greene, Achebe, Conrad, and Naipaul to get to the heart of the matter and confront one another in the heart of darkness.

The grandson recognized similar themes in this story to the ones developed in Thomas's novel, but noticed also a greater maturity in the style of writing. Flipping through all the writing Jhansi had given him, he couldn't decide what to read. As he was still being drawn to "Slightly South of the Equator," he stumbled upon a poem titled "The Wedding Feast"—a religious poem that explored an ancient Eastern Christian idea that the devil had been tricked by Christ, something the Western tradition of Christianity was not so comfortable with since it made Christ out to be a trickster. The rhythm and themes attracted him:

Have you heard about that Wedding Feast
So long ago that stunned the beast?
As soon as water turned to wine
He feared he had but little time

To tempt and scare and spread his lies
To foster filth and painful sighs
That legion panicked one by one
For now the Groom had finally come

And come he did with power and might
Dispelling darkness with his light
Six jars of stone obeyed his call
And into wine, water did fall

The Bride rejoiced and gleamed with joy
Could this King be her little boy?
Whose Glorious Hour came round at last
Defeating Darkness, future, past

But we the guests gaze on in fear
For as that Glorious Hour drew near
There was no Glory to be seen
As they did crucify their King

He mounts his wedding bed in pain
Delighted demons curse his name
Women wail, soldiers mock
Pathetic Shepherd with his flock

They mock the miracle of the Wine
They bask in shame; on blood they dine
Taunts and curses open flood
Water to wine, now wine to blood

And as the Spear his heart did reach
The Beast prepared his victory speech
"The Wedding Wine's run out," he cried
"It seems your Bride and Groom have lied"

"They've lied about this wedding feast
For who's the victor if not the beast?"
He laughed and cursed, "The king is dead
The Groom's in the tomb of his wedding bed"

But as he uttered this one last lie
The Groom in the tomb let out a sigh
"Roll back the stone, discard the shroud"
The Groom's ascending on Heaven's cloud

Bewildered, shocked, the beast looked on
Three days later, a hopeful dawn
"The stone's rolled back, how could this be?
An Incestuous Groom has deceived me?"

"Deceived yourself" the truth to tell
Mimetic Violence, the sound of hell
The old dark cycle crushed at last
The awful sound has finally past

"You tricked yourself in that awful hour
For Violence is not the only power
There's a language that you will never speak
Gentle, Patient, Kind and Meek"
The King returned to claim his Bride
Who huddled near his deep-pierced side
They drank the water turned to wine
Rejoicing in a banquet fine

And when the time to toast drew near
The Groom proclaimed in voice so clear
"The Beast has lied; his world's a sham
The True Wedding Feast is the Feast of the Lamb"

He finally read one last poem, which Thomas had written for his children and wherein he acknowledged his great debt to one of his favorite poets when he wrote at the bottom of the page, "Inspired by Robert Louis Stevenson's poem 'Good Night.'" The title of Thomas's poem was "Good Morning":

We hear the sound of the cock crow twice
And smell the aroma of the coffee nice;
The dawn approaches the morning comes
It storms our room like long-lost chums!
Must we arise indeed?
Well then let's get up like men
And face with courage and no trace of fear
The awful class of Mrs. Drear
Good morning Mother, Father, Sun
They stole away all our summer fun
There's nothing left but lines and bad books
Tons of homework and nasty looks

Nearly two weeks passed before he called Jhansi and asked her to come and collect the material. She wanted to ask him whether he'd decided to write the introduction or not, but his manner on the phone prevented conversation. Half an hour later she was in his apartment standing exactly in the place she'd stood before.

"I'm sorry, but I've decided not to write the introduction to the novel."

"Why?" she pleaded.

"I have my reasons. Here's the manuscript. I read it thoroughly, not once, but twice. And here is the rest of the material, a good deal of which I have also read. Good day, miss. I must be going. I have an appointment."

She left in all confusion as he politely showed her the way out. She'd wanted to speak with him, but he had again blocked any exchange. Before she knew it, she was sitting on the mat in her house brooding over what had happened.

"Why didn't I at least ask him if he liked it, or if, in his judgment, any of it had merit? Poor Thomas will be so disappointed. All that effort! All those words—over ninety thousand in all. For what? For whom? Oh, Thomas, I want to be there to comfort you when you find out," she said to herself.

All night she worried about how to break the news to him. She began even to blame herself.

Perhaps I didn't present myself properly, she thought. *Or maybe the way I introduced Thomas as an author was wanting. How am I going to tell him?*

For many months, she had literally lived for his phone call, and now she was dreading it. It came at last.

"Meena, hurry up and get your sister from the roof! He's on the phone," her mother cried out.

"Let me talk to him, Mother, just for a moment," Meena pleaded.

"No child. It's long distance. Go get your sister now, and stop wasting time."

Jhansi came running down the stairs, past their secret place, where she'd placed flowers every morning since he'd left, forcing it to take on the status of a shrine. She burst into the house and grabbed the phone from her mother.

"Hello. How are you?"

"Fine, Jhansi, yourself?"

"Fine, thank God."

"Your family well?"

"Everyone's fine."

"How are Sister and the children?"

"Just fine, praise God. Are you all ready, Jhansi?"

"I think so; what about you?"

"I think so too. Tell me about the book. Did you meet him?"

"Uh . . . yes . . . I did."

"Did he like it? What did he say? What was he like?"

"Thomas," she whispered.

"What is it, Jhansi?"

"He has declined," she barely managed to say, nearly choking on her words.

"Why?"

"He didn't say."

"Did he like it? Did he say he thought it had some merit?"

"He said nothing except that he had his own reasons."

Thomas was dead quiet.

"Don't worry, sweetheart," Jhansi said. "Some people wouldn't know good writing if it slapped them in the face. There are plenty of important people who would jump at the chance of writing an introduction to such a fine piece of work."

"You're very kind, my love."

"And I am very right too. We'll just—"

"Jhansi, did you like it? Please tell me the truth."

She paused then said, "No. I didn't like it. I adored it. And I adore you."

"Honest?"

"Honest to God."

"Then that's enough for me; no need to publish any of it. After all, I write for you. If you liked it, I'm satisfied. I mean, it would have been nice to have someone from Narayan's family say something positive about the novel, since, although I dedicated it to you, I wrote it in his memory."

"Do you suspect he knows about it, Thomas?"

"I don't know about that. I've never tried communicating with him; he doesn't know me. But I have found myself at times praying for the repose of his soul, and at other times asking for his help."

"But he's not a saint to ask for his intercession."

"How do we know? In my heart of hearts, I think he can hear me. And I think his good friend, Mr. Greene, can hear me too. Lately, in fact, as I near the completion of my vow, I find myself constantly calling upon Mr. Greene's intercession."

"Which vow is that?"

"I'll tell you later."

"Do you really think they intercede for you?"

"I don't know, really, but I do look forward to the day we'll be able to meet in heaven, provided I'm not damned to eternal hell."

"Don't even say it!"

"Well, it's always a possibility, you know; freedom is no joke. We are so radically free that we can even choose to go to hell."

"Stop talking about hell, damn it!"

"Exactly! That's exactly what we must do. We must damn it."

"Damn what?"

"Damnation. We must damn damnation! And there is only one way to do so. We must believe in and love a God, as Greene has taught me, who died not only for what was good and beautiful—that is too easy, even men do that—but to believe in and love a God who died for the 'halfhearted and the corrupt', now that's spectacular."

"O my dear. I miss you, my lord. So what now?"

"I'm sorry, could you repeat? The line is not clear; it's breaking up."

"I said, what about the book?"

"Well, I don't know; it's just a book."

"But I thought it was to be the book of books," she argued. "And you wanted many to read it."

"A plan is a plan, but life is life. You can't say everything in one book. In fact, you can't say everything in a thousand books. No one can say everything. And the depth of one's life, even a superficial life, can never be totally captured in writing."

"But you put your very soul into it."

"You're my soul, Jhansi. You're the soul of my soul. I did want many people to read it, but if you've read it, that's enough. I did want to do a lot more in it, but it didn't come together."

"Like what?"

"Oh, I'll tell you later. We'd better hang up now."

"No. Please. Don't hang up. Just tell me briefly."

"Well, I wanted to develop the theme of love after death. I wanted to show in what sense death is a kind of divine mercy that we ought to be grateful for, but again, I just didn't have the time and energy to pull it all together."

"Wait a second," she said with a puzzled tone in her voice. "I thought death was a divine punishment for the original sin."

"It was. It is. But it's a merciful punishment. God's wrath is always wrapped up in love; you know that. You see, I had wanted to devote an entire section to the meaning of the words in the sacred Scriptures, "Then the Lord God said: See! The man has become like one of us, knowing what is good and bad! Therefore, he must not be allowed to put out his hand to take fruit from the tree of life also, and thus eat of it and live forever. The Lord God therefore banished him from the Garden of Eden, to till the ground from which he had been taken. When he expelled the man, he settled him east of the Garden of Eden; and he stationed the cherubim and fiery revolving sword to guard the way to the tree of life."

"How do you remember all those quotes?"

"Well, I've taught it for years."

"I won't keep you long, but at least tell me what you mean by a merciful punishment?"

"Didn't you get it? If God had left them in the Garden, they would have eventually eaten from the tree of life and would have lived forever."

"What's wrong with living forever? I thought this was what God wanted since he did not make death."

"Nothing is wrong with living forever, of course. But they'd already eaten from the tree of the knowledge of good and evil. They would have lived forever in the state of knowing evil."

"But this is what made them like God, isn't it? God knows evil, and he's just fine."

"But man isn't God."

"But you say in your book that God wants man to become God."

"He does, but he wants man to become God with God, not without him. Becoming God without God is a curse and God didn't want man to live forever in a cursed state. Thus, he banished him from the Garden out of love and deigned that he should die, that he should go back to the ground from which he came."

"Now I see why you couldn't pull everything together."

"Oh, this is not all. I wanted to show the connection between this and Shakespeare's Othello, who 'loved not wisely, but too well,' and Pope's famous poem 'Eloisa to Abelard.' And all, mind you, in the overall context of love after death, which necessarily deals with love's sacred order, the Blessed Trinity, and with personal identity before, during, and after earthly existence."

"Oh Lord," cried Jhansi. "Maybe it's better you stopped when you did."

"But that's not it," said Thomas passionately, forgetting that the call was costing him a fortune. "You see, I wanted to show the great contrast between heroic literature and religious literature. The constant theme of the former is that life is followed by death and that all earthly glory finally leads to the tragedy of the grave. But the invariable theme of the latter is the exact opposite: death ultimately leads to new life. You see, Jhansi, my dear, this life is really an integral part of heaven, and, since the fall of man, the pain we experience here has become a necessary part of the purification that gets us ready for heaven, just as pain has become a necessary part of pleasure. We don't fully enjoy our food unless we are hungry, right?"

"Like I said, I think it's better you stopped when you did."

"I didn't really decide to stop; it just happened, very much like our life will stop at death, I suppose, or it ought to."

"What do you mean?"

"Well, I believe genuinely that we must never decide when the moment of death will be. It's a sacred moment, just like the moment of birth. Life is a great gift, and so is death. We have no right to take our own life. May God have mercy somehow on all those who have done so."

There was silence now until Jhansi finally said, "So what shall I do with the manuscript?"

"The manuscript?" Thomas sighed deeply.

"What shall we do with the book now?" she prompted him.

"All right. I know," Thomas said after another deep sigh. "Listen carefully, my love. Take it to the South Indian town of Malgudi. It's not far from you. Wait for a rainy day. Take the main road to the center of the town, where you will find a little pet shop that specializes in selling ferocious pet peacocks and overly moody monkeys. Directly behind the shop, you'll find an ancient sidewalk heading due north. Make sure to notice the raindrops dancing inside the cracks of the crooked sidewalk. Recite the poem 'The Rain,' the one we composed together in Bangalore, remember? At dusk, when it stops raining, take the path to the very end where it hooks up to a much smaller dirt path gradually winding around to the east. As soon as the river comes into view, you'll see the last lonely rays of reddish-orange sunlight reflecting off the water. Look to the south and you'll notice a deserted shrine in the middle of the field. It's a shrine to Shiva. He's sitting cross-legged in childlike serenity, eyes closed, hands open and upright as if ready to receive an offering. Take a deep breath; smell the aroma of the damp earth and the clean, wet mud. Go down to the river and bathe; by this time, it will be dark. Don't be afraid; nobody will see you except the full moon melting the darkness as she eagerly rises over the eastern mountains just as you are descending into the river. Leave the book on the bank of the river while you bathe. I'll be bathing too. After bathing, make sure you wear the turquoise blue sari. Take up the book and walk slowly to the shrine where next to the left foot of the great Shiva you'll find a few fagots of wood just waiting to offer themselves up in loving sacrifice. Light a fire, warm yourself, and begin your meditation. Listen carefully for that long-forgotten music of the spheres. Once you hear it, take the book into your lovely hands, and put it on the flames. Burn it completely, place the ashes in his hands, and then prepare yourself, my gracious Ganga, to climb up into the depth of space between the stars and the beyond, which lays hidden in his divinely entangled locks of matted hair."

INDEX OF FOREIGN WORDS:

Amma (in Tamil) Mama
Baba (in Arabic) Daddy
Elbee (in Arabic) my heart
Habeebe (in Arabic; masculine) my beloved
Habeebatee (in Arabic; feminine) my beloved
Hyatee (in Arabic) my life
Rakshas (in Hindi) mythical forces of evil
Dahl (in Tamil) Southern Indian soup-porridge
Kadhala (in Tamil) sweetheart, beloved
Khuda Hafez (in Persian) God be with you

A free eBook edition is available with the purchase of this book.

To claim your free eBook edition:

1. Download the Shelfie app.
2. Write your name in upper case in the box.
3. Use the Shelfie app to submit a photo.
4. Download your eBook to any device.

Shelfie

A free eBook edition is available with the purchase of this print book.

CLEARLY PRINT YOUR NAME ABOVE IN UPPER CASE

Instructions to claim your free eBook edition:
1. Download the Shelfie app for Android or iOS
2. Write your name in **UPPER CASE** above
3. Use the Shelfie app to submit a photo
4. Download your eBook to any device

Print & Digital Together Forever.

Snap a photo

Free eBook

Read anywhere

The Morgan James Speakers Group

We connect Morgan James published authors with live and online events and audiences whom will benefit from their expertise.

Morgan James makes all of our titles available
through the Library for All Charity Organizations.

www.LibraryForAll.org

Printed in the USA
CPSIA information can be obtained
at www.ICGtesting.com
JSHW022215140824
68134JS00018B/1075